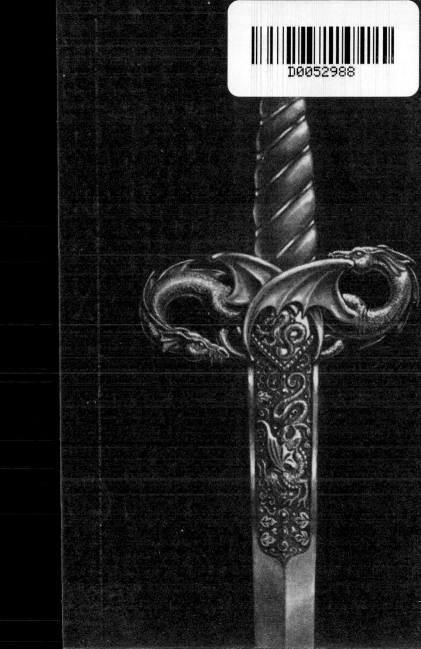

THE FIRST BOOK OF SWORDS

FRED SABERHAGEN

TOR

A TOM DOHERTY ASSOCIATES BOOK

A TOR Book

Published by Tom Doherty Associated, Inc.
8-10 West 36th Street
New York, NY 10018

First mass market printing, April 1984

ISBN: 812-55-298-9
Can. Ed. 812-55-299-7

Printed in the United States of America

THE FIRST BOOK
OF
SWORDS

PROLOGUE

In what felt to him like the first cold morning of the world, he groped for fire.

It was a high place where he searched, a lifeless, wind-scoured place, a rough, forbidding shelf of black and splintered rock. Snow, driven by squalls of frigid air, streamed across the black rock in white powder, making shifting veils of white over layers of gray ancient ice that was almost as hard as the rock itself. Dawn was in the sky, but still hundreds of kilometers away, as distant as the tiny sawteeth of the horizon to the northwest. The snowfields and icefields along that far edge of the world were beginning to glow with a reflected pink.

Ignoring cold and wind, and mumbling to himself, the searcher paced in widening circles on his high rugged shelf of land. One of his powerful legs was

deformed, enough to make him limp. He was searching for warmth, and for the smell of sulphur in the air,
for anything that might lead him to the fire he needed.
But his sandalled feet were too leathery and unfeeling
to feel warmth directly through the rocks, and the
wind whipped away the occasional traces of volcanic
fumes.

Presently the searcher concentrated his attention on
the places where rock protruded through the rough
skin of ice. When he found a notable bare spot, he
kicked, stamped with his hard heels, at the ice around
its rim, watching critically as the ice shattered. Yes,
here was a place where the frost was a trifle less hard,
the grip of cold just a little weaker. Somewhere down
below was warmth. And warmth meant, ultimately,
fire.

Looking for a way down to the mountain's heart, the
searcher moved in a swift limp around one of its
shoulders. He had guessed right; before him now
loomed a great crevice, exhaling a faintly sulphurous
atmosphere, descending between guardian rocks. He
went straight to that hard-lipped mouth, but just as he
entered it he paused, looking up at the sky and once
more muttering something to himself. The sky, brightening with the impending dawn, was almost entirely
clear, flecked in the distance with scattered clouds. At
the moment it conveyed no messages.

The searcher plunged down into the crevice, which
quickly narrowed to a few meters wide. Grunting,
making up new words to groan with as he squeezed
through, he steadily descended. He was sure now that
the fire he needed was down here, not very far away.
When he had gone down only a little way he could
already begin to hear the dragon-roar of its voice, as it
came scorching up through some natural chimney
nearby to ultimately emerge he knew not where. So he
continued to work his way toward the sound, moving

among a tumble of house-sized boulders that had been thrown here like children's blocks an age ago when some upper cornice of the mountain had collapsed.

At last the searcher found the roaring chimney, and squeezed himself close enough to reach in a hand and sample the feeling of the fire when it came up in its next surge. It was good stuff this flame, with its origin even deeper in the earth than he had hoped. A better fire than he could reasonably have expected to find, even for such fine work as he had now to do.

Having found his fire, he climbed back to the wind-blasted surface and the dawn. At the rear of the high shelf of rock, right against the face of the next ascending cliff, was a place somewhat sheltered from the wind. Here he now decided to put the forge. The chosen site was a recess, almost a cave, a natural grotto set into the cliff that towered tremendously higher yet. Out of this cave and around it, more fissure-chimneys were splintered into the black basalt of the face, chimneys through which nothing now rose but the cold howling wind, drifting a little snow. The searcher's next task was to bring the earthfire here somehow, in a form both physically and magically workable; the work he had to do with the fire meant going deeply into both those aspects of the world. He could see now that he would have to transport and rebuild the fire in earth-grown wood—that would mean another delay, here on the treeless roof of the world. But minor delays were unimportant, compared with the requirement of doing the job right.

From the corner of his eye, as he stood contemplating his selected forge-site, he caught sight of powers that raced airborne across a far corner of the dawn. He turned his head, to see in the distant sky a flickering of colors, lights that were by turns foul and gentle. Probably, he thought to himself, they are only at some sport that has nothing at all to do with me or my work. Yet he remained standing motionless, watching those sky-colors and muttering to himself, until the flying powers were gone, and he was once again utterly and absolutely alone.

Then he clambered down the surface of the barren mountainside, moving methodically, moving swiftly and nimbly despite one twisted leg. He continued going down for almost a thousand meters, to the level where the highest real trees began to grow. Having reached that level he paused briefly, regarding the sky once more, scanning it in search of messages that did not come. Wind, trapped and funneled here between the peaks, blasted his hair and beard that were as thick and wild as fur, whipped at his scorched garments of fur and leather, rattled the dragonscales he wore as ornaments.

And now, suddenly, names began to come and go in his awareness. It was as if he saw them flickering like those magical powers that flew across the sky. He thought: I am called Vulcan. I am the Smith. And he realized that descending even this moderate distance from the upper heights had caused him to start thinking in human language.

To get the size and quantity of logs he wanted for his fire, he had to go a little farther down the slope. Still the highest human settlements were considerably below him. The maplike spread of farms and villages, the sight of a distant castle on a hill, all registered in his perception, but only as background scenery with no immediate significance. His mind was on the task of gathering logs. Here, where the true forest started, finding logs was not difficult, but they tended to be from twisted trees, awkwardly shaped. It occurred to the Smith that an ax, some kind of chopping tool, would be a handy thing to have for this part of the job; but the only physical tools he had, besides his hands, were those of his true art, and they were all back at the site he'd chosen for his forge. His hands were all he really needed, though, clumsy though they could sometimes be with wood. If a log was too awkward, he simply broke it until it wasn't. At last, with a huge bundle that even his arms could scarcely clasp, he started back up the mountainside. His limp was a little more noticeable now.

During his absence the anvil and all his other ancient metal-working tools had arrived at the forge-site, and were dumped there in glorious disorder. Vulcan put down his firewood, and arranged everything in an orderly array around the exact place where he had decided that the fire should be. When he had finished, the sun was disappearing behind the east face of the mountain that towered above his head.

Pausing briefly to survey what he had done so far, he puffed his breath a little, as if he might be in need of rest. Now, to go down into the earth and bring up fire. He was beginning to wish he had some slaves on hand, helpers to handle some of these time-consuming details. The hour was approaching when he himself would have to concentrate almost entirely upon his real work. He longed to see the metal glowing in the forge, and feel a hammer in his hand.

Instead, gripping one five-meter log under his arm like a long spear, he descended for the second time into the maze of crevices that ran beneath the upper mountain. Through this maze he worked his way back toward the place where fire and thunder rose sporadically through convoluted chimneys. This time he approached the place by a slightly different route, and could see the reflected red glow of earthfire shining from ahead to meet him. That glow when it encountered daylight seemed to wink, as if in astonishment at having found this place of air so different from the lower hell in which it had been born.

At one neck in this crevice the rocks on either side

pinched in too much to let pass the Smith and his log together. He set down the log, and laid hands on the rocks and raged at them. This was another kind of work in which his hands were clumsy. Their enormous hairless fingers, like his sandalled feet, were splayed and leathery. His skin was everywhere gray, the color of old smoke from a million forge-fires. Now, with his effort against the rocks, the sandals on his huge feet pressed down on other rocks, dug into pockets of old drifted snow, crunched and shattered ancient ice. Presently the rocks that had narrowed the crevice gave way to the pressure of his hands, splitting and booming and showering fragments.

With a satisfied grunt, Vulcan the Smith took up his log again. One final time he paused, looking up at what could be seen from here of the day's clear sky—only a narrow tracery of blue. Then he went quickly on his way.

When he pushed one end of his log into the roaring chimney, the earthfire caught promptly and deeply in the wood. The log became a blazing torch when the Smith pulled it back from the inferno-fissure and tossed it spinning in the shadowed air. Its rosin popped and snapped with hot, perfumed combustion. Vulcan laughed, pleased with the forge-fire he had caught; then he tucked the log under his arm and quickly climbed again.

He built up his forge-fire quickly on the spot he had prepared for it. Now his anvil, a tabletop of ancient and enchanted iron, had to be positioned levelly and solidly in just the right spot relative to the fire. This took time. As he worked with the anvil, adjusting its position in small increments, the Smith decided that he'd have to make at least one more trip downslope for fuel before he'd be able to start his real work. After he'd begun that in earnest, he'd want no interruptions.

His eye fell on the waiting bellows. The sight made

him frown. Yes, it would be very good, perhaps essential, to have some helpers.

The more he thought about it the more obvious it seemed. Yes, human help would be necessary at some stage, given the peculiar nature of this job. He now had earthfire burning in earth-grown wood, with the clean upper air of earth to lend its spirit to the flame. Opposed to this, in a sense, was the unearthly metal that he was going to work. At one side of the grotto, sky-iron waited, a lump of it the size of a barrow. It was so heavy that the Smith grunted when he took it up into his arms to look it over carefully. He could feel the interior energies of it waiting, poised in their crystalline layers, eager to be shaped by his art. He could feel the ethereal, unearthly magic of the stuff—yes, even crude-looking as it was, slagged and pitted on all sides by the soft fist of air that had caught and eased the madness of its fall, slowing the fall until mere crashing instead of vaporization had resulted when the mass struck earthly rock at last. Yes, the metal itself would bring enough, maybe more than enough, of the unearthly to the project.

Human sweat and human pain were going to be indispensible. The catalyst of human fear would help to refine the magic too. And even human joy might be put to use—if the Smith could devise any means by which that rare essence might be extracted.

And when the twelve blades had been forged at last, when he could raise them straight and glowing from the anvil—why, for their quenching, human blood would doubtless be best . . .

The keening pipe-music and the slow drum were borne to Mala's ears by the cool night breeze, well before the few dim lights of Treefall village came into her view between the trees ahead. The sounds of mourning warned her that at least some part of the horrible tale that had reached her at home was probably true. She murmured one more distracted prayer to Ardneh, and once again impatiently lashed with the ends of the reins at the flanks of the old riding-beast she straddled. Her mount was an elderly creature, unused to such harsh treatment, and to long night journeys in general. When it felt the sting of the reins it skipped a step, then slowed down in irritation. Mala in her impatience thought of leaping from its back and running on ahead, groping her own way along the lightless and unpaved road. But already she had almost reached her destination; now she could hear the cackling of the village fowl ahead as they sensed her approach. And now the first lighted windows were coming into view amid the trees.

Presently, on a main street every bit as small and narrow as the only street of her own town, Mala was dismounting under a million stars, whose light made gray and ghostly giants of the Ludus Mountains looming just a few kilometers to the east. Autumn nights in this high country grew cold, and she was wearing a shawl over her regular garb, a workingwoman's homespun trousers and loose blouse.

The music of mourning was coming from a building that had to be the village hall, for it was the largest structure in sight, and one of the few lighted. Mala tied up her animal at a public hitching rack that was already crowded. Moving lightly, though her joints felt stiff from the long ride, she trotted the few steps to the hall. Her hair was long, dark, and curly, the loveliest thing about her physical appearance. Her face was somewhat too broad to be judged beautiful by most people's standards; her body also was broad and strong, vibrant with youth and exercise.

Her quick step carried her onto the shadowed porch of the hall before she realized that a man was standing there already. He was in shadows, not far from the

curtained doorway through which candlelight and music
came out, along with the murmur of many voices and
the soft thump of dancing feet. His bearded face was
unfamiliar to Mala, but he had a certain look of
importance; he must, she thought, be one of the elders
here.

To simply rush past an elder without acknowledg-
ing his presence would have been impolite, and Mala
halted, one foot in the shadow cast by the rising
moon. "Sir, please, can you tell me where Jord the
blacksmith is?" Since courtesy required speech of her,
she would not waste the words, but instead try to use
them to accomplish her urgent search.

The man did not answer her immediately. Instead,
he only looked in her direction as if he had not clearly
heard, or understood. As he turned his face more fully
toward Mala, she saw that he was stunned by some
great pain or grief.

She spoke to him again. "I'm looking for Jord, the
smith. We were—we are to be married."

Understanding grew in the tormented face. "Jord?
He still breathes, child. Not like my son—but both of
them are in there."

Mala put aside the curtain of hides that half-closed
the doorway, and went through, to enter the most
crowded room that she had ever seen in her seventeen
years of life. She guessed wildly that forty people,
perhaps even more, were gathered here in one place
tonight. Yet the hall was big enough for the crowd,
even big enough to have at its center a sizable area free
of crowding. In that central area stood five rude biers,
each covered with black fabric, expensive candles burning at the head and foot of each. On each bier a dead
man lay draped with ritual cloths; on several of the
bodies the cloths were not enough to hide the marks of
violence.

Near the foot of the central bier was a single chair.

Jord was sitting in it. Mala's first glance at him made
her gasp, confirming as it did another aspect of the
evil story that had reached her in her own village: the
right arm of her betrothed now ended a few centimeters below the shoulder. The stump was tightly
wrapped, in fresh, well-tended bandages, lightly spotted with the bleeding from beneath. Jord's beard-
stubbled face was aged and shrunken, making him
look in Mala's eyes like his own father. In his light hair
there was a gray streak that she had never noticed
before. His blue eyes were downcast, staring almost
witlessly at the plank floor, and the dancers' feet that
trod it slowly a pace or two away from him. The ring
of village women who danced so slowly to the dirge
went round the biers and chair, their feet hitting the
floor softly in time to the drum, slow-beaten back in
the rear of the large hall.

And outside the dancing ring, the other mourners—
yes, there might really be forty of them—mingled and
socialized, wept, joked, chatted, prayed, ate and drank,
meditated or wailed in loss just as their spirits moved
them, each in his or her own cycle of behavior. There
was a priest of Ardneh, recognizable by his white suit,
comforting an old woman who shrieked above all
other sounds her agony of grief. Most of the crowd
looked like folk of this village, as was only natural—
the story had said that all the dead men were from
here, as was Jord. Mala could recognize some of the
faces in the crowd, from her earlier visits here to meet
Jord and his kinfolk. But most of the people were
unknown to her, and a few of them were dressed
outlandishly, as if they might have come from far
away.

Still standing near the doorway, looking over shoulders and between shifting bodies, Mala breathed a
prayer of thanksgiving to Ardneh for Jord's survival;
and yet, even as she prayed, she felt a new pang of

inner anguish. The man she was going to marry had been changed, drastically and terribly, before she had ever had the chance to know him in his full health and strength and youth. Then as if trying to reject that thought she tried to step forward, meaning to hurry to Jord at once. But the thick press of bodies held her back.

At this moment she had the impression of an odd, momentary pause in the room—but it must have been only a seeming in her mind, she was not used to crowds, and when she looked at the faces in the crowd around her they were all doing just what they had been doing a moment earlier. But in that moment of pause, the hide curtain draping the doorway behind Mala had been put aside by someone else's hand. Amid the din of music and grief and conversation there was no way she could have heard that soft movement, but she did feel the suddenly augmented breath of the cold wind that at night here slid down from the mountains.

And then in the next moment a man's hand came to rest on Mala's arm—not insinuatingly, not harshly either, but just as if it had a right to be there, like the hand of a father or an uncle. But he was none of those. His face was entirely concealed by a mask, made of what looked like dark, tooled leather. The mask surprised Mala, but only for a moment. A few times in her life before, at wakes and funerals, she had seen men wearing masks. The explanation was that feuds could be exacerbated, friendships and alliances sometimes strained, if a man whose opinion mattered were seen to be mourning openly for the enemy of a friend or ally; while at the same time, some conflicting rule of conduct might require him to do so. A mask allowed its wearer's identity to be ignored by those who did not wish to know it, even if it were not really kept a secret.

The masked man was somewhat on the short side, and well enough dressed in simple clothing. And Mala thought that he was young. "What has happened, Mala?" His voice, close to her ear, was almost a whisper.

He knew her; so he was most likely some distant relative of Jord's. Or, thought Mala, noting the short sword at his belt, he might even be some minor lord or knight, one who had perhaps at some time been served by Jord as smith or armorer.

And the masked man must have come here from some distance, and must have just arrived, not to know already what had happened. In the face of such ignorance Mala stumbled over words, not so much trying to repeat the story as she had heard it as trying to find some reasonable explanation of the horror. But an explanation was hard to find.

She tried: "They . . . all six of them . . . they were called by a god to go up on the mountain. Then . . . "

"Which god's call did they follow?" The quiet voice was not surprised by talk of gods; it wanted to nail down the facts.

One of the men who had been standing in front of Mala, unintentionally blocking her path to Jord, turned round at that. "They answered Vulcan's call. No doubt about it, the god chose them himself. I heard him—so did half the village—more than half. Vulcan himself came down here from the mountain in the night and called the six men out by name. The rest of us just lay low in our beds, I can tell you. Next day, when none of the six had come back yet, we gathered here in the hall and wondered. The women kept egging us on to find out what had happened, and eventually some of us started climbing . . . it wasn't pretty, what we found there, I can tell you."

"And what," the masked man asked, "if they had chosen not to follow Vulcan's call?" The light in the hall was too uncertain, the shadows too heavy, for

Mala to be able to tell if his hands looked like those of a worker or of a man highborn. The hair emerging from his jacket's cowl was dark, with a hint of curl, giving no clue about his station. Perhaps it was this very indeterminateness in his appearance that first raised in Mala's mind a suspicion that seemed to come out of nowhere: *I wonder if this could be the Duke himself.* Mala had never actually seen the Duke, but like thousands of his other subjects who had not seen him either she knew, or thought she knew, certain things about him. One of the most intriguing of these things was that he was supposed to go out in disguise from time to time, adventuring and spying among his people. According to other information, he was still a relatively young man; and it was also said that he was physically rather small.

Jord, Mala thought, might have worked for the Duke at one time. Or some of the dead men on the biers might have. That could explain why the Duke had shown up here tonight . . . she told herself that she was making things up, but still . . . there were some stories told about the Duke's cruelty, on occasion, but then, Mala supposed, such stories were told about almost all powerful folk. Even if they were true, she thought, they didn't preclude the possibility that Duke Fraktin might sometimes take a benevolent interest in these poor outlying villages of his domain.

The solid citizen who had turned round to speak was plainly not entertaining any such exalted idea of the masked man's identity. Instead, he was looking him over as if not much impressed with what he saw, small sword or not. The citizen snorted lightly at the masked man's question, and shook his head. "When a god calls, who's going to stop and argue? If you want to know more about it, better ask Jord."

Jord had not noticed Mala yet. The brawny, young-old man with one arm and one bandaged stump still sat on his chair where ritual had placed him, almost as if he were one of the dead himself.

Mala heard the solid citizen saying: "His arm's still up there on the mountain, but he brought his pay for it back with him." Without trying to understand what this might mean, she pushed her way between the intervening bodies and ran to Jord. Inside the slow ring of dancers, Mala went down on one knee before the man she had pledged to marry, clutching at his one hand and at his knees, trying to explain how sorry she was for what had happened to him, and how she had come to him as quickly as she could when the news of the horror reached her.

At first Jord said nothing in return, but only looked at Mala as if from a great distance. Gradually more life returned to his face and in a little while he spoke. Later, Mala was never able to remember exactly what either of them said in this first exchange, but afterwards Jord could weep for his friends' lives and his own loss, and Mala was able to comfort him. Meanwhile the dancing and feverish festivity went on, punctuated only by outbursts of grief. Looking back toward the entrance from her place near the center of the hall, Mala caught one more glimpse, between bodies, of the man in the tooled leather mask.

"All will be well yet, lass," Jord was able to say at last. "Gods, but it's good to have you here to hug!" And as Mala stood beside him he gripped her fiercely around the hips with a huge, one-armed blacksmith's hug. "I'm not yet destroyed. I've been thinking it out. I'll sell the smithy here and buy a mill elsewhere. There's one in Arin I can get . . . if I hire a helper or two, I can run a mill with one hand."

Mala said things expressing agreement, trying to sound encouraging. Closing her eyes, she hoped devoutly that it would be so. She told herself that when Jord healed he'd be a young man again, and he'd regain some part of his old strength. Being wed to a one-armed man would not be so bad if he were still a man of property . . . and now two small children, widower Jord's by his previous marriage, came out of the crowd to lean possessively against their father's legs, and distract Mala from her other cares by staring at her.

The hands of the small boy, Kenn, began to play absently with the rough cloth wrapping a long, thin object that stood leaning against his father's chair. Mala, without really giving it thought, had assumed this object was some kind of aid provided for the crippled man, a crutch or possibly a stretcher. Now that she really looked at the bundle she could see that it was certainly not long enough for either. Nor was there any obvious reason for a crutch or a stretcher to be wrapped up; nor, for that matter, did it appear that Jord would be likely to benefit from either one.

Jord saw what she was looking at. "My pay," he said. Gently he eased his son's small hands from the wrapped thing. "Not yours yet, Kenn. In time, in time. Not yours to have to worry about, Marian." And with a huge finger he brushed his tiny daughter's cheek. Then he grabbed the upper end of the bundle firmly in his large fist, and raised it in the air and shook it, so that the rough wrappings fell free except where his grip had caught them. People on all sides were turning to look. The blade was a full meter long, and straight as an arrow, with lightly fluted sides. Both edges keened down to perfect lines, invisibly sharp.

"What? Who? . . . " Mala could only stumble helplessly.

"Vulcan's own handiwork." Jord's voice was rough and bitter. "This is for me, and for my son after me. This is my pay."

Mala marveled silently. In the version of the story that she had heard in her own village, an obviously incomplete version, there had been nothing about a sword . . . Jord's pay? Even in the comparatively dim candlelight the steel had a polished look. Mala's keen eyes could pick out a fine, faint mottled patterning along the flat of the blade, a pattern that seemed to lead deep into the metal though the surface was flawlessly smooth.

The chain of dancers had slowed almost to a stop. Their faces wore a variety of expressions, but all were turned, like many in the crowd beyond, to look at the blade.

"My pay," said Jord again, in the same harsh voice, that carried through the sudden relative quiet. "So Vulcan told me, when he had taken off my arm." He shook the sword in his inexpert hand. "My arm, for this. So the god said. He called this 'Townsaver.'" The bitterness in Jord's voice was great, but still impersonal, the kind of anger a man might express against a thunderstorm that had destroyed his crops. His hand was beginning to quiver with his weakness now, and he lowered the sword and started trying to wrap it up again, a job in which he needed Mala's help.

"I must get something finer than this cloth to keep it in," he muttered.

Mala still didn't know what to say or think. The sword bewildered her, she couldn't guess what it might mean. Jord's pay, from Vulcan? Pay for what? Why should the god have wanted a man's right arm? And why a sword? What would a blacksmith, or any commoner, have to do with such a weapon?

She would have to discuss it all with Jord later, in detail. Now was not the time or place. Now the dance and the noise around them had picked up again, though at a lesser level of energy.

"Mala?" Jord's voice held a new and different note.

"Yes?"

"The dance will be ending soon. I must stay here, they're going to do some more healing spells and

ritual. But maybe you'd better be going along now."
Jord was lying back weakly in his chair, letting his
eyes close.

Mala understood. When a wake-dance like this one
ended, there usually followed a final phase of the
evening's community action: those mourners who were
free to do so would pair off, man with woman, youth
with girl, and go out into the fertile fields around the
house or village, there to lie coupled in the soil from
which the harvests came. Death would be, if not
mocked, in some sense negated by that other power,
just as old, of life-creation. Mala was still an unmarried
woman, still free, in a strict interpretation of the rules,
to join in the night's last ritual. But as her wedding
was only two days off, it would be unseemly for her to
do so with anyone but her betrothed. And Jord was
still oozing blood, barely able to sit up in his chair.

She said: "Yes, I'll be going. Tomorrow, Jord, I'll see
you then." Now she would have a long ride back to her
own village, or else she would have to try to find some
place in this village to stay the night. She didn't feel
confident about Jord's kinfolk here, how well they
liked her, how welcome she'd be made to feel in their
houses. Perhaps, except for the two small children,
they didn't even know yet that she'd arrived. In accord-
ance with custom, the marriage had been arranged by
family elders on both sides, and there had been no
long acquaintance between families.

Mala had liked Jord himself well enough from their
first meeting. She had raised no objection when the
match was made, and had no real objection to going
on with it now; in fact his maiming had roused in her
a fiercely increased attachment. But at the same
time . . .

The center of the hall, with its burden of dead and
wounded, seemed to her to stink of death and suffering and defeat. Mala gripped Jord once more, by his

hand and his good shoulder, and turned away from him. Other people who like Mala were unable or unwilling to stay, were also leaving now. She went out through the hide-hung doorway with a small group of these. The group thinned rapidly, and somehow by the time she reached the hitching rack she was alone in the dark street. She took hold of her beast's reins to untie them.

"It is not over," said the calm, soft voice of the masked man, quite near at hand.

Mala turned slowly. There were only the massed stars to see him by, with the moon behind a cloud. He was alone, too, holding one hand outstretched to Mala if she wished to take it. Around them other couples passed in the dark street, moving anonymously out toward the fields.

Almost nine months had passed before Mala saw the dark leather mask and its wearer again, and then only among the other images of a drugged dream. She was traveling with her husband Jord to another funeral (this for a man who'd undoubtedly been her most eminent kinsman, a minor priest in the Blue Temple), and she'd got as far as a large Temple of Ardneh, almost two hundred kilometers from the mill and home, before the first unmistakable labor pains had started.

This being her firstborn, Mala hadn't been able to interpret the advance signs properly. Still, she could hardly have arranged to be in a better location no matter how carefully she'd planned. The Temples of Ardneh were in general the best hospitals available on the entire continent—for most folk they were actually the only ones. Many of Ardneh's priests and priestesses were concerned with healing, accustomed to dealing with childbirth and its complications. They knew drugs, and some healing magic, and in some cases they even had access to certain surviving technology of the Old World, enough of it to make possible the arcane art of effective surgery.

It was near sunset when Mala's labor began in earnest. And at sunset music began to be heard in that Temple, music that as it happened was not greatly different from what had been played at that village funeral eight and a half months earlier. It may have been the similar drumbeat that helped to bring that masked face back in dreams. The drumbeat, and of course Mala's fervent but so far utterly secret suspicion that the father of her firstborn was not Jord but rather that man whose face she'd never seen without its mask. Over the past few months she'd tried to find out what she could about Duke Fraktin, but apart from confirming his reputation for occasional cruelty, for occasional excursions among the common people in disguise, for wealth, and for magical power, she knew very little more now than she had before.

Tonight, lying in an accouchement chamber halfway up the high pyramidal Temple, Mala was questioned, in her lucid intervals between pain and druggings, about her dreams. Jord had been sent dashing out on some make-work errand by the midwife-priestess, who now asked Mala with brisk professional interest—and some evident kindness, too—exactly what she had dreamed about when the last contractions came. The drugs and spells reacted with pain directly, turning it into dreams, some happy and some not.

Mala described the masked man to the priestess as well as she could, his stature, hair, dress, short sword, and mask, all without saying when or where or how she had encountered him in real life. She added: "I think . . . I'm not sure why, but I think it may be Duke Fraktin. He rules all the region where we live." And there was a secret pride in Mala's heart, a pride that perhaps became no longer secret in her voice.

"Ah, I suppose the dream is a good omen, then."
But the priestess sounded faintly amused.

"You don't think it was the Duke?" Mala was suddenly anxious.

"You know more about it than I do, dear. It was
your dream. It might have been the Emperor, for all I
know."

"Oh, no, he didn't look like that. Don't joke." Mala
paused there, her drugged mind working slowly. Everyone had heard of the Emperor, in jokes and anecdotes
and sayings; Mala had never seen him, to her knowledge, but she knew that he was supposed to wear a
clown's mask and not a gentleman's. When the priestess had mentioned that relic-title there had sprung
into Mala's mind all of the town-louts, all the loafing
practical jokers, that she had ever seen or known in
any village. And next she thought of a certain real
clown who for years had been appearing at fairs and
festivals with a sad, grotesque face painted over his
own features. Not that it had ever occurred to her that
any of those men might really be the Emperor. In the
anecdotes and jokes the Emperor was a very old man
who was forever arguing an absurd claim to rule a
vast domain, claiming tribute from barons and dukes,
grand dukes and tyrants, even kings and queens. In
some of the stories the Emperor was fond of pointless
riddles. (*And what if they had chosen not to follow
Vulcan's call*? echoed here, unpleasantly, in Mala's
spinning head.) And in some of the stories he played
practical jokes, some of which were appreciated as
clever, by those who liked such things. There was also
a proverbial sense, in which an illegitimate child of an
unknown father, or anyone whose luck had run out,
was spoken of as a child of the Emperor.

Mala had never had reason to consider the possibility of a real man still going about in the real world
bearing that title, let alone that he might conceivably

have . . . no, she was drugged, not thinking clearly. The
Duke—or whoever it had been—had been young, and
he had certainly not worn the Emperor's clown mask.

Through the hallucinatory haze that washed over
her with the beginning of her next contractions, Mala
could hear Jord coming back. Maybe, she thought,
hopefully now, Jord was after all the baby's father.
She couldn't see Jord very clearly, but she could hear
him, panting from his quick climb up the many Temple
steps, and sounding almost childishly proud of having
successfully located whatever it was that the priestess
had sent him after. And now Mala could feel his huge
hand, holding both of hers, while he started talking
worriedly to the priestess about how his first wife had
died trying to give birth to their third child. What
would Jord think now if he knew that it might have
been the Duke . . .

And then the dream, into which this latest set of
labor pangs had been transformed, took over firmly.
There was a shrill magical chanting in new voices, the
voices of invisible beings who were marching round
Mala's bed. Jord and the priestess and all other human
beings were gone, but Mala had no time to be concerned about that, because there were too many purely
delightful things to claim all of her attention, here in
the flower garden where she was lying now . . .

The chanting rose, but other voices, in unmusical
dispute, were intruding upon it, too loudly for any
music to have covered them up. They sounded angry,
as if the dispute was starting to get serious . . .

There were flowers heaped and scattered around
Mala on all sides, great masses of blooms, including
kinds that she had never seen or even imagined before,
prodigally disposed. She lay on her back on a—what
was it? a bed? a bier? a table?—and around her,
beyond the banks of flowers, the gods themselves were
furiously debating.

She was able to understand just enough of what they said to grasp the fact that some of the gods and goddesses were angry, unhappy with some of the things that Ardneh had been doing to help her—whatever those things were. From where Mala lay, she could see no more of Ardneh than his head and shoulders, but she could tell rom even this partial view that he was bigger than any of the other deities. The face of Ardneh, Demon-Slayer, Hospitaller, bearer of a thousand other names besides, was inhumanly broad and huge, and something about it made Mala think of mill-machinery, the largest and most complex mechanism with which she was at all familiar.

She thought that she could recognize some of the others in the debate also. Notably the Smith, by the great forge-hammer in his hand, and his singed leather clothes, and above all by his twisted leg. For Jord's sake, Mala feared and hated Vulcan. Of course at the moment she was too drugged to feel very much about anyone or anything. And anyway the Smith never bothered to look at her, though he was bitterly opposing Ardneh. The argument between the two factions of the gods went on, but to Mala's perception its details gradually grew even less clear.

And now it seemed to Mala that her babe had already been born, and that he lay before her already cleaned and diapered, his raw belly bound with a proper bandage. Ardneh's faction had prevailed, at least for the time being. The baby's blue eyes were open, his small perfect hands were reaching for Mala's breast. The masked figure of his father stood in the background, and said proudly: "My son, Mark." It was one of the names Mala had discussed with Jord, one that appeared already in both their families.

"When the time comes," said the voice of Ardneh now, blotting out all other sounds (and the tones of this voice reminded Mala somehow of the voice of her dead father), "When the time comes, your first-born son will take the sword. And you must let him go with it where he will."

"His name is Mark," said the figure of the masked man in the dream. "My mark is on him, and he is mine."

And Mala cried aloud, and awoke slowly from her drugged and enchanted dream, to be told that her first-born son was doing just fine.

CHAPTER 1

One day in the middle of his thirteenth summer, Mark came home from a morning's rabbit-hunting with his older brother Kenn to discover that visitors were in their village. To judge from their mounts, the visitors were unlike any that Mark had ever seen before.

Kenn, five years the older of the two, stopped so suddenly in the narrow riverside path that Mark, following lost in thought, almost ran into him. This was just at the place where the path came out of the wild growth on the steep riverbank, and turned into the beginning of the village's single street. From this point it was possible to see the four strange riding-beasts, two of them armored in chainmail like cavalry steeds, the other two caparisoned in rich cloth. All four were hitched to the community rack that stood in front of the house of the chief elder of the village. That hitching-

25

rack was still an arrowshot away; the street of Arin-on-Aldan was longer than streets usually were in small villages, because here the town was strung out narrowly along one bank of a river.

"Look," said Mark, unnecessarily.

"I wonder who they are," said Kenn, and caught his lower lip between his teeth. That was a thing he did when he was nervous. Today had not been a good day for Kenn, so far. There were no arrows left in the quiver on his back, and only one middle-sized rabbit in the gamebag at his side. And now, this discovery of highborn visitors. The last time the brothers had come home from hunting to find the mount of an important personage tied up at the elder's rack, it had been Sir Sharfa who was visiting. The knight had come down from the manor to investigate a report that Kenn and Mark had been seen poaching, or trying to poach, in his game preserves. There were treasures living in there, hybrid beasts, meant perhaps as someday presents for the Duke, exotic creatures whose death could well mean death for any commoner who'd killed them. In the end, Sir Sharfa hadn't believed the false, anonymous charges, but it had been a scare.

Mark at twelve was somewhat taller than the average for his age, though as yet he'd attained nothing like Kenn's gangling height. If Mark bore no striking resemblance to Jord, the man he called his father, still there was—to his mother's secret and intense relief—no notable dissimilarity either. Mark's face was still child-round, his body form still childishly indeterminate. His eyes were bluish gray, his hair straight and fair, though it had begun a gradual darkening, into what promised to be dark brown by the time that he was fully grown.

"Not anyone from the manor this time," said Kenn, looking more carefully at the accoutrements of the four animals. Somewhat reassured, he moved forward into the open village street, taking an increasing interest in the novelty.

"Sir Sharfa's elsewhere anyway," put in Mark, tagging along. "They say he's traveling on some business for the Duke." The villagers might not see their manorlord Sir Sharfa more than once or twice a year, or the Duke in a lifetime. But still for the most part they kept up with current events, at least those in which their lives and fortunes were likely to be put at risk.

The first house in the village, here at the western end of the street, was that of Falkener the leatherworker. Falkener had no liking for Jord the miller or any of his family—some old dispute had turned almost into a feud—and Mark suspected him of being the one who'd gone to Sir Sharfa with a false charge of poaching. Falkener was now at work inside his half-open front door, and glanced up as the two boys passed; if he had yet learned anything of what the visitors' presence meant, his expression offered no information on the subject. Mark looked away.

As the boys slowly approached the hitching rack, they came into full view of the Elder Kyril's house. Flanking its front door like a pair of sentries stood two armed men, strangers to the village. The guards, looking back at the young rabbit-hunters, wore wooden expressions, tinged faintly with disdain. They were hard, tough-looking men, both mustached, and with their hair tied up in an alien style. Both wore shirts of light chain mail, and emblems of the Duke's colors of blue and white. The two were very similar, though one was tall and the other short, the skin of one almost tar black and that of the other fair.

As Mark and Kenn were still approaching, the Elder's door opened, and three more men came out, engaged in quiet but urgent talk among themselves. One of the men was Kyril. The two with him were expensively and exotically dressed, and they radiated an importance the like of which Mark in his young life had never seen before.

"Ibn Gauthier." Kenn whispered the name very softly. The two brothers were walking very slowly now, their soft-booted feet dragging in the summer dust as they passed the Elder's house at a distance of some twenty meters. "The Duke's cousin. He's seneschal of the castle, too."

Seneschal was a new word to Mark—he'd never heard it come up in the village current-events gossip—but if Kenn was impressed by it, he was impressed also.

The third man in the little group, a graybeard like the Elder, wore blue robes. "And a wizard," added Kenn, his whisper falling almost to inaudibility.

A *real* wizard? thought Mark. He wasn't at all sure that Kenn would know a real wizard if he saw one . . . but what actually impressed Mark at the moment was the behavior of the Elder Kyril. The Elder was actually being obsequious to his visitors, acting the same way some poor landless serf might when brought in to stand before the Elder. Mark had never seen the old man behave in such a way before. Even during Sir Sharfa's periodic visits, the knight, who was actually the master, always spoke to the old man with respect, and listened to him carefully whenever village affairs were under discussion. Today's visitors were listening carefully too—Mark could see that though he couldn't hear what was being said—but gave no evidence that they regarded the Elder with respect.

The Elder's eye now happened to fall upon the two boys who were gaping their slow way past his house. He frowned abruptly, and called to Kenn by name, at the same time beckoning him with a brisk little wave; it was a more agitated motion than Mark could remember ever seeing the Elder make before.

When Kenn stood close before him, gaping in wonder, Kyril ordered: "Go, and take down that sword that hangs always on your father's wall, and bring it directly here." When Kenn, still goggling, hesitated momentarily, the old man snapped: "Go! Our visitors are waiting."

To such a command, there could be only one possible response from any village youth. Kenn at once went pelting away down the long village street toward the millhouse at its far end. His legs, long and fast if lacking grace, were a blur of awkward angularity. Mark, poised to run after him, held back, knowing from experience that he wouldn't be able to keep up. And Mark also wanted to stay here, watching, to see what was going to happen next; and, now that he thought about it, he didn't want to have any part in simply taking down the sword, without his father's permission, from where it had always hung . . .

The three men of importance waited, gazing after Kenn, ignoring Mark who still stood twenty meters off and watched them. The blue-robed wizard—if wizard he truly was—figeted, glanced once toward Mark with a slight frown, and then away.

Kyril said, in a voice a little louder than before: "It will be quicker this way, Your Honor, than if we were all to go to the mill-house." And he made a humble, nervous little bow to the one Kenn had whispered was the Duke's cousin. It was a stiff motion, one to which the Elder's joints could hardly have been accustomed.

Now Mark began to notice that a few other villagers, Falkener among them, had started coming out of their houses here and there. There was a converging movement, very slight as yet, toward the Elder's house. They all wanted to know what was going on, but still were not quite willing to establish their presence in the street.

The man addressed by Kyril, whoever he might really be, ignored them as he might have sparrows. He

stood posing in a way that suggested he was willing to
wait a little, willing to be shown that the Elder's way
was really the quickest and most satisfactory. He asked
Kyril: "You say that this man who has the sword now
came here thirteen years ago. Where did he come
from?"

"Oh yes, that's right, Your Honor. Thirteen years. It
was then that he bought the mill. I'm sure he had
permission, all in order, for the move. He brought
children with him, and a new bride, and he came from
a village up toward the mountains." Kyril pointed to
the east. "Yes sir, from up there."

The seneschal, who was about to ask another
question, paused. For Kenn was coming back already.
He was carrying the sword in its usual corded wrapping,
in which it usually hung on the wall of the main living
room inside the house. Kenn was walking now, not
running. And he was not coming back alone. Jord, his
solid frame taller still than that of his slim-bodied
elder son, strode with him. Jord's legs kept up in a
firm pace with the youth's nervous half-trot.

Jord's work clothes were dusty, as they so often
were from his usual routine of maintenance on the
huge wooden gears and shafts that formed the central
machinery of the mill. He glanced once at Mark—Mark
could read no particular message in the look—and
then concentrated his attention on the important
visitors. Jord seemed reluctant to approach them, but
still he came on with determination. At the last moment
he put his big hand on Kenn's shoulder and thrust the
youth gently into the background, stepping forward to
face the important men himself.

Jord bowed to the visitors, as courtesy required. But
still it was to Kyril the Elder that he first spoke.
"Where's Sir Sharfa? It's to him that we in the village
must answer, for whatever we do when other highborn folk come here and—"

He who had been called the seneschal interrupted, effectively though with perfect calm. "Sir Sharfa's not available just now, fellow. Your loyalty to your manorlord is commendable, but in this case misplaced. Sir Sharfa is vassal, as you ought to know, to my cousin the Duke. And it's Duke Fraktin who wants to see the sword that you've kept hanging on the wall."

Jord did not appear tremendously surprised to hear of the Duke's interest. "I have been told, Your Honor, to keep that sword with me. Until the time comes for it to be passed on to my eldest son."

"Oh? Told? And who told you that?"

"Vulcan, Your Honor." The words were plainly and boldly spoken. Jord's calm assurance matched that of the man who was interrogating him.

The seneschal paused; whatever words he'd been intending to fire off next were never said. Still he was not going to let himself appear to be impressed by any answer that a mere miller could return to him. Now Ibn Gauthier extended one arm, hand open, rich sleeve hanging deeply, toward Kenn. The youth was still standing in the background where his father had steered him, and was still holding the wrapped blade.

The seneschal said to him: "We'll see it now."

Kenn glanced nervously toward his father. Jord must have signalled him to obey, for the lad tugged at the wrapping of the sword—a neatly woven but undistinguished blanket—as if he intended to display the treasure to the visitors from a safe distance.

The covering of the sword fell free.

The seneschal stared for a moment, then snapped his fingers. "Give it here!"

What happened in the next moment would recur in Mark's dreams throughout the remainder of his life. And each time the dream came he would experience again this last moment of his childhood, a moment in which he thought: Strange, whatever can be making a sound in the air like flying arrows?

The Elder Kyril went down at once, with the feathered end of a long shaft protruding from his chest. At the same time one of the armed guards fell, arrows in his back and ribs, his sword only a glint of steel half-drawn from its scabbard. The second guard was hit in the thigh; he got his spear raised but could do no more. The wizard went down an instant later, with his blue robes collapsing around him like an unstrung tent. The seneschal, uninjured, whirled around, drawing his own short sword and getting his back against a wall. His face had gone a pasty white.

The volley of arrows had come from Mark's right, the direction where trees and bush grew close and thick along the near bank of the Aldan. The ambushers, whoever they were, had been able to get within easy bowshot without being detected. But they were charging out of cover now, running between and around the houses closest to the riverbank. A half-dozen howling, weapon-waving men were rushing hard toward the Elder's front yard, where the victims of their volley had just fallen. Two large warbeasts sprang out of concealment just after the attacking men, but bounded easily ahead of them. One beast was orange-furred and one brindled, and both of their bodies, like those of fighting men, were partially clothed in mail. They were nearly as graceful as the cats from which half their ancestry derived.

Mark had never seen real warbeasts before, but he recognized them at once, from the descriptions in a hundred stories. He saw his father knocked down by the orange beast in its terrible passage, before Jord had had time to do more than turn toward his elder son as if to cry an order or a warning.

The seneschal was the beasts' real target, and they leaped at him, though not to kill; they must have been well trained for this action. They forced the Duke's cousin back against the front of fallen Kyril's house, not touching but confronting him, snarling and sparring just outside the tentative arc of his swordarm. When he would have run to reach his tethered riding-beast, they forced him back again. Now all four of the tethered animals at the rack were kicking and bucking, screaming their fear and excitement in their near-human voices.

Kenn, in the first instant of the attack, had turned to run. Then he had seen his father fall, and had turned back. White-faced, he stood over his father now, clumsily holding the unwrapped sword, with the blade above the fallen man as if it could be made into a shield.

Mark, who had run two steps toward home, looked back at his father and his brother and stopped. Now with shaking fingers Mark was pulling the next-to-last small hunting arrow from the quiver on his back. His rabbit-hunting bow was in his left hand. His mind felt totally blank. He comprehended without emotion that a man, the soldier who'd fallen with an arrow in his leg, was being stabbed to death before his eyes. Now the charging men, bandits or whatever they were, had joined their warbeasts in a semicircle round the beleaguered' seneschal, and were calling on him to throw down his sword and surrender.

But one of the attackers' number had turned aside from this important business, and was about to deal with the yokel who still stood holding a sword. The bandit grinned, probably at the inept way in which Kenn's hands gripped the weapon; still grinning, he stepped forward with his short spear ready for a thrust.

At that point Mark's shaking fingers fumbled away the arrow that he had just nocked. He knelt, in an uncontrolled movement that was almost a collapse, and with his right hand groped in the dust of the road for the arrow. He was unable to take his eyes from what was about to happen to his brother—

A moaning had for some moments been growing in the air, the sound of some voice that was not human, perhaps not even alive. The sound rose, quickly, into a querulous, unbreathing shriek.

It issued, Mark realized, from the sword held in his brother's hands. And a visual phenomenon had grown in the air around the sword. It was not exactly as if the blade were smoking, but rather as if the air around it had begun to burn, and the steel was drawing threads of smoke out of the air into itself.

The spearthrust came. The sound in the air abruptly swelled as the spear entered the swifter blur made by the sideways parry of the sword. Mark saw the spearhead spinning in midair, along with a handsbreadth of cleanly severed shaft. And before the spearhead fell, Townsaver's backhanded passage from the parry had torn loose the chainmail from the spearman's chest, bursting fine steel links into the air like a handful of summer flowers' fluff. The same sweep of the sword-point caught the small shield strapped to the man's left arm, and with a bonebreak snap dragged him crying into the air behind its arc. His body was dropped rolling in the dust.

Now Mark's groping fingers found his dropped arrow, and he rose with it in his hand. He could feel his own body moving with what seemed to him terrible slowness.

Townsaver had come smoothly back to guard position, the sound that issued from it subsiding to a mere purring drone. Kenn's face was anguished, his eyes were fixed in astonishment on the blade that grew out of his hands, as if it were something that he had never seen before. There was a vibration in his arms, as if he were holding something that he could not control, but could not or dared not drop.

One of the invaders, who must have been the warbeasts' master, aimed a gesture toward Kenn. Obediently the orange-furred beast turned and sprang. At that moment Mark loosed his arrow. Mark had not yet learned to reckon with the animals' speed, and the streaking furry form was out of the arrow's path before the small missile arrived. As if guided by some profound curse, Mark's arrow flew straight on between two bandits' backs, to strike the embattled seneschal squarely in the throat. Without even a cry, the Duke's cousin let go of his sword and fell.

The sword in Kenn's hands screamed, almost the way a fast-geared millsaw screamed sometimes when biting a tough log. Again it drew its smoking arc, to meet the leaping animal. One orange-furred paw leapt severed in midair, with a fine spray of blood. The same stroke caught the beast's armored torso, heavier than a man's. It went down, as Mark had seen a rabbit fall when hit in mid-leap by a slinger's stone. Mark was fumbling for his last arrow as the furred body rolled on its back with legs in the air, claws in reflex convulsions taloning the air above its belly.

Now three men had Kenn surrounded. Mark, with his last arrow nocked, was at the last moment afraid to shoot at any of them for fear of hitting his brother in their midst. He saw blades flash toward his brother, but Kenn did not fall. Kenn's eyes were still wide with bewilderment, his face a study of fear and horror. Townsaver sang vicious circles in the air around him, smashing aside brandished weapons right and left. The sword seemed to twist Kenn's body after it, so that he had to leap, turning in midair, coming down with feet planted in the reverse direction. The sword pulled him forward, dragging him in wide-stanced, stiff-legged strides to the attack.

The sound of its screaming went up and up.

The swordplay was much too fast for Mark to follow.

He saw another of the attacking men go staggering backward from the fight, the man's feet moving in a reflex effort to regain balance until his back struck a house wall and he pitched forward and lay still. Mark heard yet another man cry out, a gurgling yell for help and mercy. Mark did not see the brindled warbeast leap at Kenn, but saw the beast go running back toward the riverbank, in a limping but still terribly fast flight. It howled the agony of its wounds, even above the fretful millsaw shrieking of the sword. And now two of the invading men, weaponless, were also running away, leaving the village on divergent paths. Mark got a close look at the face of one of them, and saw wide eyes, wide mouth, an expression intent on flight as on a problem.

The other invaders were all lying in the street. Four, five—it seemed impossible to count exactly.

Mark looked up and down the street, to west and east. Only himself and his brother were still standing.

A little summer dust hung in the air, played by a quiet breeze. For a long moment, nothing else moved. Then Kenn's quivering arms began to droop, lowering the sword. The machine-whine that still proceeded from the red blade trailed slowly down into silence. And now the atmosphere around the sword no longer smoked.

The swordpoint sagged to the ground. A moment later, the whole weapon fell inertly from Kenn's relaxing fingers. Another moment, and Kenn sat down in the dust. Mark could see, now, how his brother's blood was soaking out into his homespun shirt.

Mechanically replacing his last arrow, unused, in his quiver, Mark hurried forward to his brother. Beyond Kenn, Jord still lay in gory stillness; his head looked badly ruined by the passing blow from a warbeast's paw; Mark did not want to comprehend just what he was seeing there.

Farther in the background, the blue-robed wizard was raising himself, apparently unhurt. In each hand the wizard held a small object, things of magic doubtless. His hands moved round his body, wiping at the air.

Mark crouched beside his brother and held him, not knowing what else to do. He watched helplessly as the blood welled out from under Kenn's slashed clothing. The attackers' swords had reached him after all, and more than once. Kenn's hunting shirt was ghastly now.

"Mark." Kenn's voice was lost, soft, frightened, and frightening too. "I'm hurt."

"Father!" Mark cried, calling for help. It seemed to him impossible that his father would not react, leap up, give him aid, tell him what to do. Maybe he, Mark, should run home, get help from his mother and his sister. But he couldn't just let go of Kenn, whose hand was trying to grip Mark's arm.

In front of Kenn, almost within touching distance, a dead bandit crouched as if in obeisance to his superior foe. Townsaver had taken a part of the bandit's face away, and his hands and his weapons were piled together before him like an offering. It did no good to look away. There was something very similar to be seen in every direction.

The sword itself lay in the street, looking no more dangerous now than a pruning hook, with dust blandly blotting the wet redness all along the blade.

Mark let out an inarticulate cry for help, from anyone, anywhere. He could feel Kenn's life departing, running out almost like water between his fingers.

Women were crying, somewhere in the distance.

Someone, walking slowly, came into Mark's view a little way ahead of him. It was Falkener. "You shot the seneschal," the leather-worker said. "I saw you."

"What?" For a moment Mark could not understand

what the man was saying. And now the wizard, who had been bending over the body of Ibn Gauthier, came doddering, as if in fear or weakness (though graybeard, he did not look particularly old) to where Mark was. The small objects he had been handling, whatever they were, had now been put away. With what appeared to Mark to be unnatural calm, he rested a hand on Jord's bloody head and muttered something, then reached to do the same for Elder Kyril and for Kenn. His manner was quite impersonal.

The women's crying voices were now speeding closer, with the sound of their running feet. Mark had not known that his mother could still run so fast. Mala and Marian, both of them dusty with mill-work, threw themselves upon him, hovered over their fallen men, began to examine the terrible damage.

"You shot the seneschal," said Falkener to Mark again.

This time, the hovering wizard took note of the accusation. With an oath, he grabbed the last arrow from Mark's quiver and strode away, to compare it with the shaft that still protruded from the throat of the Duke's cousin.

Other villagers were now appearing in the street, to gather around the fallen. They came out of their houses singly at first, then in twos and threes. Some, with field implements in hand, must have come running in from work nearby. The Elder was dead, the village leaderless. An uproar grew, confusion mounted. There was talk of dashing off to the manor with word of the attack, but no one actually went yet. There was more talk of organizing a militia pursuit of the attackers, whoever they had been, wherever they had gone. Wild talk of war, of raids, of uprisings, flew back and forth.

"Yes, they were trying to kidnap the seneschal. I saw them. I heard them."

"Who? Kidnap who?"

"Kyril's dead too. And Jord."

"But it was the boy's arrow that struck him down."

"Who, his own father? Nonsense!"

" . . . no . . . "

" . . . all wrong, havoc like this, must have been cavalry . . . "

" . . . no doubt that it's his arrow, I've found them on my land, near my woolbeasts . . . "

Mala and Marian had by now stripped off Kenn's shirt and were trying to bind up his wounds. It looked a hopeless task. Kenn's eyes were almost closed, only white slits of eyeball showing. Mala went to Jord's inert form, and with tears streaming from her eyes tried to get her husband to react, to wake up to what was happening around him. "Husband, your oldest son is dying. Husband, wake up . . . Jord . . . ah, Ardneh! Not you too?"

A neighbor woman hovered over Mala, trying to help. Together they put a rolled blanket under Jord's head, as if that might be of benefit.

Mark turned from them, and sat staring at the sword. Something less terrible to look at. It was as if thoughts were coming and going in his head continually, but he could not grasp any of them. Only look at the sword. Only look—

He became aware that his mother was gripping his arm fiercely, shaking him out of his state of shock. In a voice that was low but had a terrible power she was urging him: "Son, listen to me. You must run away. Run fast and far, and don't tell me, don't tell anyone, where you're going. Stay out of sight, tell no one your name, and listen for word of what's happening here in Arin. Don't think about coming home until you know it's safe. That's your arrow in the Duke's cousin's throat, however it got there. If the Duke should get his hands on you, he could have your eyes put out, or worse."

"But . . ." Mark's mind wanted to protest, to scream that none of this could be happening, that the world was not this mad. His body, perhaps, knew better, for he was already standing. His mother's dark eyes probed him. His sister Marian looked up at him from where she still crouched with Kenn's lifeless head cradled in her lap, her blue horrified eyes framed in her loose fair hair. All around, villagers were arguing, quarreling, in greater confusion than ever. Falkener's hoarse voice came and went, and the wizard's unfamiliar one.

Impelled by a sudden sense of urgency, Mark moved swiftly. As if he were watching his own movements from outside his body, he saw himself bend and gather up the sword's wrapping from where Kenn had thrown it down. He threw the blanket over the sword and gathered the blade up into it.

Of all the people in the street, only his mother and his sister seemed to be aware of what he was doing. Mala, weeping, nodded her approval. Marian whispered to him: "Walk as far as our house, then run. Go, we'll be all right!"

Mark muttered something to them both, he never could remember what, and started walking. He knew, everyone in the village knew, what Duke Fraktin had done in the past to men who'd been so unlucky as to injure any of his kinfolk, even by accident. Mark continued to move pace after pace along the once-familiar village street, the street that now could never be the same again, carrying what he hoped was an inconspicuous bundle. He walked without looking back. For whatever reason, there was no outcry after him.

When he reached the millhouse, instead of starting to run he turned inside. The practical thought had occurred to him that if he ran away for very long he was going to need some food. In the pantry he picked up a little dried meat, dried fruit, and a small loaf, unconsciously emptying his game bag of the morning's kill of rabbits in exchange. From near his bed he grabbed up also the few spare arrows that were his. Somehow, he'd remembered, out in the street, to sling his bow across his back again.

A few moments after he had entered the millhouse, Mark was leaving it again, this time by the back door. This was on the eastern, upstream side of the building, and now the mill was between him and the village street. From this point a path climbed the artificial bank beside the millwheel, which was now standing idle, and then followed the wooded riverbank out of town. Mark met no one on the first few meters of this path. If earlier there had been people fishing here, or village children playing along the stream, the excitement in the street had already drawn them away.

Now Mark did begin to run. But as soon as he started running, he could feel fear growing in him, an imagined certainty of pursuit, and to conquer it he had to slow down to a walk again. When he walked, listening carefully, he could hear no sounds of pursuit, no outcry coming after him.

He had followed the familiar path upstream for half a kilometer when he came upon the dead body of the brindled warbeast. It had plainly been trying to crawl into a thicket when it died, caught and held by the ragged fringes of its hacked chainmail snagged on twigs. Mark paused, staring blankly. The animal was a female . . . or had been, before the fight. Now . . . how had the creature managed to get this far? It looked like an example of the vengeance of a god.

CHAPTER 2

From the place where he had come upon the dead warbeast, Mark walked steadily upstream. He traveled the riverbank in that direction for another hour, still without meeting anyone. By that time he was feeling acutely conscious of the blood dried on his clothing and his hands, and he stopped, long enough to wash himself, his garments, and at last the sword as clean as possible. The washing had limited success, for by now spots of his brother's blood had dried into his shirt, and there was no getting them out by simply rubbing at them and rinsing them with water. The sword in contrast rinsed clean at once, dirt and gore sluicing from it easily, leaving the smooth steel gleaming as if it had never been used. Nor, despite all the shredded chainmail and the cloven shields, were its edges nicked or dulled.

Yes, Mark had known all his life that the sword called Townsaver was the work of Vulcan himself. He'd known that fact, but was only now starting to grasp something of its full meaning. But maybe the sword would rust . . .

Dressed again, in wet clothes, Mark hurried on. He had made no conscious decision about where he was going. The path was so familiar that his feet bore him along it automatically. He kept putting more distance between himself and his home without having to plan a route. From hunting and fishing trips he knew the way so well here that he thought he'd be able to keep on going confidently even after dark. At intervals he waded into the shallow stream, crossing and recrossing it, sometimes trudging in the water for long stretches. If the Duke's men were going to come after him with keen-nosed tracking beasts, it might help . . .

He feared pursuit, and listened for it constantly. But when he tried to picture in his mind exactly what form it would take, it looked in his imagination rather like the militia that Kenn had had to join and drill with periodically. That was not a very terrifying picture. But of course the pursuit wouldn't really be like that. It might include tracking beasts, and aerial scouts, and cavalry, and warbeasts too . . . again Mark saw, with the vividness of recent memory, the mangled body of the catlike creature that had tried like some hurt pet to crawl away and hide . . .

His thoughts never could get far from the burden that he was carrying, the awkward bundle tucked at this moment under his right arm, wrapped up in a blanket newly stained. Townsaver, let the gods name it whatever they liked, hadn't really saved the town at all. Because it was not the town that the intruders had been trying to attack. They had been after the eminent visitor, and nothing else. (And here Mark wondered again just what a *seneschal* might be.)

Mark supposed that the intruders had been bandits, planning a kidnapping for ransom—everyone knew that such things happened to the wealthy from time to time. Of course as a rule they didn't happen to members of the Duke's family. But perhaps the bandits hadn't known just who their intended victim was, they'd seen only that he must be rich.

And the victim had come to the village in the first place only because of the sword itself; that was what he had wanted to see and hold, what he would probably have taken away with him if he could. If only he had . . .

The killing of Jord and of Kyril had probably been completely accidental, just because they'd been standing in the bandits' way. And the bandits had attacked Kenn only because he was holding the sword, and had gone on holding it. Mark, struggling now against tears, recalled how his brother had looked like he wanted to throw the weapon down, and couldn't. The sword had taken over, and once that happened there had been nothing that Kenn could do about it.

So, if the sword hadn't entered into it, Mark's brother and father would both be still alive. And the Elder Kyril too. And probably even the Duke's cousin would be alive and well cared for in his abductors' hands, to be sent home as soon as a ransom was paid—or, perhaps more likely, released with abject apologies as soon as the kidnappers found out who he was. Yes, the sword had destroyed warbeasts and bandits. But it had also brought ruin upon the very town and people that its name suggested it might have saved . . .

On top of all the other deeper and more terrible problems that it caused, it was also a damned awkward thing to carry. And the more time that Mark spent carrying it, the more maddening this comparatively minor difficulty became. He continually tried to find a safe and comfortable way to hold the thing while he walked with it. In a way his mind welcomed this challenge, as an escape from the consideration of difficulties infinitely worse.

After he washed the sword he tried for a little while carrying it unwrapped, but that quickly became uncomfortable too. The only halfway reasonable way to carry a naked sword, particularly one as keen-edged as this, was in hand, as if you were ready to fight with it. Mark wasn't ready to fight, and didn't want to pretend he was. More importantly, the weight borne that way soon made his wrist and fingers ache.

Careful testing assured him that the edges were still sharper than those of any other blade, knife or razor that he'd ever held; if he were to try to carry this weapon stuck through his belt, his pants would soon be down around his ankles. And, to Mark's vague, unreasonable disappointment, it was soon obvious that the sword was not going to rust because of its immersion in the river. The brilliant steel dried quickly, and in fact to Mark's fingertip felt very slightly oily. With a mixture of despair and admiration he stared at the finely mottled pattern that seemed to lead on deeper and deeper into the metal, under the shiny surface smoothness.

Before he'd walked very far after the washing, he had paused to rewrap the sword in the still-wet cloth, and tied it up again, leaving a loop of cord for a carrying handle. Mark slogged on, shifting his burden this way and that. If he hung it from one hand, it banged against his legs; if he put it over one shoulder like a shovel, he could feel it threatening to cut him, right through its wrapping and his shirt. Of course, with the sword tied up like this, he wouldn't be able to use it quickly if he had to. That really didn't bother Mark. He didn't want to try to use it anyway.

Mark kept fighting against the memory of how Kenn had used the sword—or how it had used Kenn, who was as innocent as Mark of any training with such a weapon. In the militia exercises, Kenn had always practiced with the lowly infantry weapon, a cheap spear. Swords of even the most ordinary kind, let alone a miraculous blade like this one, were for the folk who lived in manorhouse and castle.

And yet . . . this one had certainly been given to Mark's father. Given deliberately, by a being who was surely of higher rank than any merely human lord.

Gods and goddesses were . . . well, what were they? It struck Mark forcibly now that he'd never met anyone but his own father who'd claimed convincingly to have any such direct contact with any deity.

Nor, it occurred to Mark now, could he remember meeting anyone who had sincerely envied Jord his treasure, considering the price that Mark's father had had to pay for it.

All this and much more kept churning uncontrollably through Mark's mind as he trudged the riverbank and waded in the stream, meanwhile listening for pursuers. From the time of Mark's earliest understanding, the sword, and the way his father had acquired it, had been among the given facts of life for him. Never until today had he been confronted with the full marvel and mystery of those facts. Always the sword, with its story, had simply hung there on the wall, like a candle-sconce or a common dish, until everyone who lived in the house had grown so used to it that it had almost been forgotten. Visitors asking about the odd bundle had received a matter-of-fact answer, one they'd perhaps not always believed. And the visitors' repetitions of the story elsewhere, Mark supposed now, had probably been believed even less often.

And Vulcan had said it was called Townsaver . . . thinking again of the town's saving, Mark had to fight back tears again. Now, as in some evil dream or story, the cursed burden of the sword had revealed itself for

the curse it truly was, and now it had come down to
him. He was the heir, the only surviving son, now that
Kenn was dead . . . he knew that Kenn was dead. The
sword was Mark's now, and Mark had to run with it,
to at least get the burden of it away from his mother
and his sister.

Mark didn't want to let himself think just yet about
where he might be running to.

His eyes were blurred with tears again. That was
bad, because now it was starting to get dark anyway,
and he was very tired, so tired that his feet were
dragging and stumbling at best, even when he could
see clearly where to put them down.

Mark stopped for a rest in a small clearing, a few
steps from the main riverbank path. Here he ate most
of the food that he'd brought along, and then went to
get a drink from the brisk rapids nearby. Already he'd
come far enough upstream to start encountering rapids,
a fact that made Mark feel even more tired. He went
back to his small clearing and sat down again. He was
simply too weary to go on any farther, at least not until
he'd had a little rest . . .

Mark woke with a start, to early sunlight mottling
its way through leaves to reach his face. At once he
started to call Kenn's name, and to look around him
for his brother, because he'd wakened with the half-
formed idea that he must have come out with Kenn on
some kind of hunting or fishing expedition. But reality
returned as soon as Mark's eyes fell on the sword,
which lay beside him in its evilly stained wrapping.
He jumped up then, a stiff-muscled movement that
startled nearby birds. When the birds had quieted
there was nothing to be heard but the murmur of the
rapids. There were no indications of pursuit as yet.

Mark finished off what little food he had left, and
too another long drink from the stream. About to push

on again, he hesitated, and, without quite knowing why, once more unwrapped the blade. Some part of his mind wanted to look at it again, as if the morning sunlight on the sword might reveal something to negate or at least explain the horror of yesterday.

There was still no trace of rust to be seen, and the sword and its wrappings were now completely dry. How should he try to carry the thing today? When Mark stood the weapon upright on the path, point down, and stood himself beside it, the sword's pommel reached as high as his ribcage. The weapon was just too long for him to carry about handily, and far too sharp . . . Mark was momentarily distracted when he looked at the decorations going round the hilt and handle, white on black. He could remember sleepy evenings at home, in the dwelling-rooms beside the creaking mill, when Jord had sometimes allowed the children to take the sword down from the wall and in his presence look it over. Sometimes the children and their mother, interested also, had speculated on what the pattern of the decorations might mean. Mark's father had never speculated. He'd never spoken much about the sword at all, even at those relaxed times. Nor had Jord ever, not in Mark's hearing anyway, said anything directly about the great trial through which the sword had come to him. Nothing about how Vulcan had taken his right arm off, or with what implement, or what explanation, if any, the god had given for what he did. That was one scene that Mark had always forbidden his own imagination to attempt.

The inlaid decoration, white on black, going round the handle of the sword, had always suggested to Mark a crenelated castle wall seen from the outside. Or perhaps it was the wall of a fortified town. Mark had heard of cities and big towns that boasted defensive walls like that, though he'd never come very close to seeing one. Castles of course were a different matter.

Everyone saw at least one of those, at least once in a while.

There was the name, of course: Townsaver. And, in one spot on the handle, just above the depicted wall, there was a small representation of what might very well be intended as a swordblade. It looked as if some unseen hand inside the town or castle were brandishing a sword . . .

Mark came to himself with a small start. How long had he been standing here on the pathway gazing at the thing? Even if this weapon was the magical handiwork of a god, he couldn't afford to spend all day gawping at it. Hurriedly he performed his simple packing-up, and once more got moving upstream.

Several times during the morning's travel that followed, the unhandy burden threatened to unbalance Mark's steps when he was wading. And it kept snagging itself by cloth or cord on bushes beside the path. That morning, for the first time, the idea suggested itself to Mark that he might be able to rid himself of the sword and not have to carry it any farther. He could find a deep pool somewhere in which to drown it, or else hide it in a crevice behind a waterfall—by now he'd come upstream far enough for waterfalls. The idea was tempting, in a way. But Mark soon rejected it. Disposing of this sword would not, could not, be as easy as throwing away a broken knife. He did not know yet, perhaps would not yet allow himself to know, what he meant to do with it finally. But he did know that something more than simply discarding it was required of him. Besides, he'd seen often enough the successful working of finding-spells, the minor enchantments of a local part-time wizard. If that country fellow could locate wedding rings down wells, and pull lost coins out of haystacks, what chance would Mark have of hiding a great sword like this one from the real wizards that the Duke must be able to command.

Toward midday, Mark cautiously moved out of the riverbank thickets, and entered high empty pasture land for long enough to stalk and kill a rabbit. He felt proud of the efficiency of this hunt, for which he needed only one clean shot. But as he released the bowstring he saw for one frightening moment the falling seneschal . . .

The food, familiar hunter's fare cooked on a small fire, helped a great deal. It strengthened Mark against the pointless tricks of his shocked imagination, against struggling in his mind with events over which he now could have no control. He told himself firmly that he should instead be consciously deciding where he was going to go.

But he had still reached no such decision when he finished his meal, put out his little fire, and moved on. He knew that if he continued to follow the river upstream for another full day, he'd be quite close to the village in which his father had grown up . . . the place where Jord had worked as a two-armed blacksmith, and from which he'd been summoned one dark night by a god, to trade his right arm for this cursed weapon. Mark felt sure that village was not where he was really headed now.

All right, he'd wait to think things out. He'd just keep going. When plans were really needed, they'd just have to make themselves.

As the sky began to darken with the second nightfall of Mark's journey, he looked up through the screen of riverbank trees to see the glow of sunset reflected on the slowly approaching mountains. Those mountains were near enough now to let him see how steep and forbidding their slopes were—especially up near the top, up there where gods and goddesses, or some of them anyway, were said to dwell. The darkness of the

sky deepened, and the pink glow faded from even the
highest peaks. Then Mark saw what he'd seen only a
time or two before in all his life: sullen, glowing red
spots near the summits, what folk called Vulcan's
fires. Those fires as he saw them now were still so far
away as to be part of another world.

When it was fully dark, Mark burrowed into a thicket,
and contrived for himself a kind of nest to sleep in. For
a moment that evening, just as he was dozing off, he
thought that he heard his father's voice, calling to
him, with some urgent message . . .

Throughout the next day, Mark continued as before
to work his way upstream. The way grew steeper, the
going slower, the land rockier and rougher, the country
wilder, trees scarce and people even more so. On that
day, though he peered more boldly than before out of
the riverside thickets, Mark only once saw distant
workers in a field, and no one else except a single
fisherman. He was able to spot the fisherman in time
to detour round him without letting the man suspect
that anyone else was near.

That afternoon, two full days since he'd fled his
home, Mark saw certain landmarks—a distant temple
of Bacchus, an isolated tabletop butte—that assured
him he was now quite near the village in which his
father had been born. Some few of his father's kinfolk
still lived there, and it was necessary now for Mark to
think about those relatives. The angry riders of the
Duke might well have reached them already, might
have established a watch over every house in all the
land where they thought the fugitive would be likely to
turn for help. And now, for the first time, one clear
idea about his destination did come to Mark: safety
for him could lie only outside the Duke's territory, in
that strange outer world he'd never visited.

But there was something else, besides distance and
dangers, that still lay between him and that possibility

of safety. He had, he discovered now, a sense of terrible obligation, connected of course with the sword. The obligation was unclear to him as yet, but it was certain.

Mark held to his course along the river, and did not approach his father's old village closely enough to see what might be going on there. On what he could see of the nearby roads, there were no swift riders, no signs of military search; and his repeated scanning of the sky discovered no flying beasts that might be looking for him. But Mark kept mainly to the concealing thickets, and traveled quickly on.

When the last sunset glow had died on the third evening of his flight, he raised his eyes again to the mountains ahead of him. Again he saw, more plainly now than ever before, the tiny, fitful sparks of Vulcan's fires.

On this third night the air of the high country grew chill enough to keep Mark from sleeping soundly. He wrapped himself in the sword's covering, but built no fire, for fear of guiding his still hypothetical pursuers to him. The next morning, wet from a light drizzle, he climbed wearily on. The country round him grew ever wilder, more alien to what he knew. He continued to follow the river as it carved its way across a high plain, then up among a series of broken foothills. Mark's head felt light now, and his stomach painfully empty. On top of each shoulder he had a sore red spot, worn by the cord from which the sword was slung.

Near midday, with timberline visible at what appeared to be only a small distance above him, Mark came upon a small shrine to some god he did not recognize. He robbed it of its simple offerings, dried berries and stale bread. As he ate he tried to compose a prayer to the anonymous god of the shrine, explaining what he'd done, pleading his necessity. He might not have bothered with the prayer were he not getting so close to the gods' high abode. Even here, so close, he was not entirely sure that the gods had either the time or the inclination to notice what happened at small shrines, or to hear small prayers.

Maybe tomorrow he'd be high enough on the mountain to get some direct divine attention. At any previous time in Mark's life, such a prospect would have frightened him. But, as it was, the shock that had driven him from his home still insulated him against the theoretical terrors that might appear tomorrow.

Not far above the shrine, the Aldan had its origin in the confluence of two brooks, both of which flowed more or less out of the north. At their junction Mark tried his luck at fishing, and found his luck was bad. He grubbed around for edible roots, and came up with nothing that he could eat. He searched for some fresher berries than the shrine had provided, and found a few that birds had spared. If any human dwelling had been in sight he would have tried his skill at burglary or begging to get food. But there was no such habitation to be seen on any of the vast hills under the enormous sky, and Mark was not going to turn aside now to look for one.

He spent the fourth night of his journey, sleeping little, amid a tumble of huge rocks at timberline. Tonight the lights of Vulcan's forge-fires appeared to Mark to be almost overhead, startlingly near and at the same time dishearteningly far above him. Near midnight some large animal came prowling near, staying not far beyond the glow of a small fire that Mark had built in a sheltering crevice. When he heard the hungry snuffling of the beast he unwrapped Townsaver and gripped the hilt of the weapon in both hands. No sound came from the blade, and the air around it remained clear and quiet. Mark could feel no hint of magical protection in its steel, yet in the circumstances the simple weight and razorsharpness of it were a considerable comfort.

In the morning there were no animals of any kind in sight, nor could Mark even find a significant track. The air at dawn was bitter cold but almost windless. During the night Mark had wrapped himself again in the sword's cloth, but now he swathed the weapon again and tied it for carrying. Then he climbed, heading up between foothills, following a dry ravine, moving now on knees that quivered from his need for food. Once he was moving, he was no longer quite sure just how he'd spent the night just past, whether he'd slept at all or not. It seemed to him quite possible that he'd been walking without a pause since yesterday.

Shortly he came upon a small spring, that gave him good water to drink. He took this discovery as a good omen, drank deeply, and pressed on.

All streams were behind him now, as far as he could tell. He kept following what looked like an ill-defined trail up through the ravine. Often he wasn't sure that he was really following a trail at all. By now he was unarguably on the slopes of the mountain itself, but so far the climbing was not nearly as difficult as he had feared that it might be. There were no sheer cliffs or treacherous rockslides that could not be avoided. Even so, the going soon became murderously hard because of sheer physical exhaustion.

Mark considered ways to lighten the load that he was carrying. But it consisted of only a few things, none of which he felt willing yet to leave behind. The idea that he might be able to discard the sword, somehow, along the way had itself already been discarded. The sword was connected with his goal, and it would go with him to the end. At one point, with his head spinning, he did decide to divest himself of bow and quiver. But he changed his mind and went back for them before he'd gone ten steps.

The climb became a blur of weariness and hunger.

At some timeless bright hour near the middle of the day Mark was jarred back to full awareness of his surroundings by the realization that he'd run into a new feature of the mountain. Just ahead was the bottom of a cliff face, very nearly vertical, a surface that he was never going to be able to climb . . . gradually he understood that there was no need for him to try.

He was standing on a high, irregular shelf of black rock, with the wind howling around him. But the day was still clear, and the afternoon sun on his back was comfortingly warm. The sun had warmed the black rocks here considerably, even if the deeper shadows still held patches of snow, and there was a chill in the wind that played endlessly in the fantastic chimneys of the cliff. Mark stood still for a time, still holding the sword and bearing his other burdens, slowly getting his breath back after the long climb. In some of the chimneys he could hear a roaring that was deeper than the wind, a noise that he thought was coming up from somewhere far below.

Mark was wondering which of the chimneys might hold fire, when his attention was caught by a place he saw at the rear of the rocky shelf, just at the angle where the clifface went leaping up again. There were signs of old occupancy back there. Mark's eye was caught by scattered, head-sized lumps of some black and gnarled substance. The lumps were of an unfamiliar, off-round shape. He went to one and prodded it with the soft toe of his hunter's boot. The object was hard, and very massive for its size. Mark slowly understood that the lumps were metal or ore that had been melted and then reformed into rough blobs.

He stood now in the very rear of a shallow half-cave in the face of the rising cliff, in a place where the sun struck now and the wind was baffled. Here there were old, cold ashes, from what must have been a very large wood fire. The ashes looked too old, Mark thought, to have any connection with the fires he'd seen up here during the last few evenings. Anyway, he'd assumed, from the stories he'd heard, that what people called the lights of Vulcan's forge were something to do with earthfire, volcanic, whether or not it was the god in person who raised and tended them. Yet plainly someone had once built a large blaze, deliberately, here in this broad depression in the rock floor against the cliff. The stain of its smoke still marked the natural chumney above. The tone of the old soot was a different darkness from that of the rock itself.

In front of the abandoned fireplace Mark slumped to his knees, then let himself sink back into a sitting position. The air up here was thin, and stank of sulphur. It frosted the lungs and gave them little nourishment. At least his stomach had now ceased its clamoring for food; he had reached an internal balance with his hunger, a state almost of comfort . . . with a mental snap he came back to full alertness, finding himself sitting quietly on stone. Had he just started to fall asleep, or what?

He didn't see what difference it would make if he did doze off for a rest. But no, there was something to do, something to be decided, now that he was here. He ought to see to that first, think about it a little at least. He'd come up here for some vital reason . . . ah yes, the sword. When he had warmed himself a little more, he'd think about it.

Still sitting in the faint sun-warmth of the high, sheltered place, Mark slowly began to notice how much unburned wood was lying about nearby. There were large chips and roughly broken scraps, and the half-burnt ends of logs that must once have been too big for a man to lift. He realized that he needed heat. He wanted a fire, and so he painfully began to gather and arrange wood in the old fireplace.

It should have been an easy matter to build a fire

using this available material, but weakness made it hard. Drawing his hunter's knife, Mark tried to shave tinder and fine kindling but his hands were shaky, and the blade slipped from the half-frozen wood. He tried the sword and found the task much easier despite its weight and size. With the sword held motionless, its point resting on the ground and the hilt on his bent knee, Mark could draw any chunk of wood against the edge and take off shavings as thin and fine as he wanted. Then when he had his tinder and his kindling ready, his flint struck a fat spark from the rough flange of the sword's steel hilt.

The fire caught from that first spark. It burned well—almost magically well, Mark thought. Larger fragments soon fed it into respectable size and crackling strength. Then, after he'd rested and warmed himself a little more, he took his hunter's cup and gathered some snow from a shaded crevice, to melt and heat himself some water for a drink. Now, if only he had a little food... Mark cut that thought off, afraid the hunger pangs would start again.

He sat on the rocky ground with the unwrapped sword beside him, sipping heated water. And found himself staring at large symbols, markings so faint that he hadn't noticed them at first, painted or somehow outlined on the rock of the shallow cave's rear wall. Several of the symbols had been partially obscured by the old stains of smoke. There were in all about a dozen of the signs, all of them drawn with inhumanly straight, geometrical sides; and the lines of one of them, Mark realized, formed the same design that appeared on the hilt of the sword. He took up the sword again and looked at it carefully to make sure.

After that he continued to stare at the wall-signs, with the feeling that he was on the verge of extracting some important meaning from them, until he was distracted by a sound. It was not the wind, or his own fire, but the deep chimney-roaring, louder than before, rising below the never-quite-ceasing whine of wind. It was too breathlessly prolonged to be the voice of any animal or human. The furnaces of Vulcan, Mark thought. The forge-fires. Whatever they really were, they were burning still, somewhere near to where he was sitting. And this old wood-fire place in front of him was . . . that thought would not complete itself.

Mark's sun-shadow on the face of the cliff before him was reaching higher, and he knew that behind him the sun was going down. He thought: I won't live through this night up here; the cold if nothing else will kill me. But in spite of approaching death—or perhaps because of it—he felt a strong and growing conviction that he was going to see Vulcan soon. And somehow neither death nor the gods were terrible; the shock of watching his father and his brother die still numbed Mark's capacity for terror. Now he understood that ever since he'd picked up the sword from the village street he'd been meaning to confront Vulcan with it. To confront him, and . . . and maybe that would be the end.

Trying to gain strength, Mark built up his fire again, with larger chunks of wood. Then he curled up in front of it, as if he could absorb its radiant energy like food. Again he had the sword's cloth wrapped round his own body as a blanket.

The next time he awoke, he was cold and stiff, and the world was totally dark around him except for a million stars and the brightly winking embers of his fire. Slowly and painfully Mark turned over on his bed of rock, twisting his aching body to get the nearly-frozen half of it toward the fire. His face and the backs of his hands felt tender, as if they'd been almost scorched when the flames were high. But they began to freeze as soon as they were turned away from the remaining warmth. Mark knew he ought to make himself stand up, move his arms and walk, and then build up the fire again. He knew it, but he couldn't seem to get himself in motion. Deep in the middle of his body he could feel a new kind of shivering, and now he was almost completely sure that he was going to die tonight. Still the fact had very little importance.

Get up and tend the fire, and it will save you.

Startled, Mark raised his head, croaked out a half-formed question. The words had come to him as if in someone else's voice, and with the force of a command. He could not recognize the voice, but it made a powerful impression. Now, once he'd moved his head, the rest was possible. He sat up, rubbing his arms together, preparing himself for further effort. Now his arms were able to move freely. And now he forced himself to rise, swaying on stiffened knees, but driving his legs, torso, everything into activity. Half-paralyzed with cold and stiffness still, he gathered more wood and fed the flames when he had blown them back to life.

Then Mark lay down near the new flames, wrapping himself in the blanket again. He rubbed his face. When he took his hands down from his eyes, a circle of tall, silent figures was standing around him and the fire. They were too tall to be human. Mark, too numb to feel any great shock, looked at what he could see of the faces of the gods. He wondered why he could not recognize Ardneh, to whom his mother prayed so much, among them.

One of the goddesses—Mark couldn't be sure which one she was—demanded of him: "Why have you brought that sword back up here, mortal? We don't want it here."

"I brought it for my father's sake." Mark answered without fear, without worrying over what he ought to say. "This sword maimed him, years ago. It's killed him now. It's killed my brother, too. It's driven me away from home. It's done enough, I'm getting rid of it."

This caused a stir and a muttering around the circle. The faces of the gods, shadowed and hard for Mark to see, turned to one another in consultation. And now the voice of a different deity chided Mark: "It was time enough, in any case, for you to be leaving home. Do you want to be a mill-hand and a rabbit-hunter all your life?"

"Yes," said Mark immediately. But even as he gave the answer, he wondered if it were really true.

Another god-voice argued at him: "The sword you have there has done hardly anything as yet, as measured by its capabilities. And anyway, who are you to judge such things?"

Another voice chimed in: "Precisely. That sword was given to Jord the smith, later Jord the miller, until you, mortal, or your brother had it from him. It's yours now. But you can't just bring it back here and be rid of it that way. Oh, no. Even leaving aside the question of good manners, we—"

And another: "—can't just take it back, now that it's been used. You can't bring a used gift back."

"*Gift*?" That word brought Mark almost to midday wakefulness. It came near making him jump to his feet. "You say a *gift*? When you took my father's arm in payment for it?"

An arm, long as a tree-limb, pointed. "This one here is responsible for taking the arm. We didn't tell him to do that." And the towering figure standing beside Vulcan (Mark hadn't recognized Vulcan till the instant he was pointed out) clapped the Smith on the back. It was a great rude slap that made Vulcan stagger on his game leg and snarl. Then the speaker, his own identity still obscure, went on: "Do you suppose, young mortal, that we went to all the trouble of having Clubfoot here make the swords, make all twelve of them for our game, never to see them properly used? They were a lot of trouble to have made."

For a game . . . a *game*? In outrage Mark cried out:
"I think I'm dreaming all of you!"

None of the gods or goddesses in the circle thought
that was worth an answer.

Mark cried again: "What are you going to do about
the sword? If I refuse to keep it?"

"None of your business," said one curt voice.

"I suppose we'd give it to someone else."

"And anyway, don't speak in that tone of voice to
gods."

"Why shouldn't I speak any way I want to, I'm
dreaming you anyway! And it *is* my business what—"

"Do you never dream of real persons, real things?"

Smoke from the fire blew into Mark's face. He choked,
and had to close his eyes. When he opened them again
the circle of tall beings was still there, surrounding
him.

"And, anyway, if we gods wish to play a game, who
are you, mortal, to object?" That got a general murmur
of approval.

Mark was still outraged, but his energy was failing.
His muscles seemed to be relaxing of themselves. He
lay weakly back on rock half-warmed by fire. Despite
all he could do, his eyelids were sagging shut in utter
weariness. He whispered: "A game . . . ?"

A female voice, that of a goddess who had not
spoken until now, argued softly: "I say that this Mark,
this stubborn son of a stubborn miller, deserves to die
tonight for what he's done, for the disrespect he's
shown, the irresponsible interference."

"A miller's son? A *miller's* son, you say?" That, for
some reason, provoked laughter. "Ah, hahaaa! . . . anyway, he's protected here by the fire that he's kindled,
using magical materials and tools. Not that he had the
least idea of what he was doing when he did it."

"What is so amusing? I still say that he must die

tonight. He must. Otherwise I foresee trouble, in the game and out of it, trouble for us all."

"Trouble for yourself, you mean."

And another new voice: "Hah, if you say he must die, then *I* say he must live. Whatever your position is in this, I must maintain the opposite."

They're just like people, Mark thought. His next thought was: I'm almost gone, I'm dying. Now the idea was not only acceptable, but brought with it a certain feeling of relief.

During the rest of the night — his gentle dying went on for a long, long time — Mark kept revising his opinion of the wrangling gang of gods who surrounded him on his deathbed. Sometimes it seemed to him that they were conducting their debate on a high level, using words of great wisdom. At these times he wanted to make every effort to remember what they said, but somehow he never could. At other times what they were saying struck him as the most foolish babble that he had ever heard. But he could not manage to retain an example of their foolishness either.

Anyway, he completely missed the end of the argument, because instead of dying he finally awoke to behold the whole vast reach of the sky turning light above the great bowl of rock that made the world. The near rim of the bowl was very near in the east, almost overhead, while the northwest portion of the rim was far, far away, no more than a little pinkish sawtooth line on the horizon. And to the southwest the rim was so distant that it could not be seen at all.

Mark was shivering again, or shivering still, when he woke up. Now he was cold on both sides. The fire was nearly out, and he immediately started to rebuild it. Somewhat to his surprise, his body moved easily. For whatever reason, he had awakened with a feeling of achievement, a sense that something important had been accomplished while he lay before the fire. Well,

for one thing, his life had been preserved, whether by
accident or through the benevolence of certain gods.
He was not at all sure of the reality of the presences
he'd seen. There was no sign of gods around him now;
nothing but the mountain and the sky, and the high,
keening wind.

Except for the obscure symbols on the wall of stone,
and the remnants of that large and ancient fire.

The need for food had now settled deep in Mark's
bones, and he thought, with the beginning of fear, that
soon he might be too weak to make his way back down
the mountain. He had to implement his final decision
about the sword before that happened; so as soon as
he had warmed himself enough to stop his shivering,
he turned his back on his renewed fire and the old
forge-place of the gods. Keeping the blanket wrapped
around himself, he slung bow and quiver on his back
again, and took up Townsaver. He carried the blade as
if he meant to fight with it.

Testing the wind, he tried to follow the smell of
sulphur to where it was the strongest. It took him only
a few moments to stumble right against what he was
looking for, in the form of a chest-high broken column
of black rock. The middle of the broad black stump
was holed out, as if it were a real treestump rotting,
and up out of the central cavity there drifted acrid
fumes, along with some faintly visible smoke. At certain moments the smoke was lighted from beneath
with a reddish glow, visible here at close range even in
broad daylight. A breath of warmth came from the
fumarole, along with something that smelled even
worse than sulphur, as foul as the breath of some
imagined monster.

Somewhere far below, the mountain sighed, and the
wave of rising heat momentarily grew great.

Mark lifted the sword. He used both hands on the
hilt, just as his brother Kenn had held it with two

hands during the fight. But no power flowed from the weapon now, and Mark could do with it as he liked. Without delaying, without giving the gods another moment in which to act, he thrust the sword down into the rising smoke and let it fall.

Father, Kenn, I've done it.

The sword fell at once into invisibility. Mark heard the sharp impact that it made on nearby rock, followed by another clash a little farther down. Holding his breath, he listened a long time for some final impact, perhaps a splash into the molten rock that an Elder had once told Mark lay at the bottom of these holes of fire. But though he listened until he could hold his breath no more, he heard no more of the falling sword.

Mark looked up into the morning sky, clear but for a few small clouds. They were just clouds, with nothing remarkable about them. He realized that he was waiting for a reaction, for lightning, for something to embody what must be the anger of the gods at what he had just done. He was waiting to be struck dead. But no blow came.

What did come instead was, in a sense, even worse. It was just the beginning of a sickening suspicion that his throwing the sword down into the volcano had been a horrible mistake. Now he had made his gesture, of striking back at the gods for what they had done to him. And what harm had his gesture done them? And what good had it done himself?

In thirteen years, Jord had never made this awful trek, had never thrown the gods' payment for his right arm back into their teeth. For whatever reason, Mark's father had kept his arm-price hanging on the wall at home instead. Never trying to use it, never trying to sell it, not bragging about it—but still keeping it. Mark had never really, until this moment, tried to fathom why.

One thing was sure, Mark's father had never tried to

rid himself of the sword.

The spell of shock that had been put on Mark in the village street by the evil magic of violence began at last to lift. He realized that he was alone upon a barren mountainside, almost too weak to move, many kilometers from the home to which he dared not return. And that he'd just done something awesome and incomprehensible, completed a mad gesture that would make him the enemy of gods as well as men.

He hung weakly on the edge of the smoking, stinking stone stump, growing sicker and more frightened by the moment, until he began to imagine that the voices of the gods were coming up out of the central hole along with the mind-clouding smoke. Yes, the gods were angry. In Mark the feeling grew of just having made an enormous blunder. The feeling escalated gradually into black terror.

Only his lack of energy saved him from real panic. Doing what he could to flee the wrath of the gods, leaning shakily on the black rocky stump, Mark started round it to reach its far side, from which the mountainside went rather steeply down. As Mark moved onto the descending slope, the stump he leaned on turned into a high crooked column, the way around it into a definite descending path.

Mark had not followed this path for twenty steps before he came upon the sword. It was lying directly in his way, right under a jagged hole in the side of the crooked chimney-column, through which it had obviously dropped out. One bounce on rock, the first impact that he'd heard, then this. Altogether the sword had fallen no farther than if he'd dropped it from the millhouse roof.

Even in that short time it had encountered heat enough to leave it scorching. Mark burned his fingers when he tried to pick it up, and had to let it drop again. He had to wait, shivering in the mountain's morning shadow, and blowing on his fingers, until the unharmed metal had cooled enough for him to handle it.

CHAPTER 3

"I am still amazed at the extent of your recent failure, Wearer-of-Blue," Duke Fraktin said. "Indeed, the more I think about it, the more amazed I grow."

The blue-robed wizard's real name was not the one by which he had just been addressed. But his real name—or, indeed, even his next-to-real name—were not to be casually uttered; not even by the lips of a duke; and the wizard was used to answering to a variety of aliases.

The wizard now bowed, though he remained seated, in controlled acknowledgement of the rebuke; he had a way, carefully cultivated, of not showing fear, a way that made even a very confident master tread a little warily with him.

"I have already said to Your Grace," the blue-robed

one responded now, "all that I can say in my own defense."

There was a small gold cage suspended from a stone ceiling arch not far above the wizard's head, and inside that cage a monkbird screamed now, as if in derision at this remark. The hybrid creature's ineffectual wings made a brief iridescent blur on both sides of its thin, furred body. But its brain was too small to allow it the power of thought, and neither of the men below it paid its comment the least attention.

Except for the slave girl who had just brought wine, the two men were quite alone. They were seated in one of the smaller private chambers of the rather grim and drafty castle that was the Duke's chief residence, and would have been thought of as his family seat if any of the duchesses he had tried out so far had succeeded in giving him some immediate family. The present Duke's great-grandfather had begun the clan's climb to prominence by taking up the profession of robber baron. He had also begun the construction of this castle. Much enlarged since those days, it clung to a modest but strategically located crag overlooking the crossing of two important overland trade routes. Trade on both highways had somewhat diminished since the days of the castle's founding, but by now the family was into other games than simple robbery and the sale of insurance on life, health, and business.

Rich wall hangings, in the family colors of blue and white, rippled silkily as a gentle breeze entered the chamber through the narrow windows let into its thick stone walls. In the Duke's father's day the women of the household had begun to insist upon some degree of interior elegance, and the hangings dated from that time. And today for some reason those rippling drapes gave the Duke a momentarily acute sense of the swiftness of time's passage—all the efforts of his ancestors had enabled him to begin his own life with great advantages, but his own decades had somehow sped past him and out of reach, and today his domain was little larger or stronger than when his father had left it to him—a gift rather unwillingly bestowed. The Duke still wanted very much to be king of the whole continent someday, but it was years since he had said as much aloud to even his closest advisers. He would have expected and feared their silent ridicule, because there was so little hope.

Until very recently, that is.

He made a small gesture of dismissal to the slave girl, who rose swiftly and gracefully from her knees, and departed on silent feet, her gauzy garments swirling. Yes, in the matter of women too he thought himself unlucky—time passed, wives appeared, were found for one reason or another unsatisfactory, and departed again. The duty he felt he owed himself, of providing his own heir for his own dukedom, was still not accomplished.

The Duke poured himself a small cup of the wine. "I think," he said to his wizard, "that if you were to try, you might find a few more words to say to me on the subject." As if in afterthought, he poured a second golden cup of wine, and handed it across; he nodded meanwhile, as if confirming something to himself. His Grace was on the small side, wiry and graying, with a hint of curl still in his forelock. On the subject of beards and mustaches, as on much else, he had never been able to make up his mind with any finality, and he was currently clean-shaven except for a modest set of sideburns. The ducal complexion was on the dark side, particularly around the eyes, which made the sockets look a little hollow and gave him a hungry look sometimes.

He prodded his wizard now: "As you have described the sequence of events to me, this young boy first shot my cousin dead, then simply picked up the sword— the sword you had been sent there to get—and walked away with it. No one has seen him since, as far as we can determine. And you made no attempt to stop his departure. You say you did not notice it."

The wizard, apparently unruffled by all this, again made his small seated bow. "Your Grace, immediately after the fight, a crowd gathered in the street. There was much confusion. People were shouting all manner of absurd things, about cavalry, invasions—the scene was far from orderly, with people coming and going everywhere. My first concern was naturally for your cousin's life, and I did all that I could to save him— alas, my powers proved inadequate. But in those first moments I did not even know whose arrow had struck him down. I assumed, reasonably, I think, that it had come from one of the attackers' bows."

"And of course when the fight was over you thought no more about the sword. Even though you'd just seen what it could do."

"Beg pardon, Your Grace, I really did not see that. When the fighting started I went to earth at once, put my head down and stayed that way. As Your Grace is very well aware, most magic works very poorly once blades are drawn and blood is shed. I was of course aware that some very potent magic was operating nearby; I know now that was I sensed was the sword. But while the fighting lasted there was nothing I could do. As soon as silence fell, I jumped up and—"

"Did what you could, yes. Which, as it turned out, wasn't very much. Well, we'll see what Sharfa has to say about these villagers of his when he gets back."

"And have you now summoned him back, Your Grace?"

"Yes, I've sent word that he should hurry, though I hate for him to cut short his other mission . . . well, he must do what he thinks best when he gets my message. So must we all. Meanwhile, let's have the miller and his wife in."

"By all means, sire. I think it a very wise decision for you to question them yourself."

"I want you to observe."

The wizard nodded silently. Duke Fraktin made another small motion with his hand. Though the two men were to all appearances alone, this gesture somehow sufficed to convey the Duke's will beyond the chamber walls. In the time that might have been needed for a full, slow breath, a spear-carrying guard appeared, ushering in two people in worn commoners' garb.

The man was tall and sturdy, and the Duke would have put his age at between thirty-five and forty. His fair hair hung over neatly bandaged temples. He had only one arm, now round the waist of the woman at his side. She was plump but still attractive for one of her class and age, a few years younger than her husband. The dark-haired woman was more than a little frightened at the moment, the Duke thought, though so far she was controlling it well. The man looked more dazed than frightened. It was only today, according to the medical reports, three days after his injury, that he'd regained his senses fully.

Duke Fraktin signed to the guard to withdraw, and then surprised the couple by rising from his chair and coming to greet them, which meant descending from the low dais upon which he and his wizard had been sitting—the wizard was no longer to be seen anywhere. The smiling Duke took the man briefly by the hand, as if this were some ceremony for the award of honors. Then, with a sort of remote possessiveness, he touched the bowing, flustered woman on the head. "So, you are Jord, and you are Mala. Have you both been well treated? I mean, by my men who brought you here?"

"Very well treated, Your Honor." The man's voice, like the expression on his face, was still a little dazed. "I thank you for the care you've given me. The healing."

The Duke waved gratitude away. Whenever quick medical care was needed, for someone whose life mattered, he had a priestess of Ardneh on retainer, and the priestess had reason to be prompt and attentive in responding to his calls. "I wish we might have saved your elder son. He fell as a true hero," the Duke said and added a delicate sigh. "Actually it is your younger son who most concerns me today."

The parents were alarmed at once. The man asked quickly: "Mark's been found?" Their reactions, the Duke thought, would have been subtly different if they had known where their child was. The Duke allowed himself another sigh.

"Alas, no," replied the Duke. "Mark has not been found. And he seems to have taken away with him a certain very valuable object. An object in which my own interest is very strong."

The woman was looking at the Duke with a strange expression on her face, and he wondered if she was attempting to be seductive. A number of women made that attempt with him, of course, and probably few of them had such beautiful black hair. Fewer still, of course, were thirty-year-old millwives with calloused hands. This one had a high opinion of her own attractiveness. Or else something else was on her mind . . .

"Isn't it possible, sir," she asked now with timid determination, "that someone else took the sword? One of those bandits?"

"I think not, Mala. Where was Mark when you saw him last?"

"In the street, sir. Our village street, right after the fight. My daughter and I came running out from the mill, when people told us that Kenn was fighting out there with the sword. When I got there, Mark was standing off to one side. I didn't think he was hurt, so I ran right to Kenn, and . . . " She gestured toward her

husband at her side. "Then, later, when I looked around
for Mark again, he wasn't there."

The Duke nodded. The daughter had given his men
a similar report; she had been allowed to remain in the
village, looking after the mill. "And when you first ran
out into the street, Mala, it was Kenn who had the
sword?"

"Kenn was already lying on the ground, Your Honor,
sir. I don't know about the sword, I never thought
about it. All I could think of then was that my husband and my son were hurt." Her dark eyes peered at
the Duke from under her fall of curly hair. Maybe not
trying to be seductive, but trying to convey some
message; well, he'd get it from her later.

The woman went on: "Your Grace has close relatives too. If you knew that they were in peril, I suppose that your first thought too would be for them."

The man glanced at his wife, as if it had struck him,
too, that she was acting oddly.

The Duke asked: "And *is* another relative of mine
now in peril, as you say?"

"I do not know, sir." Whatever the woman had on
her mind, it was not going to come out openly just
now.

"Very well," the Duke said patiently. "Now. As for
young Mark, I can understand his taking fright, and
running away, after such an experience—though I, of
course, would not have harmed him, had he stayed. I
can understand his flight, I say—but why should he
have taken along that sword?"

"I think . . . " the man began, and paused.

"Yes? By the way, Jord, would you care for a little of
this wine? It's very good."

"No thank you, sir. Your Grace, Mark must have
seen both of us fall. His older brother and myself, I
mean. So he probably thinks that I'm dead along with
Kenn. That would mean . . . I've always told my sons

that one day when I was gone the sword would be theirs. Of course I always thought that Kenn would be the one to have it some day. Now Kenn is . . . "

The Duke waited for the couple to recover themselves. In his own mind he thought he was being as gracious about it as if they were of his own rank. Courtesy and gentleness were important tools in dealing with folk of any station; he sometimes had trouble making his subordinates understand that fact. All attitudes were tools, and the choice of the correct one for each situation made a great deal of difference.

Still, he began to grow impatient. He urged the miller: "Tell me all about the sword."

"It was given me years ago, Your Grace." The miller was managing to pull himself together. "I have already told your men."

"Yes, yes. Nevertheless, tell me again. Given you by Vulcan himself? What did he look like?"

The miller looked surprised, as if he had thought some other question would come next. "Look like? That's a hard thing to describe, Your Honor. As you might expect, he's the only god I've ever seen. If it was a man I had to describe, I'd say: Lame in one leg. Carries a forge-hammer in hand most of the time—a huge forge-hammer. He was dressed in leather, mostly. Wearing a necklace made out of what looked like dragon-scales—I know that sounds like foolishness, or it would, but . . . and he was taller than a man might be. And infinitely stronger."

Obviously, thought the Duke, this was not the first time the miller had tried to find words to describe his experience of thirteen years ago. And obviously he still wasn't having much success.

"More than a man," Jord added at last, with the air of being pleased to be able to establish that much at least beyond a doubt. "Your Grace, I hope you don't misunderstand what I'm going to say now."

"I don't suppose I will. Speak on."

"From the day I met Vulcan, until now, no man—no woman either—has truly been able to frighten me. Oh, if I were to be sentenced to death, to torture, I'd be frightened, yes. But no human presence . . . even standing before the Dark King himself, I think, would not be so bad as what I've already had to do. Your Grace, you must have seen gods, you'll know what I mean."

His Grace had indeed confronted gods—though very rarely—and on one occasion the Dark King also. He said: "I take your meaning, miller, and I think you put it well, that special impact of a god's presence. So, you stood by Vulcan's forge at his command, and you helped him make the swords?"

"Then Your Grace already knows, I mean that more than one were made." The miller appeared more impressed by this than by the Duke himself or his surrounding wealth and power. "I have never met anyone else who knew that fact, or even suspected it. Yes, we made more than one. Twelve, in fact. And I stood by and helped. Smithery was my trade in those days. Not that any of the skill that made those swords was mine—no human being has skill to compare with that. And five other men from my village were called to help also—to work the bellows, and tend the fire, and so on. We had no choice but to help."

Here the woman surprised the Duke again, this time by interrupting, with a faint clearing of her throat. "Does Your Grace remember ever visiting that village? It's called Treefall, and it's almost in the mountains."

Duke Fraktin looked at the woman—yes, definitely, he was going to have to see her alone, later, without her husband. Something was up. "Why, I suppose I may have been there," the Duke said. The name meant nothing to him.

He faced the man again. "No, Jord, I don't suppose you had much choice when Vulcan ordered you to help him. I understand that unfortunately none of the five other men survived."

"Vulcan used 'em up, sir. He used their bodies and their blood, like so many tubs of water, to quench the blades."

"Yet you he spared . . . except of course that he took your arm. Why do you suppose he did that?"

"I don't remember that part at all well, Your Grace . . . might I sit down? My head . . . "

"Yes, yes. Pull up one of those chairs for him, Mala. Now Jord. Go on. About when you made the swords."

"Well, sir, I fainted. And when I woke again, my right arm was gone. A neat wound, with most of the bleeding stopped already. And my left hand was already holding Townsaver's hilt. And Vulcan bent over me, as I was lying there, and he said . . . "

"Yes, yes?"

"That now the sword was mine to keep. Townsaver. The Sword of Fury, he called it too. To keep and to pass on as inheritance. I couldn't understand . . . I hurt like hell . . . and then he laughed, as if it were all nothing but a great joke. A god laughing makes a sound like—like nothing else. But it has never been a joke to me."

"No, I suppose not." The Duke turned and stepped back up onto his dais, and poured himself another small cup of wine. When he looked down at the jeweled hilt of the fine dagger at his belt, his hand itched to toy with it, but he forebore. At this moment he wanted to do nothing, say nothing, in the least threatening. He asked mildly: "How many swords did you say that Vulcan forged that day?"

"I don't think I said, Your Grace, but there were twelve." The miller looked a little better, more in control of himself, since he'd been allowed to sit down. "Would you believe it?" he almost smiled.

"I would believe it, since you say so, and you are an

honest man. I would know if you were lying. Now,
about these other eleven swords. It is very very important that their existence should be kept very quiet. No
one outside this room is to hear of them from you. My
good people, what do you suppose I should do to make
sure of that?"

The man looked to be at a loss. But the woman
stepped forward smoothly. "You should trust us, Your
Grace. We won't say a word. Jord's never mentioned
those other swords until now, and he won't. And I
won't."

The Duke nodded to her slowly, then switched
his attention back to the man. "Now, smith, miller,
whatever—what happened to those other eleven
swords?"

A helpless, one-armed shrug. "Of that, sire, I have
no idea."

"Did Vulcan name them, as he named your sword?
What were they like? Where did they go?"

Again Jord made a helpless motion. "I know none
of those things, Your Grace. I never got a good look at
any of those other swords, at least not after the early
stages of the forging. I saw twelve white-hot bars of
steel, waiting for Vulcan's hammer—that was when I
counted 'em. Later I was too busy to think, or care—
and later still, I had my bleeding stump to think
about. I couldn't . . . "

"Come, come, Jord. You must have seen more than
that. You were right there, the whole time, weren't
you?"

"I was, sir, but . . . Your Grace, I'd tell you more if I
could." Jord sounded desperate.

"Very well, very well. Perhaps you will remember
more about those swords. What else did Vulcan say to
you?"

"I don't know what all he might have said, Your
Grace. He gave me orders, told me what to do, I'm

sure. I must have understood what he was saying then, but I never could remember afterwards."

"You do remember seeing those twelve white-hot steel bars, though. Were they all alike?"

"All meant to be straight blades, I think. Probably much like the one that I was given. Weapons never were my specialty."

"Ah." The Duke sipped at his wine again, and paced the room. He took thought, trying to find the cleverest way to go. "The sword that you were given. How was it decorated?"

"The blade, not at all, sir. Oh, there was a very fine pattern right in the steel, such as I've never seen elsewhere. But that was, as I say, in the very metal itself. Then there was a rough steel crossguard, no real decoration there either. And then the handle above was straight and black, of some material I didn't recognize; sometimes I wondered if it was from the Old World. And on it was a fine white pattern of decoration."

"What did this pattern represent?"

"I puzzled often about that, sir. It might have been a crenelated wall, like on a castle or a town." And the woman nodded agreement to what her husband said.

The Duke asked: "Do you suppose that you could sketch it for me?"

"I'll have a try, sir." The man sounded reasonably confident.

"Later. Now, you were a smith yourself. Regardless of whether weapons were ever your specialty, I take it that this sword was of such beauty that you must have realized it would be worth a lot of money, even leaving aside any magical properties it may have had. Did it never enter your head to sell it?"

The man's face hardened at that. "Beg pardon, Your Grace. I didn't think it had been given me to sell."

"No? Didn't Vulcan say that it was yours, to do with as you liked?"

"He said it was mine, sir. But until it came time for me to pass it to my sons. That was said very definitely, too."

"I'm curious, Jord. What did you think your son would do with it, when it came to him? Just keep it on the wall, as you did?"

"I don't know, sir."

The Duke waited a little, but nothing more came. He sighed. "A pity. I'd have given you a very handsome price, if you'd brought the thing to me. I still will, of course, should the blade ever happen to come into your control again. If, for example, your son should bring it back. Or if, perhaps, you should look through the woods and find it where he dropped it. I'll give you a good price and ask no questions."

The man and woman looked at each other, as if they wished they could take advantage of the Duke's generosity.

The Duke sat in his chair, leaning forward. "Just realize that, sooner or later, in one way or another, I'll have that sword." He leaned back, brightening. "And I do want to give your son a substantial reward, for trying his best to defend my cousin—as did your older son, indeed. So before I forget—" And from a pocket the Duke produced a golden coin; it spun brightly toward Jord in a practiced toss.

Dazed or not, Jord caught the reward deftly in his huge workman's hand. He stood up, and he and his wife both bowed in gratitude.

As if it had never occurred to him to ask the question before, the Duke inquired: "Where do you suppose young Mark is now? Have you perhaps some relatives in another village, where he might have gone?"

"We have kin in Treefall, Your Grace." It was the woman who answered. Again she was mentioning that village, again with an odd but subtle emphasis in her voice. Yes, he'd have to see her alone soon.

Jord said: "We've told your men already about all our relatives, sire . . . Your Grace, when can we go home? I'm worried about our daughter, left alone."

"She'll be all right. I have people in the village now, keeping an eye on things . . . you have no other children living, besides that daughter and Mark?"

"None, sir," said the woman. High child mortality was common enough. She added: "Your Grace has been very good to us. To provide healing for my husband, and now money."

"Why, so I have. But why not? You are good people, faithful subjects. And when your young boy is found, I mean to be good to him as well. There's a story being told by a neighbor of yours, as doubtless you're aware, that it was Mark's arrow that felled my cousin. Even if that should be so, Mark would not be punished for it—you understand me? If it were so, the evil hit would have happened by accident—or possibly as the result of an evil spell, worked by some enemy. My wizards will find out who did it." And His Grace glanced at the empty-looking chair beside his on the dais. "But I do hope, I hope most earnestly, that your young one is doing nothing foolish with that sword. It has power far beyond anything that he might hope to control or even to understand. I would protect him from disaster if I could. But of course I cannot protect him if I don't know where he is."

The faces of both parents, the Duke decided, were still those of helpless sufferers, not those of schemers trying to decide whether a secret should be told or not. He sighed once more, inwardly this time, and made a gesture of dismissal. "Jord, go make that drawing for me, of the decorations on the sword. Tell the men in the next room what I want you to do, they'll get you what you need. Mala, stay here, I want to hear your story once again."

The spear-carrying guard had reappeared. And in a moment Jord, having made an awkward bow toward the Duke, was gone.

The woman waited, looking out from under her dark curls.

"Now, my dear, you wanted to tell me something else."

She was not going to pretend otherwise. But still she seemed uncertain as how best to proceed. "I spoke of that village, sire. Treefall. The place my husband comes from."

"Yes?"

"I thought, Your Honor, that I had encountered you there one night. Thirteen years ago. At a funeral. The very night that the five men slain by Vulcan were being waked, and my husband prayed for—though he would not be my husband till two days later—and healing magic worked to help him recover from the awful wound—"

"Ah." The Duke pointed a finger. "You say you *thought* you had encountered me? You did not know? You would not remember?"

"The man I met, my lord, wore a mask. As I know the mighty sometimes do, when they visit a place beneath their station."

"So. But why should you think this masked man was me? Had you ever seen me before?"

"No sir. It was just that I had heard—you know how stories go round among the people—heard that you sometimes appeared among your people wearing a mask of dark leather . . ." Mala evidently realized that her words sounded unconvincing. "I had heard that you were not very tall, and had dark hair." She paused. "It was a *feeling* that I had." Pause again. "There were funeral rites that night. I went with the masked man to the fields. Nine months later, my son Mark was born."

"Ah." The Duke looked Mala over thoughtfully, looked her up and down, squinting a little as if trying to remember something. "Folk out in the villages do say, then, that sometimes I go abroad disguised."

"Yes, Your Grace, many say that. I'm sure they mean no harm, they just—"

"But this time, folk were wrong. You understand?"

Mala's dark eyes fell. "I understand, Your Grace."

"Your husband, does he—?"

"Oh no sir. I've never told him, or anyone, about the masked man."

"Let it remain so," said Duke Fraktin. And again he made a gesture of dismissal.

The woman hesitated marginally. Then she was gone.

The Duke turned toward the wizard's chair, which once again was visibly occupied. He waited for its occupant to comment.

The first thing that the Blue-robed one said was: "You did not consider using torture, Your Grace?"

"Torture at this time would be foolish. I'll stake my lands that at this moment neither of them knows where their brat has gone—or where my sword is, either. The woman, at least, would hand the sword over to me in a moment if she could. I think the man would, too, if it came to an actual decision. And when they find themselves safely home again in a day or two, with my gold in their hands—they'll want more. The word will go out from them that their son should come home. Word spreads swiftly across the countryside, Blue-Robes—I've been out there among them and I know. When their child hears that his parents are home, safe, rewarded by me—there's a good chance that he'll bring home the sword. If he still has it, if we haven't found him already. But on the other hand if we begin with pointless torture, he'll hear about that too. What chance then that he'll come home voluntarily?"

"Your Grace knows best, of course. But that man's a stiff-necked one, underneath his meekness. I have the impression that he was holding something back."

"You are a shrewd observer, Blue-Robes. Yes, I agree, he was. But I don't believe it's anything central to our purpose. More likely something that passed between him and the god, years ago."

"Then, sire—?"

"Then why not get it out of him. Indeed." And Duke Fraktin sighed his delicate sigh. "But—it may not be his to tell. Have you considered that possibility?"

"Your Grace?"

"Are we *sure*, Blue-Robes—are we really sure—that we want to know everything that a god has said should be kept secret?"

"I must confess, sire, that your subtlety is oftentimes beyond me."

"You think I'm wrong. Well, later, perhaps, I'll put the whole family on racks or into boots." The Duke was silent for a few moments, thinking. "Anyway, he's a man of property—he's not going to take to the hills and leave his mill to be confiscated. Not unless we frighten him very clumsily."

"And the woman, sire?"

"What about her?"

"The time she spoke of, thirteen years ago, that was before I came into your service. There was no basis in fact for what she said? I ask because a magical influence may sometimes be established through intimacy."

"You heard what I told her." The Duke was brusque. The wizard bowed lightly. "And what about the young boy, sire? When he is found?"

The Duke looked at his advisor. "Why, get the sword from him, of course, or learn from him where it is, or at the very least where he last saw it."

"Of course, sire. And then, the boy?"

"And then? What do you mean, and then? He killed

my cousin, did he not?"

The wizard bowed his little bow, remaining in his chair. "And the village, my lord — the place where such an atrocity was permitted to happen?"

"Villages, Blue-Robes, are valuable assets. We do not have an infinite supply of them. They provide resources. Vengeance must never be more than a tool, to be taken up or put down as required. One boy can serve as an example, can serve better that way, perhaps, than in any other. But a whole village — " And Duke Fraktin shook his head.

"A tool. Yes, sire."

"And a vastly more powerful tool is knowledge. Find out where that sword is. Even finding out whose men those were who tried to kidnap my cousin would be better than mere vengeance."

CHAPTER 4

Getting down from the high mountains was difficult, when your legs were increasingly weakened by hunger, and your head still felt light from hunger, volcanic fumes, altitude, and confrontation with the gods. Getting down still wasn't as difficult, though, as going up had been.

Even carrying the sword was easier now, as if Mark had somehow got used to it. No, more than that, as if it had in some way become a part of him. He could rest its bundled weight on his shoulder now without feeling that he was going to be cut, or swing it at his side without expecting that its awkward weight would trip him up.

He could even contemplate, more or less calmly, the fact that his father and brother were dead, his mother and sister and home out of his reach, perhaps forever.

His old life was gone, the gods had agreed on that much at least. But he still had his own life, and the open road ahead, to carry him away from the Duke's vengeance. And the sword.

To find his way down the mountain, Mark simply chose what looked like the easiest way, and this way kept leading him obligingly farther and farther to the south. South was fine with Mark, because he thought that the shortest route out of Duke Fraktin's territory probably lay in that direction.

He seemed to remember hearing also that the lands of Kind Sir Andrew, as the stories called him, were in that direction too. There were a number of stories told about Sir Andrew, all very different from those told about the Duke. Mark supposed that he would willingly have gone south anyway, but the prospect of entering the realm of a benign ruler made it easier to contemplate leaving home permanently behind.

Anyway, his present problems kept him from worrying a great deal about his future. Survival in the present meant avoiding Duke Fraktin's search parties, which he had to assume were looking for him; and it also meant finding food. In this latter respect, at least, Mark's luck had turned. The first stream he encountered on his way down the mountain, a bright small torrent almost hidden in its own ravine, surprised him by yielding up a fish on his first try with his pocket line and his one steel hook. Dried brush along the watercourse provided enough fuel for a small fire, and Mark caught two more fish while the first was cooking. He ate his catch crudely cleaned and half cooked, and went on his way with his strength somewhat renewed.

By now, most of the daylight hours had passed. Looking back, Mark could see that the whole upper two-thirds of the mountains had been swallowed by clouds. He'd got down just in time, no doubt, to save his life from storm and cold. Darkness was gathering

fast, and when he came to a small overhang in the
bank of the stream he decided to let it shelter him for
the night. He tried fishing again, without success. But
he found a few berries, and made himself a small
watchfire as darkness fell.

During the night there were rain showers enough to
put out his fire, and the bank offered him no real
protection against the weather. But the deep, bitter
cold of the high altitudes was moderated here; Mark
shivered, but survived. Dawn came slowly, an indirect
brightening of an overcast sky. For Mark the clouds
were reassuring—the Duke's menagerie was said to
include flying beasts of some degree of intelligence,
that he sent out on spy missions from time to time.
Again in the morning Mark fished without catching
anything. Then he got moving, picking and eating a
few more berries as he went. He continued to follow
down the channel of the leaping, roaring stream until
the way became too difficult. Then he left the streambed
to strike out across a less difficult slope.

His chosen way gradually revealed itself as a real
path. The trail was very faint at first, but after he'd
followed it for half an hour its existence was undeniable.
Switchbacking through a field strewn with great
boulders, it led him in another hour to a primitive
road, which also tended to the south as well as down.

The road's twin ruts showed that it had once been
used by wheeled vehicles. But it was reassuringly
empty of all signs of present traffic, and Mark continued to follow its twistings among the foothill outcrop-
pings and rockslides. Within a few kilometers it joined
a north-south way, much wider and better defined,
upon which some effort at road-building had once
been expended.

Mark turned onto this highway, still heading south.
Presently he came upon evidence of recent use, freshly
worn ruts and beast-droppings no more than a day

old. His sense of caution increased sharply. The Duke's men and creatures, if they really were searching for him, were likely to be near.

Trying to make himself inconspicuous, Mark left the road and trudged along parallel with it at some fifty meters' distance. But the rocky terrain not only slowed him down, it threatened to completely destroy his hunter's boots, whose soft soles were already badly worn by climbing on rock. To save his feet he soon had to go back to the comparative smoothness of the road.

For half an hour longer he kept going, alert for anything that looked or smelled like food, and wondering when the newly threatening rain was going to break. He glanced back frequently over his shoulder, worried about the Duke's patrols.

And then suddenly he was indeed being overtaken, by two mounted men. Obviously they had already spotted Mark, but at least they were not soldiers. Their riding-beasts were only trotting, giving no impression of actual pursuit. Still they were quickly catching up. The men were both in commoners' dress, very little different from Mark's own. Both were young, both spare and wiry of build. And both wore long knives sheathed at their belts, a detail that Mark supposed was common enough out here in the great world. He thought, as they drew near, that their faces were reassuringly open and friendly.

"Where to, youngster?" The man who spoke was riding a little in advance of the other. He was also slightly the bigger of the two, and carrying a bigger knife. Both men smiled at Mark, the one in the rear thereby demonstrating that he had lost a fair number of his teeth.

Mark had, while walking, prepared an answer for that question, in case it should be needed. "To Sir Andrew's Green," he said. "I hear there's to be a fair." It was common knowledge that Sir Andrew had one every year, military and economic conditions permitting.

The two men glanced at each other. They'd slowed their mounts now, to just match Mark's steady marching pace. "Fairs are fun," agreed the one who had already spoken. "And at Sir Andrew's gates would be a pleasant place to bide, in these times of unrest." He studied Mark. "You'll have some kin there, I suspect?"

"Aye, I do. My uncle's an armorer in the castle." This answer, too, had been thought out in advance. Mark hoped it would put him in the shadow of the distant Sir Andrew's kind protection—for whatever that might be worth.

It was still the same man who did the talking. "An odd-looking bundle you've got there under your arm, lad. Might you be taking along a sword, for your uncle to do some work on it?"

"Yes, that's it." Was it reasonable that the man had guessed, simply from looking at the bundle, what it contained? Or had a general search been ordered, rewards posted, for a fugitive boy carrying a sword? Mark turned his eyes forward and kept on walking.

The talking man now urged his riding-beast ahead of Mark, then turned it crossways to the road, blocking Mark's path, and reined it to a halt. "I'll take a look at your sword," he said, and his voice was still as easy and as friendly as before.

If ever the time had been when wordplay with these two might have helped Mark's cause, that time was obviously past. He skipped into a run, ignoring their cries for him to stop. Bending low, he ran right under the belly of the leader's mount, making the animal whine and rear. Its master was kept busy for a moment, trying to do no more than retain his seat. Meanwhile, the second man, urging his own steed forward, found his companion in the way. Before the two could get themselves untangled Mark had a good running start and was well off the road.

The idea that he might be able to run faster if he threw away the sword never occurred to him, even though its awkward weight joggled him off balance and slowed him down. He held it under one arm and ran as best he could. Two large boulders loomed up just ahead—if he were to dash between them, the men would never be able to follow him mounted. The trouble was that just on the other side of the boulders, open country stretched away indefinitely. They'd ride around the obstacle easily and catch him in the open, before he'd had a long enough run to make him gasp.

Mark feinted a dart between the rocks, then instead tossed his sword up atop the highest one and scrambled up after it, using hands and feet nimbly on tiny projections from the rock. The boulder was more than two meters high, with a flat top surface where his sword had landed. Up here he'd have good footing, and room to stand and swing the sword, though not much more. As his pursuers came cantering, outraged, up to the rock, Mark was relieved to be able to confirm his first impression that they were carrying no missile weapons, slings or bows. And the side of the boulder where he'd scrambled up, steep as it was, appeared to be the least difficult to climb; it wouldn't be easy for them to come at him from two directions.

The men were both roaring at him angrily. Even mounted as they were, their heads were no higher than the level of Mark's feet. Ignoring their noise, he tugged at the cord that bound the bundle. The sword seemed almost to leap out of its wrappings, as if it were eager to be used. Still no sound came from it, no sense of power flowed; it balanced well in Mark's two-handed grip, but remained heavy and inert.

The men below fell silent as he held up the blade. He was ready to use it if he had to, his stomach clenching now like a fist, with feelings worse than hunger. The men were jockeying their mounts back-

ward now, executing a minor retreat. Their faces as
they looked at the sword showed that they were
impressed—and also, Mark thought, that they were
not surprised.

"Put it down, kid," urged the man who did the
talking. The other as if in agreement emitted a braying
sound, and Mark understood that this man had somehow lost his tongue. Mark had heard the same kind of
an unpleasant sound before, from the mouth of a man
who was said to have spread nasty stories about the
demise of the father of the present Duke.

"Just toss it down to us, young one," the speaker
said, his tone encouraging. "We'll take it and go on our
way, and you can go on yours." The speaker smiled.
He sounded as if he might even believe what he was
saying, at least while he was saying it.

Mark said nothing. He only held the sword, and
tried to be ready for what would come. The terror he
had known on the mountain, after throwing away the
sword, did not return now, though the weapon in his
hands still felt devoid of power.

His enemies were two, and they were men full
grown. Both of them had now drawn their knives,
functional-looking weapons worn with sharpening and
use. Yet the two men did not immediately try to swarm
up onto the rock. Instead they still watched the sword.
They remained at a little distance, still mounted, con-
ferring between themselves with quick signs and
whispers.

Then the one who could speak rode right up to the
rock again. "Get down here right now, kid." His voice
was now hard and tough, utterly changed from what
it had been. "If I have to come up there after you, I'll
kill you."

Mark waited.

The man, moving with an appearance of great
purpose, swung himself lithely out of his saddle and

onto the side of the boulder at the place where Mark had climbed. But when Mark standing atop the great rock took a step toward him with lifted sword, he hastily dropped to the ground and backed away.

They know what sword I have here, thought Mark. They know what it can do. The Duke has spread the word, and he's offering a reward. But still the weapon in Mark's hands felt totally dead. Was there some incantation he had to utter, something he had to do to call out the magic? What had Kenn been saying, doing, just before the fight? Mark thought that a less magical person than his brother had probably never lived.

If the two men were not going to leap bravely to the attack, neither were they about to give up. Both mounted again, they rode side by side all around the rocks where Mark had taken his position, scouting out his strongpoint. They took their time about making a complete circle of the boulders, pausing now and then to exchange a whisper and a nod.

Mark watched them. He could think of nothing else to do. He still had his bow slung on his back, and a few arrows left. But, looking at the men's faces, marking how their eyes kept coming back to the sword, he felt it would be a bad mistake to put it down. It was their fear of the sword that held them back.

As if he had been reading Mark's thought, the speaker called to him suddenly: "Put it down, boy, and let's talk. We're not meaning to do you any harm."

"If that's so, then put your own blades down and ride away. This one is mine."

Presently the two did sheathe their knives again, and rode away a little distance toward the road, and Mark's heart dared to rise. But as soon as the pair were out of easy earshot they stopped for another conference. This one lasted for several minutes. Mark could see the gestures of the speechless man, but could not read their meaning. And Mark's heart sank again when the two dismounted, tied their animals to a bush as if preparing for a long stay, and then strolled back in his direction. Now the speechless one, moving with a casualness that would not have fooled a child half Mark's age, ambled on past the high rocks. Soon, with a very casual turn at some meters' distance, he had put himself on the opposite side of the high rocks from his friend and the road.

Meanwhile the talking man was trying to keep Mark's attention engaged. "Youngster, there's a reward offered for that sword you got. We could talk about splitting it between us. You know, half for you and half for us. And you to go on free, of course."

The first rock thrown by the speechless one missed Mark by a wide margin. Actually the speaker on the road side of the rocks had to step out of the way of it himself. Mark could see in the speaker's face how he winced, out of embarrassment at his partner's clumsiness. Mark had to turn halfway round, to make sure that he was able to dodge the second thrown stone. Then he had to face back toward the road again, because the man who talked had once more drawn his knife, and was gamely trying again to scramble up the rock.

As Mark moved forward to counter this frontal attack, a third thrown stone went past his head, a little closer than the previous two. The climber, once more seeing Townsaver right above his head, dropped off the boulder's flank as he had before. Again Mark spun around, in time to dodge another missile.

A sound that had begun some time ago now registered in his attention, growing louder. It was the rumble of wagon wheels, drawing nearer with fair speed. And now the wagon came into sight, moving southbound on the road, pulled by two loadbeasts and approaching at a brisk pace. On the wagon's cloth sides large symbols were rather crudely painted. Mark had seen

the wagons of tinkers, priests, and peddlers decorated
with signs meant for advertisement and magic, but
never signs like these. Dancing on his boulder, he had
no time to puzzle about meanings now, but sang out
for help as loudly as he could.

An open seat at the front of the wagon held three
people, the one in the middle being a young woman.
All three faces were turned toward the fight, but for a
moment it appeared that the wagon was going to rush
straight on past. It did not. Instead the driver, another
wiry man somewhat older than Mark's assailants,
cried out to his team and reined in sharply on one
side. The vehicle had already passed the rocks, but
now it swerved sharply and came back, leaving the
road in a sharp, tilting turn.

When the man at the foot of the rock saw this, he
set up his own cry for aid. "Help! We got us a runaway
and a thief treed here. There's a reward, that's a stolen
weapon he's got in his hands."

His voiceless associate, running back from the far
side of the rocks, grunted and waved his arms, achiev-
ing nothing but a short distraction. While Mark, in
outrage momentarily greater even than his fear, yelled:
"Not so! It's mine!"

The wagon had braked to a halt in a swirl of dust, a
pebble's toss from where Mark stood. The wiry man
who gripped the reins now had his eyes raised judg-
matically toward Mark, thinking things over before he
acted. The girl in the middle of the seat had straight
black hair, cut short, and a round, button-nosed, somehow impertinent face, looking full of life if not exactly
pretty. On the other side of her, the seat sagged under
a heavy-set youth who wore a minstrel's plumed cap,
and a look of no great intelligence upon his almost
childish face. In his thick fingers this youth was nursing
a lute, which instrument he now slowly and carefully
put back into the covered rear portion of the wagon.

In the momentary silence, a thin whining sound arose from somewhere, to fade out again as abruptly as it had begun. Mark's hopes soared for an instant; but the sound, whatever it had been, had not proceeded from the sword.

His enemy who could speak still urged the wagon-driver: "Help us get him down, and we'll split the reward."

Mark pleaded loudly: "I'm no runaway, they're trying to rob me. This sword is mine."

"Reward?" asked the wiry driver. He squinted from one to another of the two men on foot.

The spokesman nodded. "Split 'er right down the middle."

"Reward from who?"

"Duke Fraktin himself."

The driver nodded slowly, coming to his conclusion. He looked up once more at the anguished Mark, then shook his head. "Fetch out the crossbow, Ben—go on, do it, I say."

The crossbow produced by the large youth from inside the wagon was bigger than any similar weapon in Mark's limited experience. He could feel his inward parts constricting at the very sight of it. Ben cocked it with a direct pull, not using stirrup or crank, and without apparent effort. Then he loaded a bolt into the groove, and handed the weapon to the driver.

"Now," said the driver, in his most reasonable voice yet. And with a faint smile he laid his aim directly on the man who was standing closest to his wagon. "You and your partner, mount up. And ride away."

The man who was looking at the wrong end of the crossbow turned color. He made a tentative motion with his knife, then put it back into its sheath. He stuttered over an argument, then gave it up in curses. Meanwhile his speechless companion stood by looking hangdog.

Ben's hands now held a formidable cudgel, and the look on his childish face was woeful but determined. The young woman, her expressive features all grimness now, had brought out a small hatchet from somewhere.

"Of course," remarked the wagon-driver distantly, "if you two don't want your mounts, we sure could use 'em."

The two he was confronting exchanged a look between them. Then they stalked to where they'd left their animals, and mounted. With a look back, and a muttering of curses, they rode off along the road to the northeast.

The muscular youth called Ben let out a tremulous sigh, a puffing of relief, and tucked his club away. The driver carefully watched his two opponents out of sight; then he handed the crossbow back to Ben, who carefully unloaded it, easing the taut cords.

Mark looked more closely at the driver now, and was reminded vaguely of the militia drillmaster he'd once heard shouting commands at Kenn and a hundred others. But there was kindness in the driver's voice as he said: "You can put the sword down now, boy."

"It's mine."

"Why, surely. We don't dispute that." The driver had blue eyes that tended to squint, a nose once broken, and a thick fall of sandy hair. The muscular youth, looking friendly and overgrown, was regarding Mark with sympathy. As was the pert girl, who had put away her hatchet. Mark carefully set the sword down on the rock at his feet and rubbed his fingers, which were cramped from the ferocity with which he'd gripped the hilt. "Thank you," he said.

The driver nodded almost formally. "You're welcome. My name is Nestor, and I hunt dragons to earn my bread. This is Barbara sitting next to me, and that's my apprentice, Ben. You look like maybe you could use a ride somewhere."

Again the keening, moaning sound rose faintly. Mark thought that he could locate it now inside the wagon; some kind of captive animal, he thought, or a pet.

"My name is Einar," said Mark. It was a real name, that of one of his uncles, and another answer that he'd thought out ahead of time. And now, because his knees had started to tremble, worse than ever before, he sat down on the rock. And only now did he notice how dry his mouth was.

And only after he'd sat down did it sink in: *I hunt dragons* . . .

"We can give you a ride, if you're agreeable," Nestor was saying. "And maybe a little something to munch on as we travel, hey? One advantage of a wagon, you can do other things while you keep moving."

Mark pulled himself together and rewrapped the sword. Then with it in hand he slid down from atop the boulder.

"Can I take that for you?" asked Nestor, reaching down from the elevated seat. Mark had made his decision, and handed up the sword; Nestor put it back inside the wagon. Then one of Ben's thick-fingered hands closed on Mark's arm, and he was lifted aboard as if he were a babe.

Barbara had made room on the seat for Mark by going back into the comparatively dim interior of the wagon. She was fussing about with something there, in a place crowded with containers, bales, and boxes.

Nestor already had the loadbeasts pulling. "Going south all right with you, Einar?"

"I was headed that way." Mark closed his eyes, then opened them again, because of images of knives. He could feel his heart beating. He let things go, and let himself be carried.

CHAPTER 5

Riding the wagon's jouncing seat, Mark was startled out of an incipient daze by the return of the squealing noise. This time it came insistently, from close behind him. He looked back quickly. Barbara, crouching in the back of the wagon, had just removed a cloth cover from a small but sturdy wooden cage. Inside the cage—by Vulcan's hammer and Ardneh's bones!—was a weasel-sized creature that could only be a dragon. Mark had never seen one before, but what else could be as scaly as a snake and at the same time be equipped with wings?

Seeing Mark turn his head, Barbara smiled at him. She delayed whatever she was doing with the dragon long enough to hand Mark a jug of water, and then, when he'd had a drink, a piece of fruit. As he bit into that, she got busy feeding the dragon, handing it something that she fished out of a sizable earthen crock. Mark faced forward again, chewing.

Ben had a different, smaller jug in hand. "Brandy?"

"No thanks." Mark had never tasted strong drink of any kind before, and didn't know what effect it might be likely to have on him. He'd seen a village man or two destroyed by constant heavy drinking. Ben—who was getting a frown from Nestor—stowed away the jug.

"Is that blood on your shirt, Einar?" Barbara called from the rear. "You all right?"

"No m'am. I mean, yes it is, but it's old. I'm all right."

Ben's curiosity was growing almost visibly. "That's sure some sword you got."

"Yes," agreed Nestor, who was driving now at a brisk pace, mostly concentrating on the road ahead, but frequently looking back. "Real pretty blade there."

"I had it from my father." If his hearers believed that, Mark expected them to draw the wrong conclusion from it. No one would be much surprised to find a nobleman's bastard out on the road, hiking in poverty, carrying along some gift or inheritance that was hard to translate to any practical benefit. Now Mark repeated the story about his armorer-uncle being in the employ of kind Sir Andrew. He couldn't be sure how much his audience believed, though they nodded politely enough.

Ben wagged his large head sympathetically. "I'm an orphan myself. But it don't worry me any more." From behind the seat he pulled out the lute he had been holding earlier, and strummed it. Mark thought that it sounded a little out of tune. Ben went on: "I'm really a minstrel. Just 'prenticing with Nestor here till I can get a good start at what I really want to do. We got an agreement that I can quit any time I'm ready."

Nestor nodded as if to confirm this. "Good worker," he remarked. "Hate to lose you when you go."

Ben strummed again, and began to sing:

> *The song was . . .*
> *No, this song is*
> *The ballad of gallant young Einar*
> *Who was walking as free as . . .*

The singer paused. "Hard to find a rhyme for that name." He thought for a moment and tried again:

> *Young Einar was walking the roads*
> *As free as a lark one day*
> *Along came two men*
> *Who wanted . . .*

"That's not quite how it ought to go," Ben admitted modestly, after a moment's thought.

"Must be hard to play while we're bouncing," said Barbara understandingly. There had in fact been one or two obvious wrong notes.

Mark was thinking that Ben's was not really one of the best singing voices he'd ever heard, either. But no one else had any comment about that, and he sure wasn't going to be the first to mention it.

Throughout the rest of the day Nestor kept the wagon rolling pretty steadily. He showed his wish for concealment by expressing his satisfaction when a belt of fog engulfed the road for a kilometer or so. He was always alertly on watch, and he had Barbara and Mark take turns riding in the rear of the wagon, next to the dragon's cage, keeping an eye out to the rear — for the soldiers of the Duke, Mark assumed, though Nestor never actually said so. From inside the covered, swaying cage, the unseen small dragon squealed intermittently. It reminded Mark of the odd noise that a rabbit would sometimes let out when an arrow hit it.

Beside the cage was the earthen crock, with a weighted net for a top, that held live frogs. Mark was told that these were the dragon's food, and he fed it one or two. Its tiny breath, too young to burn, steamed at his hand. Its toy eyes, doll-eyes, glittered darkly.

"When do we leave Duke Fraktin's territory?" Mark asked at one point in the afternoon. By now the foot-hills had been left behind, and the road was traversing firmly inhabited land under a cloudy sky. Fields almost ready for harvest alternated with woodlands and pastures. Nestor had driven through one small village already.

"Sometime tomorrow," said Nestor shortly. "Maybe sooner." The fog had lifted completely now, and he was busier than ever being sharp-eyed. When Mark asked some more questions about the dragon, he was told that they were taking it to the fair on Sir Andrew's green, where it ought to earn some coin as an exhibit. It would also, Mark gathered, serve to advertise Nestor's skill in the hunt. Sir Andrew was a Fen Marcher, which meant he had territory abutting the Great Swamp. He and some of his tributary towns, Mark was told, had chronic dragon problems.

Mark, thinking about it, had trouble picturing one man, however strong and skilled and brave, just going out and hunting dragons as if they were rabbits. From the stories he'd heard, real dragon hunts were vast enterprises involving numbers of trained beasts and people. And Nestor might be brave and skilled, but he didn't look all that strong. Ben, of course, looked strong enough for two at least.

As the afternoon passed, Nestor drove more slowly, and appeared to be even more anxious about seeing what was on the winding road ahead of him. Passing a pack-toting peddler who was coming from the other direction, he slowed still more to ask the man a question: "Soldiers?"

The wink and faint nod that he got in return were apparently all the answer Nestor needed. He turned off the road at the next feasible place, and jounced across an unfenced field to a side lane.

"Just as soon not meet any of the Duke's soldiers," he muttered, as if someone had asked him for an explanation. "There's a creek down this way somewhere. Maybe the water's low enough to ford. On the other side's Blue Temple land, if I remember right."

There was no problem in finding the creek, which meandered across flat and largely neglected farmland. Locating a place where it could readily be forded was somewhat harder. Nestor sent Ben and Barbara to scout on foot, upstream and down, and eventually succeeded. Once on the other side, he sighed with relief and drove the wagon as deep as possible into a small grove, not stopping till he was out of sight of Duke Fraktin's side of the stream. Then he announced that it was time to set up camp. Ben and Barbara immediately swung into a well-practiced routine, tending the loadbeasts and starting to gather some wood for a fire.

As Mark began to lend a hand, Nestor called him aside. "Einar, you come with me. We need some more frogs for the dragon, and I've a special way of catching them that I want to show you."

"All right. I'll bring my bow, maybe we'll see a rabbit."

"It'll be getting dark for shooting. But fetch it along."

From the back of the wagon Nestor dug out what looked like Mark like a rather ordinary fishnet, of moderately fine mesh. On the wooden rim were symbols that Mark supposed might have some magical significance, though often enough such decorative efforts had no real power behind them. With Nestor carrying the net beside him, Mark trudged into the trees, an arrow nocked on his bow. They followed the general slope of the land back down to the creek bed.

As they walked, Nestor asked: "Einar, what's your uncle's name? The one who's armorer for Sir Andrew. I might know him."

"His name's Mark." At least he said it quickly; this was one answer he hadn't thought out in advance.

"No. I don't know him." A cloudy twilight was oozing up out of the low ground. They had reached the creek-bank without spotting any rabbits or other game, and Mark put away his bow and arrow.

"Anyway," said Nestor, "that sword of yours didn't look like it needed a lot of work." He was studying the stream as he spoke, and it was impossible to tell from his voice what he was thinking. Stepping carefully now from one stone to another, he worked his way out near the middle of the stream, where he positioned his net in a strong flow of water, catching the wooden frame on rocks so it would be held in place. He straightened up, stretching his back, still seeming to study the water's flow. "Didn't you say that your uncle was going to work on it?"

Mark hesitated, finally got out a few lame words.

Nestor did not seem to be paying very close attention to what he said this time. "Or, maybe you've given some thought to selling your sword at the fair. That would be a good time and place, if you mean to sell it. Honest business dealings are more likely under Sir Andrew's eye than elsewhere. There might even be one or two people there who could buy such a thing."

"I wouldn't know how to sell it. And anyway, I wouldn't want to. It was my father's." All of that was the truth, which made it a relief to say.

"A sword like that, I suppose it must have some special powers, as well as being beautiful to look at." Nestor was still gazing at the stream.

Mark was silent.

Nestor at last looked at him directly. "Would you get

it now? Bring it here, and let me have a look at it?"

Mark could think of no decent way to refuse. He turned away wordlessly and trudged back to the wagon. He could grab his sword when he got there and run away again; but sooner or later he was going to have to trust someone.

He found Ben and Barbara engaged in what looked like a tricky business. They had removed the dragon's cage from the wagon and were cleaning the cage while its occupant shrilled at them and tried to claw and bite them. They looked at Mark curiously when he climbed into the wagon, and again when he emerged with his wrapped sword in hand. But they said nothing to him.

Darkness was thickening in the grove when Mark brought the sword back to Nestor, who was sitting on a rock beside the stream and appeared to be lost in meditation. But the wiry man roused quickly enough, took the sword on his lap and undid its wrappings carefully. There was still enough light for a fairly close inspection. Nestor sighted along the edge of the blade, and then tried it with a leaf. Brushed lightly along the upright edge, the leaf fell away in two neat halves.

With one finger Nestor traced the subtle pattern on the hilt. Then, acting as if he had reached a decision, he let Mark hold the sword for a moment and got to his feet. Lifting his net from the water, he peered into the mass of small, struggling creatures it had captured. The net held, thought Mark, a surprising weight of swimming and crawling things; perhaps the magical symbols round the rim really were effective.

Nestor plunged his hand into the mass, pulled out one wriggling thing, and let the rest sag back into the water. "Baby dragon," he said, holding up a fistful of feebly squirming gray for Mark's inspection. There were no wings, and the creature was vastly smaller than the one back in the cage. "You find 'em in a lot of the streams hereabouts. There's a million, ten million, hatched for every one that ever grows big enough to need hunting."

Then he surprised Mark by taking Townsaver back again. Nestor held the blade extended horizontally, flat side up, and on that small plain of metal he set the hatchling dragon. Freed of his grip, it hissed an infinitesimal challenge, and lashed a tiny tail. Nestor rotated the blade, slowly turning it edge-side up; somehow the creature continued to cling on. Its scales, though no bigger than a baby's fingernails and paper-thin, could protect it from that cutting edge. It hissed again as the sword completed a half-rotation, once more giving the dragon a flat space to rest upon.

Nestor contemplated this result for a moment, as if it were not at all what he had been expecting. Then with a small flick of his wrist he dashed the tiny creature to the ground; and in the next moment he killed it precisely with the sword, letting the weight of the weapon fall behind the point. Nestor handled the sword, thought Mark, as if it had been in his hand for years.

"One less to grow up," said Nestor, turning his thoughtful gaze toward Mark. With the sword point still down in the soil at his feet, he leaned the hilt back to Mark, giving the sword back. "First dragon this sword has ever killed, do you suppose?"

"I suppose," said Mark, not knowing what the question was supposed to mean. He began wrapping the weapon up again.

"Your father didn't hunt them, then. What did he do with this sword? Use it in battle?"

"I . . ." Suddenly Mark couldn't keep from talking, saying something to someone about it. "My brother did, once. He was killed."

"Ah. Sorry. Not long ago, I guess? Then the sword, when he used it, didn't . . . didn't work very well for him?"

"Oh, it worked." Mark had to struggle against an unexpected new pressure of tears. "It worked, like no other sword has ever worked. It chopped up men and even warbeasts—but it couldn't save my brother from being chopped up too."

Nestor waited a little. Then he said: "You were trying to use it today yourself. But—after I got there at least—nothing much seemed to be happening."

"I couldn't feel any power in it. I don't know why." At some point the thought had occurred to Mark that the limitation on the sword's magic might be connected with its name. But he didn't want to go into that just now. He didn't want to go into anything.

"Never mind," said Nestor. "We can talk about it later. But this design on the handle. Did your father, brother, anyone, ever tell you what it was supposed to mean?"

None of your business, thought Mark. He said: "No sir."

"Just call me Nestor. Einar, when we reach Sir Andrew's . . . well, I don't suppose I have to caution you to keep this sword a secret, until you know just what you want to do with it."

"No sir."

"Good. You carry it, I'll bring the net."

Back at the wagon, they sorted out not only a catch of frogs for dragon-food, but a few fish to augment the dinner of beans, bread, and dried fruit that Barbara was preparing. It turned out that Ben was roasting some large potatoes under the fire as well, and for the first time in days Mark could eat his fill.

After dinner, when the immediate housekeeping chores had been taken care of, Ben got out his lute and sang again. Both Nestor and Barbara, for some reason, chose this time to make their personal trips into the woods.

"Hard day tomorrow," Nestor announced when he

returned. And, indeed, everyone was yawning. The captive dragon had already been put back inside the wagon, and the dragon-hunter retired there now. Barbara shortly followed, after looking at Mark's boots and vowing that she would soon mend or replace them for him. After throwing out a quantity of bedding, and emerging once more to make sure that Mark had got his share of it, she went in again and closed the flap.

The rainclouds that had threatened earlier had largely blown away, and now some stars were visible. Ben and Mark bedded down in the open, on long grass at a small distance from the dying fire. Wrapped in the extra blanket Barbara had given him, Mark was more comfortable than he'd been since leaving home. He was better fed, also, And very drowsy. His sword was safe in the wagon, and in a way he enjoyed being free of its constant presence at his side. Yet sleep would not come at once.

He heard Ben stirring wakefully.

"Ben?"

"Yah."

"Your master really hunts dragons? For a living?"

"Oh yes, he's very good at it. That's what our sign painted on the wagon means. Everyone in the parts of the country where there are dragons knows what a sign like this means. This isn't really dragon country here. Just a few little ones in the streams."

"I thought that the only people who hunted dragons were . . . "

"Castle folk? I think Nestor was a knight once, but he don't talk about it. Just the way he acts sometimes. Some highborn people hunt 'em, and others just pretend to. And both kinds hire professionals like Nestor when they have to, to hunt or to help out. There's a lot of tricks to hunting dragons." Ben sounded fairly confident that he knew what the tricks were.

"And you help him," Mark prodded.

"Yeah. In two hunts now. Last hunt, we were able to catch that little one alive, as well as killing the big one we started after. Both times I stood by with the crossbow, but I didn't do much shooting. Nestor killed 'em both. Neither of them were very big dragons, but they were in the legged phase, of course. Bigger than loadbeasts. You know?"

"Yeah, I guess." What Mark knew, or thought he knew, about dragons was all from stories. After hatching, dragons swam or crawled around on rudimentary legs for about a year, like the one Nestor had netted, while large birds, big fish, and small land predators took a heavy toll of them. The ones that survived gradually ceased to spend a lot of time in the water, grew wings of effective size, and started flying. They continued as airborne predators until they were maybe four or five years old, by which time they'd grown considerably bigger than domestic fowl. A little more growth, and they supposedly became too big to fly.

Once their wings were no longer used, they withered away. The dragons resumed an existence as belly-crawling, almost snakelike creatures—so far their legs hadn't kept up with the growth of the rest of their bodies—though of course they too were on a larger scale than before. In this, called the snake phase, they were competitors of the largest true snakes for food and habitat.

When they were ready for the next phase—Mark wasn't sure how many years that took—dragons grew legs, or enlarged their legs, rather in the manner of enormous tadpoles. This legged phase was, from the human point of view, the really dangerous period of a dragon's life. Now, as omnivores of ever-growing size and appetite, they stalked their chosen territory, usually marshland or with marsh nearby. They ravaged crops and cattle, even carrying off an occasional man, woman, or child. Mark could vaguely remember hearing of one more phase after the legged one, in which the beasts after outgrowing any possible strengthening of their legs became what were called great worms, and again led a largely aquatic life. But of this final phase, Mark was even less sure than of the rest.

"Sure," he added, not wanting to seem ignorant.

"Yeah," Ben yawned. "And both times, Nestor followed the dragon into a thicket, and killed it with his sword." Ben sounded as if he were impressed despite himself. "Did your father hunt dragons too?"

"No," said Mark, wondering why everyone should think so. "Why?"

"I dunno," said Ben. "Just that, now that I think about it, your sword looks a whole lot like the one that Nestor uses."

CHAPTER 6

Putting aside an arras of blue and white, and signalling his blue-robed wizard to follow him, Duke Fraktin entered a concealed and windowless chamber of his castle, a room well guarded by strong magic. An eerie Old World light, steadier than any flame, came alive as the men entered, shed by flat panels of a strange material hanging on the walls. The light fell brightly on the rear wall of the chamber, which was almost entirely taken up by a large map. Painstakingly drawn in several colors, and lettered with many names, this map depicted the entire continent of which the Duke's domain was no more than a tenth part. Some areas of the map were largely blank, but most of it was firmly drawn, showing both the lines of physical features and the tints of political control. Behind those trusted contours and colors lay decades of aerial reconnaisance

113

by generations of flying creatures, some reptiles, some birds, others hard to classify by species, but all half-intelligent.

On one of the side walls, near the map, there hung a mask of dark, tooled leather, with a cowled jacket on a peg beside it.

But Duke Fraktin's present concern was not with any of these things. Instead he stopped in front of a large table, on which rested a carved wooden chest, itself the size of a small coffin. He signalled to his wizard that he wished this chest to be opened.

Accordingly the wizard laid both hands upon its lid, whereupon there rose from the chest a faint humming, buzzing sound, as of innumerable insects. In response to this sound the wizard muttered words. Apparently it was now necessary to wait a little, for the conversation between the two men went on with the chest still unopened, the magician's hands still resting quietly on it.

"Then does Your Grace still believe that these attackers were common bandits? Such do not commonly include warbeasts in their armament."

"No," agreed the Duke gently. He was looking at the map now, without really paying it much attention. "Nor do they commonly attempt to kidnap any of my relatives."

"Then it would seem, sire, that they were not simply bandits."

"That had occurred to me."

"Agents, perhaps, of the Grand Duke?"

"Basil bears me no love, I'm sure of that. And of course he too may have learned of the existence of the swords, and he may be trying now to gather them all into his own hands, even as I would have them all in mine . . . hah, Blue-Robes, how I wish I knew how many all across the continent are playing the same game. I presume your latest divinations still indicate that the magic blades at least are not scattered all around the earth?"

"The swords are all still on this continent, Your Grace. I am quite positive of that. But as to exactly where, in whose possession . . ."

The Duke's darkening mood sounded in his voice. "Yes, exactly. And there's no telling how many know of them by now. Bah. Kings and princes, queens and bandits, priests, scoundrels and adventurers of every stripe . . . bah, what a fine mess."

"At least Your Grace has had a chance to get in on the game. You were not left in ignorance that it is taking place."

"Game, is it?" The Duke snorted. "You know I have small tolerance for games. But I must play, or be swallowed up, when others gain the power of the swords. And you need not remind me any more that I have your skill at divination to thank for my awareness of the game, late as it comes; I've thanked you for that already. Gods, I wonder whose men those were. The Margrave's, you suppose? They didn't even seem to know or care about the sword, at least according to the descriptions of events we have."

The wizard, his hands stroking the carven lid of the wooden chest, coughed. It was a sound as delicate and diplomatic as the Duke's habitual sigh. "I think not the Margrave's, sire. Perhaps they could have been agents of the Queen of Yambu?"

The Duke, nagged by irritation on top of worry, flared up sullenly, then recovered. "Have I not told you never to speak of that . . . but never mind. You are right, we must consider Yambu also, I suppose. But I do not think it was her . . . no, I do not think so."

"Perhaps not . . . then we must face the possibility, Your Grace, that they were agents of the Dark King himself. I did find it odd that a mere miller should have mentioned that august name."

"I would say that this one-armed Jord is not your ordinary miller. But then, the commons in general are not nearly so ignorant of their rulers and their rulers' affairs as those rulers generally suppose."

"Just so, sire." The wizard nodded soothingly. "We have then primarily to consider Grand Duke Basil, Queen Yambu—and Vilkata himself. While remembering, as Your Grace so wisely points out, that there are still other possibilities."

"Yes." But now the Duke's attention was straying, drawn by a thought connected with the huge map. His gaze had lifted to the map, and had come to rest at an unmarked spot near the eastern limit of his own domain and of the continent itself, right at the inland foot of the coastal range that was labeled as the Ludus Mountains. Right about there, somewhere, ought to be the high village—what had the woman named it? Treefall, that was it—from which the god had conscripted his human helpers, keeping them for a night and a day of labor, death, and mutilation. It now struck Duke Fraktin as absurd that the village where such an enigmatic and almost incredible event had taken place should not even be marked on his map.

The woman had asked him . . . no, she had as much as told him that he, the Duke, had been there, and had fathered a bastard on her there, the night after Jord's maiming, in one of those hill country funeral rites. The Duke knew something about those.

A bold story indeed for any woman to make up out of nothing. Still, the fact was that the Duke could remember nothing like that happening, and he had, as a rule, a good memory. A better memory, he thought, for women than for most things. Of course he couldn't recall everything from thirteen years ago. Exactly what had he been doing at that time—?

The insect-buzzing sound had died away. The wizard pushed up the lid of the huge box. Both men stared at the fine sword that was revealed inside, nesting in a lining of rare and fantastically beautiful blue fur. The sword had not been brought to the Duke in any such sumptuous container as this; in fact it had arrived, wrapped for concealment, in the second-best cloak of a Red Temple courtesan.

The clear light from the Old World wall panels glinted softly on mirror steel. Beneath the surface of the blade, the Duke's eye seemed to be able to trace a beautiful, finely mottled pattern that went centimeters deep into the metal, though the blade was nowhere a full centimeter thick.

Putting both hands on the hilt, the Duke lifted the sword gently from the magical protection of the chest. "Are they ready out on the terrace?" he asked, without taking his eyes from the blade itself.

"They have so indicated, Your Grace."

Now the Duke, holding the sword raised before him as if in ritual, led the way out of the blind room behind the arras, across a larger chamber, and through another doorway, whose curtains were stirred by an outdoor breeze. The terrace on which he emerged was open to the air, and yet it was a secret place. The view was cut off on all sides by stone walls, and by high hedges planted near at hand. On the stone pavement under the gray sky, several soldiers in blue and white were waiting, and with them one other man, a prisoner. The prisoner, a middle-aged, well-muscled man, wore only a loincloth and was not bound in any way. Yet he was sweating profusely and kept looking about him in all directions, as if he expected his doom to spring out at him at any moment.

The Duke trusted his wizard to hold the sword briefly, while he himself quickly slipped a mail shirt on over his head, and put on a light helm. Then he took back the sword, and stood holding it like the experienced swordsman that he was.

The Duke gestured toward the prisoner. "Arm him, and step back."

Most of the soldiers, weapons ready, retreated a step or two. One tossed a long knife, unsheathed, at the prisoner's feet.

"What is this?" the man demanded, his voice cracking.

"Come fight me," said the Duke. "Or refuse, and die more slowly. It is all one to me."

The man hesitated a moment longer, then picked up the knife.

The Duke walked forward to the attack. The prisoner did what he could to defend himself, which, given the disparity in arms and armor, was not much.

When it was over, a minute later, the Duke wiped the long blade clean himself, and with a gesture dismissed his troops, who bore away with them the prisoner's body.

"I felt no power in it, Blue-Robes. It killed, but any sharp blade would have killed as well. If its power is not activated by being carried into a fight, then how can it be ordered, how controlled? And what does it do?"

The wizard signed humbly that he did not know.

The Duke bore the cleaned blade back into the concealed room behind the arras, and replaced it in the magically protective chest. Still his hand lingered on the black hilt, tracing with one finger the thin white lines of decoration. "Something like a castle wall on his sword, the fellow said."

"So he did, Your Grace."

"But here I see no castle wall. Here there's nothing more or less than what we've seen in the pattern since that woman brought me the sword a month ago. This shows a pair of dice."

"Indeed it does, Your Grace."

"Dice. And she who brought it to me from the Red

Temple said that the soldier who left it with her had been wont to play, and win, at dice." Annoyingly, that soldier himself was dead. Stabbed, according to the woman's story, within a few breaths of the moment when he'd let the sword out of his hands. The killers who'd lain in wait for him had evidently been some of his fellow gamblers, who were convinced he'd cheated them. Duke Fraktin had sent Sir Sharfa, one of his more trusted knights, out on a secret mission of investigation.

"Am I to cast dice for the world, Blue-Robes?"

The wizard let the question pass as rhetoric, without an answer. "No common soldier, Your Grace, could have carried a sword like this about with him for long. It would certainly have come to the attention of his officers, and then . . . "

"It would be taken from him, yes. Though quite likely not brought here to me. Ah well, it's here now." And the Duke, sighing, removed his finger from the hilt. "Tell me, Blue-Robes, is it perhaps something like our lamps, some bit of wizardry left over from the Old World? And is the miller's tale of how he came by it only a feverish dream that he once had, perhaps when his arm was amputated, perhaps after he'd caught it clumsily in his own saw or his own millstones?"

"I am sure Your Grace understands that none of those suggestions are really possible. Much of the miller's tale is independently confirmed. And we know that the Old World technologists made no swords; they had more marvelous ways to kill, ways still forbidden us by Ardneh's Change. They had in truth the gun, the bomb . . . "

"Oh, I know that, I know that . . . but stick to what is real and practical, not what may have happened in the days of legend . . . Blue-Robes, do you think the Old World really had to endure gods as well as their nonsense of technology? Ardneh, I suppose, was really there."

"It would seem certain that they did, Your Grace. Many gods, not only Ardneh. There are innumerable references in the old records. I have seen Vulcan and many others named."

The Duke heaved a sigh, a great sincere one this time, and shook his head again. As if perhaps he would have liked to say, even now, that there were no gods, or ought to be none, his own experience notwithstanding.

But here was the sword before him, an artifact of metal and magic vastly beyond the capabilities of the humans of the present age. And it had not been made in the Old World either. According to the best information he had available, it had been made no more than thirteen years ago, in the almost unpeopled mountains on the eastern edge of his own domain. If not by Vulcan, then by whom?

Gods were rarely seen or heard from. But even a powerful noble hardly dared say that they did not exist. Not, certainly, when his domain adjoined the Ludus Mountains.

CHAPTER 7

Mark awoke lying on damp ground, under a sky much like that of the day before, gray and threatening rain. Still, blanketed and fed, he was in such relative comfort that for a moment he could believe that he was dreaming, back in his own bedroom at the mill, and that in a moment he might hear his father's voice. The illusion vanished before it could become too painful. There was Ben, a snoring mound just on the other side of the dead fire, and there was the wagon. From inside it the little dragon had begun a nagging squall, sounding almost like a baby. No doubt it was hungry again.

And now the wagon shook faintly with human stirrings inside its cover; and now Ben sat up and yawned. Shortly everyone was up and moving. For breakfast Barbara handed out stale bread and dried fruit. People munched as they moved about, getting things packed up and ready for the road. Preparations were made quickly, but fog was closing in by the time everything was ready to travel. With the fog, visibility became so poor that Nestor entrusted the reins to Ben, while he himself walked on ahead to scout the way.

"We're near the frontier," Nestor cautioned them all before he moved out. "Everybody keep their eyes open."

Walking thirty meters or so ahead, about at the limit of dependable visibility, Nestor led the wagon along back lanes and across fields. Before they had gone far, they passed a gang of someone's field workers, serfs to judge by their tattered clothes, heading out with tools in hand for the day's labor. When these folk were greeted, they answered only with small waves and nods, some refusing to respond at all.

Shortly after this encounter Nestor called a halt and held a conference. He now admitted freely that he was lost. He thought it possible that they might not have crossed the frontier last night after all—or that they might even have recrossed it to Duke Fraktin's side this morning. Mark gathered that the border here-abouts was a zig-zag affair, poorly marked at best, and in places disputed or uncertain. However that might be, all they could do now was keep trying to press on to the south.

The four people in and around the wagon squinted up through fog that appeared to be growing thicker, if anything. They did their best to locate the sun, and at last came to a consensus of sorts on its position.

"That way's east, then. We'll be all right now."

With Nestor again walking a little ahead of the wagon, and Ben driving, they crossed a field and jolted into the wheel-ruts of another lane. Time passed. The murky countryside flowed by, with a visibility now of no more than about twenty meters. Nestor was a ghostly figure, pacing at about that distance ahead of the wagon.

More time passed. Suddenly, seeming to come from close overhead, there was a soft sound, quickly passing, as of enormous wings. Everyone looked up. If there had been a shadow, it had already come and gone, and no shape was revealed in the bright grayness. Mark exchanged looks with Barbara and Ben, both of whom looked just as puzzled as he felt. No one said anything. Mark's impression had been of something very large in flight. He had certainly never heard anything like it before.

Nestor, who had heard it too, called another halt and another conference. He didn't know, either, what the flying thing might have been, and now he was ready to curse the fog, which earlier he had welcomed. "It's not right for this part of the country, this time of the year. But we'll come out of it all right if we just keep going."

This time Nestor stayed with the wagon and took over the driving himself. The others remained steadily on lookout, keeping watch in all directions as well as possible in the fog.

The lane on which they were traveling dipped down to a small river, shallow but swiftly flowing, and crossed it in a gravel ford. Nestor drove across without pausing. Mark supposed that this was probably another bend of the same stream that they'd just camped beside, and that this crossing might mean a new change of territory. But no one said anything, and he suspected they were all still confused about whose lands they were in.

Slowly they groped their way ahead, through soupy mists. The team, and the dragon as well, were nervous now. As if, thought Mark, something more than mere fog were bothering them.

There was the river again, off to the right. The road itself moved here in meandering curves, like a flatland stream.

Suddenly, from behind the wagon and to the left, there came the thudding, scraping, distinctive sound of riding-beasts' hard footpads on a hard road. It sounded like at least half a dozen animals, traveling together. It had to be a cavalry patrol.

The dragon keened loudly.

"Halt, there, the wagon!"

From somewhere a whip had come into Nestor's hand, and he cracked it now above the loadbeasts' backs, making a sound like an ice-split tree. The team started forward with a great leap, and came down from the leap in a full run. So far today they had not been driven hard, and their panic had plenty of nervous energy for fuel.

"Halt!"

The order was ignored. Only a moment later, the first arrows flew, aimed quite well considering conditions. One shaft pierced the cloth cover of the wagon above Mark's head, and another split one of the wooden uprights that supported the cloth.

"Fight 'em!" roared Nestor. He had no more than that to say to his human companions, but turned his energy and his words, in a torrent of exhortation and abuse, toward his team. The loadbeasts were running already as Mark had never known a team to run before. Meanwhile inside the wagon a mad scramble was in progress, with Ben going for the crossbow and Mark for his own bow and quiver. Mark saw Barbara slipping the thong of a leather sling around one finger of her right hand, and taking up an egg-shaped leaden missile.

Looking out from the left front of the wagon with bow in hand, Mark saw a mounted man swiftly materializing out of the mist. He wore a helmet and a mail shirt, under a jerkin of white and blue, and he rode beside the racing team, raising his sword to strike at its nearest animal. Mark quickly aimed and loosed an arrow; in the bounding confusion he couldn't be sure of the result of his own shot, but the crossbow thrummed beside him and the rider tumbled from his saddle.

The caged dragon, bounced unmercifully, screamed. The terrified loadbeasts bounded at top speed through the fog, as if to escape the curses that Nestor volleyed at them from the driver's seat. It seemed to Mark that missiles were sighing in from every direction, with most of them tearing through the wagon's cloth. Someone outside the wagon kept shouting for it to halt. Ben, in the midst of recocking his crossbow, was almost pitched out of the wagon by a horrendous bounce.

Mark saw Barbara leaning out. Her right arm blurred, releasing a missile from her sling in an underhand arc. One of the cavalry mounts pursuing stumbled and went down.

The patrol had first sighted the wagon across a bight of the meandering road, and in taking a short cut to head it off had encountered some difficult terrain. This had provided the wagon with a good flying start on a fairly level stretch of road. But now the faster riders were catching up.

"Border's near!" yelled Nestor to his crew. "Hang on!"

We know it's near, thought Mark, but which direction is it? Maybe now Nestor really did know. Mark loosed another arrow, and again he could not see where it went. But a moment later one of the pursuing riders pulled up, as if his animal had gone lame.

Another bounce, another tilt of the wagon, bigger than any bounce and tilt before. This one was too big. Mark felt the tipping and the spinning, the wagon hitting the earth broadside, with one crash upon another. He thought he saw the dragon's cage, still intact, fly past above his spinning head, all jumbled with a stream of bedding, and a frog-crock streaming frogs. He hit the ground, expecting to be killed or stunned, but soft earth eased the impact.

Aware of no serious injury, he rolled over in grass and sand, the ground beneath him squelching wetly. Nearby, the wagon was on one side now, with one set of wheels spinning in the air, and the team still struggling hopelessly to pull it. Meanwhile what was left of the cavalry thundered past, rounding the wagon on both sides, charging on into thickets along the roadside just ahead. Mark could catch just a glimpse of people there, who looked like Ben and Barbara, fleeing on foot.

The dragon was still keening, inside its upended but unbroken crate beside the wagon.

On all fours, Mark scrambled back into the thick of the spilled contents at the wagon's rear. He went groping, fumbling, looking for the sword. He let out a small cry of triumph when he recognized Townsaver's blade, and thrust a hand beneath a pile of spilled potatoes for the hilt. He had just started to lift the weapon when he heard a multitude of feet come pounding closer just behind him. Mark turned his head to see men in half-armor, wearing the Duke's colors, leaping from their mounts to surround him. A spearman held his weapon at Mark's throat. Mark's hand was still on the sword, but he could feel no power in it.

"Drop it, varlet!" a soldier ordered.

—and overhead, out of the mist, great wings were sighing down. And the caged dragon's continuous keening was answered from up there by a creak that might have issued from a breaking windmill blade—

Another inhuman voice interrupted. This one was a basso roar, projecting itself at ground level through the mists. Mark's knees were still on the ground, and through them he could feel the stamp of giant feet, pounding closer. A shape moving on two treetrunk legs, tall as an elder's house, swayed out of the fog, two forelimbs raised like pitchforks. Striding forward faster than a riding-beast could run, the dragon closed in on a mounted man. Flame jetted from a beautiful red cavern of a mouth, the glow of fire reflecting, resonating, through cubic meters of the surrounding fog. The man atop his steed, five meters from the dragon, exploded like a firework, lance flying from his hand, his armor curling like paper in the blast. Mark felt the heat at thirty meters' distance.

Without pausing, the dragon altered the direction of its charge. It snorted, making an odd sound, almost musical, like metal bells. Once more it projected fire from nose and upper mouth. This time the target, another man on beastback, somehow dodged the full effect. The riding-beast screamed at the light brush of fire, and veered the wrong way. One pitchfork-forelimb caught it by one leg, and sent it and its rider twirling through the air to break their bodies against a tree.

All around Mark, men were screaming. He saw the Duke's men and their riding-beasts in desperate retreat.

The dragon changed the direction of its charge again. Now it was coming straight at Mark.

Nestor, at the moment when the wagon tipped, had tried to save himself by leaping as far as he could out from the seat, to one side and forward. He did get clear of the crash, landed on one leg and one arm, and managed to turn the flying fall into an acrobat's tumbling roll, thanking all the gods even as he struck that here the earth was soft.

Soft or not, something struck him on the side of the head, hard enough to daze him for a moment. He fought grimly to stay free of the descending curtain of internal darkness, and collapsed no farther than his hands and knees. He was dimly aware of someone— Ben, he thought it was—bounding past him, into

nearby thickets promising concealment. And there went
a pair of lighter, swifter feet, Barbara's perhaps.

In the thick fog, cavalry came pounding near. Beside
Nestor in the muck, partially buried in it even as he
was, there was a log. He let himself sink closer to it,
trying to blend shapes.

The cavalry swept past with a lot of noise, then
was, for the moment, gone. Nestor scrambled his way
back toward the tipped wagon. He had to have the
sword. Whatever else happened, he wasn't going to
leave that for the Duke.

When he reached the spill, he found the sword at
once, as if, even half-dazed, he had known where
Dragonslicer must be. With the familiar shape of the
hilt tightly in his grip, and the sound of the returning
cavalry in his ears, Nestor moved in a crouching run
back toward the thickets. He hoped the others were
getting away somehow.

Once among the bushes, Nestor crouched down
motionless. Once more, in the fog, cavalry went pounding blindly past him, towards the wagon. He jumped
up and ran on again. A moment later, a hideous,
monstrous bellowing filled the air behind him. It
sounded like the grandfather of all dragons, and the
noise it made was followed by human screams.

Nestor ran on. He had his dragon-killing sword in
hand, but he wasn't about to turn back and risk his
neck to use it to save his enemies. Now, with the
dragon providing such great distraction, he could calculate that his chances of getting away were quite
good. Behind him the sounds of panic and fighting
persisted. Possibly the Duke's patrol could be strong
and determined enough to fight a dragon off. Nestor
kept going, angling away from the direction he thought
he'd seen Ben and Barbara take—time enough, later,
to get his crew back together if they'd all survived.

In the fog, the bank of the creek appeared so suddenly in front of Nestor that he almost plunged into the water before he saw it. He hadn't been expecting to encounter the stream right here, but here it was, across his path, and maybe he was getting turned around again—small wonder, in this pea soup.

Now Nestor deliberately stepped into the thigh-deep water and started wading. He wanted to put some more distance between himself and the fighting. If the soldiers drove the dragon off or killed it, they might still come this way looking. The uproar slowly faded with distance. It was peculiar, because this wasn't the country where you'd normally expect to find big dragons . . . any more than you'd expect a fog like this . . .

—wings translucently thin, but broad as a boat's sails, were coming down at him from above, breaking through puffs of low pearly mist—what in the name of all the gods?—

For a moment Nestor, still knee-deep in water and gazing upward, literally could not move. He thought that no one had ever seen the like of the thing descending on him now. Those impossible wings had to be reptilian, which meant to Nestor that the creature they supported had to be some subspecies of dragon. The reptilian head was small, and obviously small of brain, grotesquely tiny for such large wings. The mouth and teeth were outsized for the head, and looked large enough to do fatal damage to a human with one bite. The body between the wings was wizened, covered with tough-looking scales, the two dangling legs all scales and sinew, with taloned feet unfolding from them now.

It was coming at Nestor in a direct attack. He stood his ground—stood his muck and water rather—and thrust up at the lowering shape. With any other weapon in hand he would have thought his chances doubtful at best, but with Dragonslicer he could hardly lose.

Only at the last moment, when it was too late to try

to do anything else, did he realize that the sound he
always heard when he used this sword was not sounding now, that this time the sensation of power with
which it always stung his arm was absent.

Even shorn of magic, the blade was very sharp, and
Nestor's arm was strong and steady. The thrust slid
off one scale, but then sank in between two others,
right at the joint of leg and body. Only in that moment
did Nestor grasp how big the flying creature really
was. In the next instant one of the dragon's feet, its
leathery digits sprouting talons, as flexible as human
fingers, stronger than rope, came to scoop Nestor up
by the left arm and shoulder. The embrace of its other
leg caught his right arm and pinned it to his body,
forcing the sword-hilt out of his grasp, leaving the
sword still embedded in the creature's flesh between
its armored scales. The violence with which it grabbed
and lifted him banged his head against its scaly breast,
a blow hard enough to daze him again.

He knew, before he slid into unconsciousness, that
his feet had been pulled out of the water, that nothing
was in contact with his body now but air and dragon
scales. He felt the rhythm of the great wings working,
and then he knew no more.

Even as the enormous landwalker charged at Mark,
a shrill sound burst from the sword in his right hand.
The sound from the sword was almost lost in the roar
that erupted from the dragon's fiery throat, and the
pulsed thunder of its feet. But the sword's power
could be felt as well as heard. Mark was holding the
hilt in both hands now, and energy rushed from it up
into his hands and arms, energy that aligned the blade
to meet the dragon's rush.

The sword held up Mark's arms, and it would not
let him fall, or cower down, or even try to step aside.
He thought, fleetingly: *This is the same terror that*

Kenn felt. And helplessly he watched the great head bending near. From those lips, that looked as hard and rough as chainmail, and from those flaring nostrils, specks of fire drooled. The glowing poison spurted feebly, from a reservoir that must have been exhausted on the cavalry. Mark could feel the bounce and quiver of the soft earth with each approaching thud of the huge dragon's feet. And he saw the pitchfork forelimbs once more raised, to swipe and rend.

The head came lowering at Mark. It was almost as if those forge-fire eyes were compelled to challenge the light-sparks that now flecked the sword, springing as if struck from the metal by invisible flint. The sword jerked in a sideways stroke, driven by some awesome power that Mark's arms could only follow, as if they were bound to the blade by puppet-strings.

The one stroke took off the front quarter of the dragon's lower jaw. The dragon lurched backward one heavy step, even as a splash of iridescent blood shot from its wound. Mark felt small droplets strike, an agony of pinhead burning, on his left arm below his sleeve, and one on his left cheek. And the noise that burst from the dragon's throat behind its blood was like no other noise that Mark had ever heard, in waking life or nightmare.

In the next instant, the dragon lurched forward again to the attack. Even as Mark willed to twist his body out of the way of the crushing mass the sword in his hands maintained a level thrust, holding his hands clamped upon its hilt, preventing an escape.

Mark went down backward before that falling charge. He fell embedded in cushioning mud, beneath the scaly mass. In mud, he slid from under the worst of the weight; he could still breathe, at least. Finally the sword released his hands, and he felt a monstrous shudder go through the whole mass of the dragon's body, which then fell motionless.

The pain had faded from the pinprick burns along his arm, but in his left cheek a point of agony still glowed. He tried to quench it in mud as he writhed his way toward freedom. Only gradually did he realize that he had not been totally mangled, indeed that he was scarcely injured at all. The falling torso had almost missed him. One of the dragon's upper limbs made a still arch above his body, like the twisted trunk of an old tree.

He was still alive, and still marveled at the fact. Some deep part of his mind had been convinced that a magic sword must always kill its user, even if at the same time it gave him victory.

The scaly treetrunk above Mark's body began to twitch. Timing his efforts as best he could to its irregular pulsation, he worked himself a few centimeters at a time out from under the dead or dying mass. He was quivering in every limb himself, and now he began to feel his bruises, in addition to the slowly fading pain of the small burn. Still he was unable to detect any really serious injury, as he crawled and then hobbled away from the corpse of the dragon into some bushes. The only clear thought in his mind was that he must continue either to try to hide or to run away, and at the moment he was still too shaken to try to run.

Sitting on the muddy ground behind a bush, he realized gradually that, for the moment at least, no danger threatened. The dragon had chased the cavalry away, and now the sword had killed the dragon. He had to go back to the dragon and get the sword.

Standing beside the slain monster he couldn't see the sword. It must still be buried where his hands had last let go of it. It must still be hilt down in mud, under the full weight of more than a thousand kilograms of armored flesh.

Going belly down in mud again, Mark reached as far as possible in under the dead mass. He could just touch the sword's hilt, and feel through it a faint, persistent thrum of power. The blade was hilt-deep in the dragon; though Mark could touch the weapon, it seemed impossible without moving the dragon to pull it out.

Mark was still tugging hopelessly at the handle when he heard Ben's voice, quiet but shaken, just behind him.

"Bigger'n any dragon I ever saw . . . where's Nestor?"

Mark turned his head halfway. "I don't know. Help me get the sword out, it's stuck in, way down here."

"You see what happened? I didn't." Without waiting for an answer, Ben planted his columnar legs close beside the plated belly of the beast, then raised both hands to get leverage on one of the dragon's upper limbs, which appeared to be already stiffening. Grunting, he heaved upward on the leg.

Mark tugged simultaneously at the sword's handle, and felt it slide a few centimeters toward him. "Once more."

Another combined effort moved the hilt enough to bring it out into full view. When Ben saw it, he bent down and took hold—there was room on that hilt for only one of his hands. One was enough. With a savage twist he brought the blade right out, cutting its own way through flesh and scale, bringing another flow of blood. The colors of the blood were dulling quickly now.

As soon as Ben had the sword free, he dropped it in the mud, and stood there rubbing the fingers of the hand with which he'd pulled it out. "I felt it," he muttered, sounding somewhat alarmed. He didn't specify just what it was he'd felt.

"It's all right," said Mark. He picked up the weapon and wiped it with some handy leaves. His hands were and remained black with mud, but, as before, the sword was clean again with almost no effort at all.

Mark became motionless, staring at the hilt. It showed no castle wall, but the white outline of a stylized dragon.

Ben wasn't looking at the sword, but staring at Mark's face. "You got burned," Ben said softly. "You must have been close. Where's Nestor?"

"I haven't seen him. Yes, I was close. I was the one who held the sword. This sword. But this isn't mine. Where's mine?" As he spoke, Mark rose slowly to his feet. His voice that had been calm was on the verge of breaking.

Ben stared at him. There was a sound nearby, and they both turned quickly to see Barbara. She was as muddy and bedraggled as they were, carrying her hatchet in one hand, sling in the other.

"Where's Nestor?" she asked, predictably.

Haltingly, his mind still numbed by the fact that his sword was gone, Mark recounted his version of events since the wagon had tipped over. They looked at him, and at the sword; then Barbara took the weapon from his hands, and pressed gently with the point right on the middle of one of the dragon's thickest scales. There was a spark from the steel. With a faint, shrill sound, the blade sank in as into butter.

Mark said: "That looks almost exactly like my sword, but it must be Nestor's. Where's mine?" The feeling of shock that had paralyzed him was suddenly gone, and he ran to search amid the jumbled contents of the wagon. He couldn't find the sword there, or anywhere nearby. The others followed him, looking for Nestor, but he was not to be found either, alive or dead. They called his name, at first softly, then with increasing boldness. The only bodies to be found were those of soldiers, mangled by the landwalker before it had been killed.

"If he's gone," said Mark, "I wonder if he took my sword?"

He might have, by mistake, they decided—no one thought it would make sense for Nestor to take Mark's weapon and deliberately leave his own behind.

"But where'd he go?"

"Maybe the soldiers got him. And the other sword."

"They were in a blind panic, just getting out of here. The ones who're still alive are running yet."

Dead riding-beasts were lying about too, and some severely injured. Ben dispatched these with his club. The team of loadbeasts was still attached to the spilled wagon, and fortunately did not appear to be seriously hurt. The human survivors, pushing together, tipped the wagon back on its wheels again, and saw that all four wheels still would roll.

While Mark continued a fruitless search for his sword, the others reloaded cargo, throwing essentials, valuables, and junk all back into the wagon. They reloaded the now empty frog-crock, and at last the tumbled dragon-cage.

Barbara paused with her hand on the cage, whose forlorn occupant still keened. "Do you suppose the big ones came after this? They must have heard it yelping."

Ben shook his head decisively. "Never knew dragons to act that way. Big ones don't care about a small one, except maybe to eat it if they're hungry, which they usually are." Ben was worried, but not about dragons. "If Nestor's gone, what're we going to do?"

Barbara said: "We've looked everywhere around here. Either he's still running, or else he got hurt or killed and washed down the river. I can't think of anything else."

"Or," said Mark, coming back toward the others in his vain seeking, "the soldiers got him after all. And my sword with him."

They all looked once more for Nestor and the sword. They even followed the river downstream for a little distance. It seemed plain that a body drifting in this stream would catch in shallows or on a rock before it had gone very far.

Still there was no sign of man or weapon.

At last Barbara was the decisive one. "If the soldiers did get him, he's gone, and if he's dead he's dead. If he's still running, well, we can't catch him when we've got no idea which way he went. We'd better get ourselves out of here. More soldiers could come back. Einar, your sword's just not here either. If Nestor's got it, and he catches up with us, you'll get it back."

"Where'll we go?" Ben sounded almost like a child.

She answered firmly: "On to Sir Andrew's. If Nestor is going to come looking for us anywhere, it'll be there."

"But what'll we say when we get there? What'll we do? Sir Andrew's expecting Nestor."

"We'll say he's delayed." Barbara patted Ben's arm hard, encouragingly. "Anyway, we've still got Nestor's sword. You can kill dragons with it if you have to, can't you? If little Einar here can do it."

Ben looked, if not frightened, at least doubtful. "I guess we can talk about that on the way."

CHAPTER 8

Two men were sitting in Kind Sir Andrew's dungeon. One, who was young, perched on a painted stool just inside the bars of a commodious whitewashed cell. The other man was older, better dressed, and occupied a similar seat not very far outside the bars. He was reading aloud to the prisoner out of an ancient book. To right and left were half a dozen other cells, all apparently unoccupied, all clean and whitewashed, all surprisingly light and airy for apartments in a dungeon. Though this level of the castle was half underground, there were windows set high in the end wall of the large untenanted cell at the far end of the row.

At a somewhat greater distance, down a branching, stone-vaulted, cross corridor, were other cells that gave evidence of habitation, though not by human beings. Sir Andrew had caused that more remote portion of his dungeon to be converted into a kind of bestiary, now housing birds and beasts of varied types, whose confinement had required the weaving of cord nets across the original heavy gratings of the cell doors and windows.

Yes, there were more windows in that wing. You could tell by the amount of light along the corridor that way. The young man on the stool inside the cell, who was currently the only human inmate in the whole dungeon, and who was supposed to be listening to the reading, kept looking about him with a kind of chronic wonder, at windows and certain other surprises. The young man's name was Kaparu—at least that was the only name he could remember for himself. He was thin-faced and thin-boned, and had lank, dark, thinning hair. His clothes were ragged, and his weathered complexion showed that he had not been an indoor prisoner for any length of recent time. He had quick eyes—quick nervous hands as well, hands that now and then rubbed at his wrists as if he were still in need of reassurance that they were not bound. Every now and then he would raise his head and turn it, distracted by the small cheerful cries that came from his fellow prisoners down the corridor.

Kaparu was no stranger to the inside of jails and dungeons, but never in all his wanderings had he previously encountered or even imagined a jail like this. To begin with, light and air were present in quite astonishing quantities. Yes, the large cell at the end of the row had real windows, man-sized slits extending through the whole thickness of the lower castle wall, like tunnels open to the bright late summer afternoon. The way it looked, the last prisoner put in there might just have walked out through the window. In through those embrasures came not only air and light, but additional cheerful sounds. Outside on Sir Andrew's green the fair was getting under way.

There was also a sound, coming from somewhere else in the dungeon, of water dripping. But somehow, in this clean, white interior, the sound suggested not dankness and slow time, but rather the outdoor gurgle of a brook. Or, more aptly, the lapping of a lake. The castle stood on a modest rise of ground, the highest in the immediate neighborhood, but its back was to a sizable lake, whose surface level was only a little lower than this dungeon floor.

Resting on the floor of the prisoner's cell, not far from the feet of his stool, was a metal dish that held a sizable fragment of bread, bread fresh from the oven today and without insects. Beside the plate, a small pottery jug held clean drinking water. At intervals the prisoner involuntarily darted a glance toward the bread, and each time he did so his left foot as if in reflex lifted a trifle from the stool-rung it was on — but in this peculiar dungeon there were evidently no rats to be continually kicked and shooed away.

And each time the prisoner turned his head to look at the plate, his gaze was likely to linger, in sheer disbelief, upon the small vase filled with fresh cut flowers, that stood beside his water jug.

The man who sat outside the cell, so patiently reading aloud from the old book, had not been young for some indeterminate time. He was broadly built, and quite firmly and positively established in middle age, as if he had no intention at all of ever growing really old. His clothing was rich in fabric and in workmanship, but simple in cut, and more than ordinarily untidy. Like his garments, his beard and mustache of sandy gray were marked with traces of his recently concluded lunch, which had obviously comprised some richer stuff than bread and water.

At more or less regular intervals, he turned the pages of the old book with powerful though ungraceful fingers, and he continued to read aloud from the book in his slow, strong voice. It was a knowledgeable voice, and never stumbled, though its owner was translating an old language to a new one as he read. Still there were hesitations, as if the reader wanted to make very sure of every word before he gave it irrevocable pronunciation. He read:

" 'And the god Ardneh said to the men and women of the Old World, once only will I stretch forth the power of my hand to save you from the end of your own folly, once only and no more. Once only will I change the world, that the world may not be destroyed by the hellbomb creatures that you in your pride and carelessness have called up out of the depths of matter. And once only will I hold my Change upon the world, and the number of the years of Change will be forty-nine thousand, nine hundred, and forty-nine.

" 'And the men and women of the Old World said to the god Ardneh, we hear thee and agree. And with thy Change let the world no longer be called Old, but New. And we do swear and covenant with thee, that never more shall we kill and rape and rob one another in hope of profit, of revenge, or sport. And never again shall we bomb and level one another's cities, never again . . . ' "

Here the reader paused, regarding his prisoner sternly. "Is something bothering you, sirrah? You seem distracted."

The man inside the cell started visibly. "I, Sir Andrew? No, not I. Nothing is bothering me. Unless . . . well, unless, I mean, it is only that a man tends to feel happier when he's outside a cell than when he's in one." And the prisoner's face, which was an expressive countenance when he wished it to be, brought forth a tentative smile.

Sir Andrew's incipient frown deepened in response. "If you think you would be happier outside, then pray do not let your attention wander when I am reading to you. Your chance of rejoining that happy, sunlit world beyond yon windows depends directly upon your behavior here. Your willingness to admit past errors, to seek improvement, take instruction, and reform."

Kaparu said quickly: "Oh, I admit my errors, sir. I do indeed. And I can take instruction."

"Fine. Understand that I am never going to set you free, never, as long as I think you are likely to return to your old habits of robbing innocent travelers."

The prisoner, like a child reprimanded in some strict school, now sat up straight. He became all attention. "I am trying, Sir Andrew, to behave well." And he gave another quick glance around his cell, this time as if to make sure that no evidence to the contrary might be showing.

"You are, are you? Then listen carefully." Sir Andrew cleared his throat, and returned his gaze to the yellowed page before him. As he resumed reading, his frown gradually disappeared, and his right hand rose unconsciously from the book, to emphasize key words with vague and clumsy gestures.

" '—and when the full years of the Change had been accomplished, Orcus, the Prince of Demons, had grown to his full strength. And Orcus saw that the god Draffut, the Lord of Beasts and of all human mercy, who sat at the right hand of Ardneh in the councils of the gods, was healing men and women in Ardneh's name, of all manner of evil wounds and sickness. And when Orcus beheld this he was very wroth. And he—' "

"Beg pardon, sir?"

"Eh?"

"That word, sir. 'Wroth.' It's not one that I'm especially familiar with."

"Ah. 'Wroth' simply means angry. Wrathful." Sir Andrew spoke now in a milder tone than before, milder in fact than the voice in which he generally read. And at the same time his expression grew benign.

Once more he returned to his text. "Where was I? Yes, here . . . 'In all the Changed world, only Ardneh himself was strong enough to oppose Orcus. Under the banner of Prince Duncan of the Offshore Islands, men and women of good will from around the earth rallied to the cause of good, aiding and supporting Ardneh. And under the banner of the evil Emperor, John Ominor, all men and women who loved evil rallied from all the lands of the earth to—' "

"Sir?"

"Yes, what?"

"There's one more thing in there I don't understand, sir. Did you say this John Ominor was an emperor?"

"Hm, hah, yes. Listening now, are you? Yes. The Emperor in those days—we are speaking now, remember, of a time roughly two thousand years in the past, at the end of what is called Ardneh's Change, and when the great battle was fought out between Orcus and Ardneh, and both of them perished—at that time, I say, no man was called emperor unless he was a real power in the world. Perhaps even its greatest power. It might be possible to trace a very interesting connection from that to the figure of mockery and fun, which today—"

"Sir?"

"Yes?"

"If you don't mind, sir. Did you say just a moment ago that Ardneh perished?"

Sir Andrew nodded slowly. "You *are* listening. But I don't want to get into all that now. The main thrust of this passage, what you should try to grasp today- . . . but just let me finish reading it. Where was I? Ha. 'In all the Changed world, only Ardneh himself—' and so forth, we had that. Hah. 'In most dreadful combat the two strove together. And Orcus spake to Ardneh, saying—'Ah, drat, why must we be interrupted?"

The prisoner frowned thoughtfully at this, before he

realized at just what point the text had been broken off. Sir Andrew had been perturbed by certain new sounds in the middle distance, sounds steadily drawing near. A shuffling of feet, a sequential banging open of doors, announced the approach of other human beings. Presently, at the highest observable turn of the nearby ascending stair, there appeared the bowed legs of an ancient jailer, legs cut off at the knees by a stone arch. The jailer came on down the stairs, until his full figure was in view; in one arm, quivering with age, he held aloft a torch (which surely had been of more use on the dark stair above than it was here) to light the way for the person following him, a woman—no, a lady, thought the prisoner.

She was garbed in Sir Andrew's colors of orange and black, and she brought with her an indefinable but almost palpable sense of the presence of magical power. She must have been a great beauty not long hence, and was attractive still, not less so for the touch of gray in her black hair, the hint of a line or two appearing at certain angles of her face.

As soon as this lady had become fully visible at the top of the stairs, she paused in her descent. "Sir Andrew," she called, in a voice as rich and lovely as her visual appearance, "I would like a little of your time, immediately. A matter of importance has come up."

Grunting faintly, Sir Andrew rose from his stool, turning as he did so to address the visitor. "It's really important, Yoldi?" he grumbled. And, a moment later, answered his own question. "Well, of course, it must be." He had long ago impressed upon everyone in the castle his dislike of being interrupted when he was at his favorite work of uplifting prisoners.

Sir Andrew went to the stair, and took the torch from the hand of the aged jailer, making a shooing motion at the man to signify that he was dismissed.

Then, holding the flame high with one arm, bearing his precious book under the other, the knight escorted his favorite enchantress back up the stairs, to where they might be able to hold a private conference.

Once they had climbed round the first turn, Dame Yoldi glanced meaningfully at the old book. "Were you obtaining a good result?" she asked.

"Oh, I think perhaps a good beginning. Yes, I know you're convinced that my reading to them does no good. But don't you see, it means they have at least some exposure to goodness in their lives. To the history, if you like, of goodness in the world."

"I doubt that they appreciate it much."

There were windows ahead now, tall narrow slits in the outer wall where it curved around a landing, and Sir Andrew doused his torch in a sandbucket kept nearby. Trudging on to where the windows let in light, he shook his head to deny the validity of Dame Yoldi's comment. "It's really dreadful, you know, listening to their stories. I think many of them are unaware that such a thing as virtue can exist. Take the poor lad who's down there now, he's a good example. He has been telling me how he was raised by demon-worshippers."

"And you believed him?" Good Dame Yoldi sounded vexed, both by the probability that the true answer to her question would be yes, and the near certainty that she was never going to hear it from Sir Andrew.

The knight, stumping on ahead, did not seem to hear her now. He paused when he reached the first narrow window, set where the stair made its first above-ground turn. Through the aperture it was possible to look out past the stone flank of the south guard-tower, and see something of the small permanent village that huddled just in front of the castle, and a slice of the great common green beyond. On that sward, where woolbeasts grazed most of the year, the annual fair had been for the past day or so taking shape.

"I should have ordered him some better food, perhaps. Some gruel at least, maybe a little meat." Sir Andrew was obviously musing aloud about his prisoner, but his distracted tone made it equally obvious that his thoughts were ready to stray elsewhere. "Crops were so poor this year, all round the edge of the Swamp, that I didn't know if we'd have much of a fair at all. But there it is. It appears to be turning out all right."

Dame Yoldi joined him at the window, though it was so narrow that two people had trouble looking out at once. "Your granaries have taken a lot of the shock out of poor years, ever since you built them. If only we don't have two bad years in a row."

"That could be disastrous, yes. Is that what you wanted to see me about? Another village delegation? Is it crops, dragons, or both?"

"It's a delegation. But not from any of the villages this time."

Sir Andrew turned from the window. "What then?"

"They've come from the Duke, and I've already cast a sortilege, and the omens are not particularly good for you today. I thought you'd like to know that before you meet these people."

"And meet them I must, I suppose. Yoldi, in matters of magic, as in so much else, your efforts are constantly appreciated." Sir Andrew leaned toward his enchantress and kissed her gently on the forehead. "All right, I am warned."

He moved to the ascending stair, and again led the way up. He had rounded the next turn before he turned his head back to ask: "What do they say they want?"

"They don't. They refuse to discuss their business with anyone else before they've seen you."

"And they exhibit damned bad manners, I suppose, as usual."

"Andrew?"

On his way up, the knight paused. "Yes?"

"Last night that vision of swords came to me again. Stacked in a pyramid like soldiers' spears in the guardroom, points up. I don't know what it means yet. But as I said, today's omens are not good."

"All right." When the stair had brought him to a higher window, Sir Andrew paused again, to catch his breath and to look out once more and with a better view over the hectares of fairground that had sprung up before his castle almost as if by magic. Jumbled together were neat pavilions, cheap makeshift shelters, professional entertainers' tents of divers colors, all set up already or still in the process of erection. The present good weather, after some days of rain, was bringing out a bigger crowd than usual, mostly people from the nearby villages and towns. The lowering sun shone upon banners and signs advertising merchants of many kinds and of all degrees of honesty, all of them getting ready to do business now or already engaged in it. Sir Andrew's towers dominated a cross-road of highways leading to four important towns, and a considerable population was tributary to him. On fine evenings, such as this promised to be, the fair would likely run on by torchlight into the small hours. The harvest, such as it was, was mostly already in, and most of those who worked the land would be able to take time out for a holiday.

The master of the castle frowned from his window, noting the booths and tables of the operators of several games of chance. Their honesty, unlike that of the other merchants, tended to be of only one degree.

"Hoy, these gamblers, gamesters." The knight's face expressed his disapproval. "Remind me, Yoldi. I ought to warn them that if any of them are caught cheating again this year, they can expect severe treatment from me."

"I'll remind you tomorrow. Though they will undoubtedly cheat anyway, as you ought to realize by this time. Now, may we get on with the important business?"

"All right, we'll get it over with." And the knight looked almost sternly at his enchantress, as if it were her fault that the meeting with the Duke's people was being delayed. He motioned briskly toward the stair, and this time she led the way up. He asked: "Who has the Duke sent to bully me this time?"

"He's sent two, one of which you'll probably remember. Hugh of Semur. He's one of the stewards of the Duke's territories adjoining—"

"Yes, yes, I do remember him, you don't have to tell me. Blustery little man. Fraktin always likes to send two, so they can spy and report on each other, I suppose. Who's the other this time?"

"Another one of the Duke's cousins. Lady Marat."

"For a man without direct heirs, he has more cousins than—anyway, I don't know her. What's she like?"

"Good-looking. Otherwise I'm not sure yet what she's like, except that she means you no good."

The pair of them were leaving the stair now, on a high level of the castle that held Sir Andrew's favorite general-purpose meeting room. He caught up with Dame Yoldi and took her arm. "I hardly supposed she would. Well, let's have them in here. Grapes of Bacchus, do you suppose there's any of that good ale left? No, don't call for it now, I didn't mean that. Later, after the Duke's dear emissaries have departed."

The emissaries were shortly being ushered in. The Lady Marat was tall and willowy and dark of hair and skin. Again, as in Dame Yoldi's case, what must once have been breathtaking beauty was still considerable—in the case of Lady Marat, thought Sir Andrew, nature had almost certainly been fortified in recent years by a touch of enchantment here and there.

Hugh of Semur, a step lower than Her Ladyship in the formal social scale, was chunkily built and much more mundane-looking, though, as his clothes testified, he was something of a dandy too. Sir Andrew recalled Hugh as having more than a touch of self-importance, but he was probably trying to suppress this characteristic at the moment.

Formal greetings were quickly got out of the way, and refreshment perfunctorily offered and declined. Lady Marat wasted no time in beginning the real discussion, for which she adopted a somewhat patronizing tone: "As you will have heard, cousin, the Duke's beloved kinsman, the Seneschal Ibn Gauthier, was assassinated some days ago."

"Some word of that has reached us, yes," Sir Andrew admitted. Having got that far he hesitated, trying to find some truthful comment that would not sound too impolite. He preferred not to be impolite without deliberate purpose and good cause.

Her Ladyship continued: "We have good reason to believe that the assassin is here in your domain, or at least on his way. He is a commoner, his name is Mark, the son of Jord the miller of the village of Arin-on-Aldan. This Mark is twelve years old, and he is described as large for his age. His hair and general coloring are fair, his face round, his behavior treacherous in the extreme. He has with him a very valuable sword, stolen from the Duke. A reward of a hundred gold pieces is offered for the sword, and an equal amount for the assassin-thief."

"A boy of twelve, you say?" The furrow of unhappiness that had marked Sir Andrew's brow since the commencement of the interview now deepened. "How sad. Well, we'll do what we must. If this lad should appear before me for any reason, I'll certainly question him closely."

The Lady Marat was somehow managing to look

down her nose at Sir Andrew, though the chair in which he sat as host and ruler here was somewhat higher than her own. "Good Cousin Andrew, I think that His Grace expects a rather more active co-operation on your part than that. It will be necessary for you to conduct an all-out search for this killer, throughout your territory. And when the assassin is found, to deliver him speedily to the Duke's justice. And, to find and return the stolen sword as well."

Sir Andrew was frowning at her fixedly. "Twice now you've called me that. Are we really cousins?" he wondered aloud. And his bass voice warbled over the suggestion in a way that implied he found it profoundly disturbing.

Dame Yoldi, seated at Sir Andrew's right hand, looked disturbed too, but also half amused. While Hugh of Semur, showing no signs but those of nervousness, hastened to offer an explanation. "Sir Andrew, Her Ladyship meant only to speak in informal friendship."

"Did she, hah? Had m'hopes up high there for a minute. Thought I was about to become a member of the Duke's extended family. Could count on his fierce vengeance to track down anyone, any child at least, who did me any harm. Tell me, will you two be staying to enjoy the fair?"

The Lady Marat's visage had turned to dark ice, and she was on the verge of rising from her chair. But Dame Yoldi had already risen; perhaps some faint noise from outside that had made no impression on the others had still caught her attention, for she had gone to the window and was looking out into the approaching sunset.

Now she turned back. "Good news, Sir Andrew," she announced in an almost formal voice. "I believe that your dragon-hunters have arrived."

Yoldi's eyes, Sir Andrew thought, had seen more than she had announced.

CHAPTER 9

Nestor, struck on the head with stunning force for the second time in as many minutes, lost consciousness. But not for long. When he regained his senses he found himself being carried only a meter or two above the surface of a fogbound marsh, his body still helplessly clutched to the breast of a flying dragon of enormous wingspan. His left shoulder and upper arm were still in agony, though the animal had shifted its powerful grip and was no longer holding him directly by the damaged limb.

He thought that the dragon was going to drop him at any moment. He knew that a grown man must be a very heavy load — five minutes ago he would have said an impossible load — for any creature that flew on wings and not by magic. And obviously his captor was having a slow and difficult struggle to gain altitude with Nestor aboard. Now the mists below were thick enough to conceal flat ground and water, but the tops of trees kept looming out of the mists ahead, and the flyer kept swerving between the trees. No matter how its great wings labored, it was unable as yet to rise above them.

From being sure that the creature was going to drop him, Nestor quickly moved to being afraid that it was not. Then, as it gained more altitude despite the evident odds, he progressed to being fearful that it would. Either way there appeared to be nothing he could do. Both of his arms were now pinned between his own body and the scaly toughness of the dragon's. He could turn his head, and when he turned it to the right he saw the hilt of the sword, along with half the blade, still protruding from between tough scales near the joining of the animal's left leg and body. The wound was lightly oozing iridescent blood. If Nestor had been able to move his right arm, he might have tried to grab the hilt. But then, at this increasing altitude, he might not.

The great wings beat majestically on, slowly winning the fight for flight. Despite the color of the creature's blood, its scales, and everything else about it, Nestor began lightheadedly to wonder if it was truly a dragon after all. He had thought that by now, after years of hunting them, he knew every subspecies that existed . . . and Dragonslicer had never failed to kill before, not when he had raised it against the real thing. Could this be some hybrid creature, raised for a special purpose in some potentate's private zoo?

But there was something he ought to have remembered about the sword . . . dazed as Nestor was, his mind filled with his shoulder's pain and the terror of his fantastic situation, he couldn't put together any clear and useful chain of thought. This thing can't really carry me, he kept thinking to himself, and kept expecting to be dropped at any moment. No flying creature ought to be able to scoop up a full-grown man and just bear him away. Nestor realized that he was far from being the heaviest of full-grown men, but still . . .

Now, for a time, terror threatened to overcome his mind. Nestor clutched with his fingernails at the scales of the beast that bore him. Now he could visualize it planning to drop him when it had reached a sufficient height, like a seabird cracking shells on rocks below. In panic he tried to free his arms, but it ignored his feeble efforts.

Once more Nestor's consciousness faded and came back. On opening his eyes this time he saw that he and his captor were about to be engulfed by a billow of fog thicker than any previously encountered. When they broke out of the fog again, he could see that at last they had gained real altitude. Below, no treetops at all could now be seen, nothing but fog or cloud of an unguessable depth. Overhead, a dazzling white radiance was trying to eat through whatever layers of fog remained. The damned ugly wounded thing has done it, Nestor thought, and despite himself he had to feel a kind of admiration . . .

When he again came fully to himself, his abductor was still carrying him in the same position. They were in fairly smooth flight between two horizontal layers of cloud. The layer below was continuous enough to hide the earth effectively, while that above was torn by patches of blue sky. It was a dream-like experience, and the only thing in Nestor's memory remotely like it was being on a high mountain and looking down at the surface of a cloud that brimmed a valley far below.

The much greater altitude somehow worked to lessen the terror of being dropped. Once more the sword caught at Nestor's eye and thought. Turning his head he observed how, with each wingstroke, the hilt of the

embedded weapon moved slightly up and down. A
very little blood was still dripping. Nestor knew the
incredible toughness of dragons, their resistance to
injury by any ordinary weapon. But this . . .

He kept coming back to it: A dragon can't carry a
man, nothing that flies is big enough to do that. Of
course there were stories out of the remote past, of
demon-griffins bearing their magician-masters on their
backs. And stories of the Old World, vastly older still,
telling of some supposed flying horse . . .

The flight between the layers of cloud went on, for a
time that seemed to Nestor an eternity, and must in
fact have been several hours. Gradually the cloud-
layers thinned, and he could see that he was being
carried over what must be part of the Great Swamp, at
a height almost too great to be frightening at all. The
cloud layer above had now thinned sufficiently to let
him see from the position of the sun that his flight was
to the southwest.

Eventually there appeared in the swamp below an
irregular small island, bearing a stand of stark trees
and marked at its edges by low cliffs of clay or marl.
At this point the dragon turned suddenly into a gentle
downward spiral. Nestor could see nothing below but
the island itself which might prompt a descent. And it
was atop one of those low, wilderness cliffs of clay
that the creature landed.

Nestor was dropped rudely onto the rough ground,
but he was not released. Before his stiffened limbs
could react to the possibilities of freedom, he was
grabbed again. One of the dragon's feet clamped round
his right leg, lifted him, and hung him up like meat to
dry, with his right ankle wedged painfully in the crotch
of a tree some five meters above the ground. He hung
there upside down and yelled.

His screams of new pain and fresh outrage were
loud, but they had no effect. Ignoring Nestor's noise,

his tormentor spread its wings and flapped heavily off the cliff. It descended in a glide to land at the edge of the swamp, some fifteen or twenty meters below. There, moving in a cautious waddle, it positioned itself at the edge of a pool. Placid as a woolbeast, it extended its neck and lapped up a drink. It continued to ignore the sword which still stuck out of its hip.

When it had satisfied its thirst, would it wish to dine? That thought brought desperation. Nestor contracted his body, trying to pull himself up within grabbing distance of the branches imprisoning his leg. But his right arm, like his whole body, was stiff and sore, and his left arm could hardly be made to work at all. The fingers of his right hand brushed the branch above, but he could do no more, and fell back groaning. Even if by some all-out contortion he were to succeed in getting his foot free, it might well be at the price of a breakbone fall onto the hard ground at the top of the cliff.

Sounds of splashing drew Nestor's attention back to the swamp. Down there the dragon had plunged one taloned foot into the swamp. Shortly the foot was brought out again, holding a large snake. Nestor, squinting into his upside-down view of the situation, estimated that the striped serpent was as thick as a man's leg. It coiled and thrashed and hissed, its fangs stabbing uselessly against the dragon's scales. The head kept on striking even after the dragon had snapped a large bite out of the snake's midsection, allowing its tail half to fall free.

Nestor drew some small encouragement from the fact that the dragon seemed to prefer snake to human flesh. He tried again, more methodically this time, to work himself free. But in this case method had no more success than frenzy.

He must have fainted again, for his next awareness was of being picked up once more by his captor. He was being held against the dragon's breast in the same way as before, and his arms were already firmly pinned. This time the takeoff was easier, though hardly any less terrifying — it consisted in the dragon's launching itself headlong from the brink of the small cliff, and gaining flying speed in a long, swamp-skimming dive that took Nestor within centimeters of the scummy water. Moss-hung trees flitted past him to right and left, with birds scattering from the trees in noisy alarm. A monkbird screamed, and then was left below.

Again Nestor faded in and out of consciousness. Again he was unsure of how much time was passing. If the damnable thing had not hauled him all this way to eat him, then what was its purpose? He was not being taken home to some gargantuan nest to feed its little ones — no, by all the gods and the Treasure of Benambra, it could not be that. For such an idea to occur to him meant that he was starting to go mad. Everyone knew that dragons built no nests and fed no young . . . and that no flying dragon was big enough to carry a grown man . . .

The clouds in the west were definitely reddening toward sunset before the flight was over. At last the creature ceased its steady southwestern flight and began to circle over another, larger, island of firm ground in the swamp. Most of the trees and lesser growth had been cleared away from a sizable area around the approximate center of the island. In the midst of this clearing stood a gigantic structure that Nestor, observing under difficult conditions, perceived as some kind of temple. It had been built either of stone, brought into the swamp from the gods knew where, or else of some kind of wood, probably magically hardened and preserved against decay. The circles of the dragon's flight fell lower, but Nestor still could not guess to which goddess or god the temple — if such it truly was — had been dedicated; there were so many that hardly anyone knew them all. He could tell that the building was now largely fallen into ruin, and that the ruins were now largely overgrown by vines and flowers.

The largest area remaining cleared was a courtyard, its stone paving still mostly intact, directly in front of what had probably been the main entrance of the temple. The flyer appeared to be heading for a landing in this space, but was for some reason approaching very cautiously. While it was still circling at a few meters' altitude, one possible reason for caution appeared, in the form of a giant landwalker that stalked out into the courtyard from under some nearby trees, bellowing its stupidity and excitement. While the flyer continued to circle just above its reach, the landwalker roared and reared, making motions with its treetrunk forelimbs as if it meant to leap at Nestor's dangling legs when they passed above. Once he thought that he felt its hot breath, but fortunately it had no hope of getting its own bulk clear of the ground.

Then a prolonged cry, uttered in a new and different voice, penetrated the dragon's noise. The new voice was as deep as the landwalker's roar, but still for a moment Nestor thought that it was human. Then he felt sure that it was not. And, when the sound of it had faded, he was not sure that it had borne intelligence of any kind, human or non-human. The basic tone of it had been commanding, and the modulation had seemed to Nestor to hover along the very verge of speech—just as a high-pitched sound might have wavered along the verge of human hearing.

Perhaps to the landwalker dragon some meaning had been clear, for the enormous beast broke off its own uproar almost in mid-bellow. It turned, with a lash of its great tail, and stamped back into the surrounding forest, kicking small trees aside.

Now the way was clear for the flying dragon, and it

lowered quickly into the clearing. Then, summoning up one more effort, it hovered with its burden, as from underneath vast trees a being who was neither dragon nor human strode out on two legs—

Nestor looked, then looked again. And still he was not sure that his sufferings had not finally brought him to hallucinations.

The being that stood below him on two legs was clothed from head to toe in long fur, a covering subtly radiant with its own energies. The suggestion was of light on the edge of vision, its colors indefinable. The figure was easily six meters tall, not counting the upraised arm of human shape that reached for Nestor now. The face was not human—certainly it was not—but neither was it merely bestial.

Despite its subtly glowing fur, the giant hand that closed with unexpected gentleness round Nestor's torso was five-fingered, and of human shape. So was the other hand that reached to pluck out delicately the sword still embedded in the hovering dragon's hip. At that, the flyer flapped exhaustedly away. As it departed, it uttered again the creaking-windmill cry that Nestor remembered hearing once before, a lifetime in the past when he had still been driving his wagon through the fog.

The enormous two-legged creature had put the sword down on the paving at its feet, and both furred hands were cradling Nestor now. And he was about to faint again . . .

But he did not faint. An accession of strength, of healing, flowed into his maltreated body from those hands. A touch upon his wounded shoulder, followed by a squeeze that should have brought agony, served instead to drain away the existing pain. A tingling warmth spread gratefully, infiltrating Nestor's entire body. A moment later, when he was set down gently on the ground, he found that he could stand and move easily. He felt alert and capable, indeed almost rested. His pains and injuries had entirely vanished. Even the thirst that had started to torment his mouth and throat was gone.

"Thank you," he said quietly, and looked up, pondering his rescuer. Although the day was almost gone, the sky was still light. The glow of daylight tinged with sunset surrounded the subtler radiance of fur, on the head of the treetall being who stood like a huge man with his arms folded, looking down at Nestor.

"I am sorry that you were hurt." The enormous voice sounded almost human now. "I did not mean you any harm."

Nestor spread his arms. He asked impulsively: "Are you a god?"

"I am not." The answer was immediate, and decisive. "What do you know of gods?"

"Little enough, in truth." Nestor rubbed at his shoulder, which did not hurt; then he dropped his gaze to the sword, which was now lying on the courtyard's pavement at his feet. "But I have met one, once before. It was less than a year ago, though by all the gods it seems at least a lifetime. Until that day, I don't suppose I ever really believed that gods existed."

"And which god did you meet that day, and how?" The huge voice was patient and interested, willing to gossip about gods if that was what Nestor wanted. Above the folded arms, the immense face was— inhuman. It was impossible for Nestor to read expression in it.

Nestor hesitated, thought, and then answered as clearly as he could, and not as he would have responded to questions put by any human interrogator. Instead, he felt himself to be speaking as simply as a child, without trying to calculate where his answers might be going to lead him.

"It was Hermes Messenger that I encountered. He

came complete with his staff and his winged boots. I was living alone then, in a small hut, away from people—and Hermes came to my door and woke me one morning at dawn. Just like that. He was carrying in one hand a sword, the like of which I'd never seen before, and he handed it over to me—just like that. Because, as he said, I would know how to use it. I was already in the dragon-hunting trade. He told me that the sword had been for far too long in the possession of people who were never going to use it, who were too afraid of it to try, though they had some idea of its powers. Therefore had Hermes taken it from them, and brought it to me instead. It was called the Sword of Heroes, he told me, and also known as Dragonslicer. He said that it would kill any dragon handily.

"Well, I soon had the opportunity to put Dragonslicer to the test, and I found that what Hermes had told me was the truth. The blade pierced the scales of any dragon that I met like so much cloth. It chopped up their bones like twigs, it found their hearts unerringly. Hermes had told me that it had been forged by Vulcan, and when I saw what it could do I at last believed him on that point also."

"And what else did Hermes say to you?"

Trying to meet his questioner's eyes was giving Nestor trouble. Staring at the giant's legs, he marked how their fur still glowed on the border of vision, even now when direct sunlight was completely gone. Night's shadows, rising from the swamp, had by now crept completely across the cleared courtyard and were climbing the front of the enormous, ruined temple.

"What else did he say? Well, when I thought he was about to turn away and leave me with the sword, I asked him again: 'Why are you giving this to me?' And Hermes answered: 'The gods grow impatient, for their great game to begin.' "

" 'Great game'?" The giant's voice rumbled down to

Nestor from above. "Do you know what he meant by that?"

"No, though I have thought about it often." Nestor forced himself to raise his head and look the other in the eye. "Do you know what he meant?"

"To guess what the gods mean by what they say is more than I can manage, most of the time. And is this sword here at our feet the same that Hermes gave to you?"

"I thought so, when I tried to kill the flying dragon with it. But, now that I think back . . ." Nestor bent quickly and picked up the sword, examining its hilt closely in the fading light. "No, it is not, though this one is very like it. A boy I met, traveling, was carrying this one. There was a fight. There was confusion. And Duke Fraktin's soldiers probably have my sword by now." Nestor uttered a small, fierce sound.

"Explain yourself." The huge dark eyes of his questioner were still unreadable, above titanic folded arms.

"All right." Nestor's sudden bitter anger over the loss of his own sword helped suppress timidity. And the longer he spoke with the giant, the less afraid of him he felt. Briefly considering his own reactions, Nestor decided that his childlike forthrightness resulted from knowing himself, like a child, completely dependent on some benevolent other. "I'll explain what I can. But is there any reason why you cannot answer a question or two for me as well?"

"I may answer them, or not. What are these questions?"

The mildness of this reply, as Nestor considered it, encouraged his boldness; and anyway, with him boldness was a lifelong habit, now beginning to reassert itself. "Will you tell me your name, to begin with? You have not spoken it yet. Or asked for mine."

There was a brief pause before the bass rumble of

the answer drifted down. "Your name I know already, slayer of dragons. And if I tell you my name now, you are almost certain to misunderstand. Perhaps later."

Nestor nodded. "Next, some questions about the creature that brought me here. I have never seen anything like it before, and I have some experience. It flew straight here to you as if it were acting on your orders, under your control. Is it truly a dragon, or some thing of magic? Did you create it? Did you send it after me?"

"It is a dragon, and I did send it. I am sorry that you were injured, for I meant you no harm. But I took the risk of harming you, for the sake of certain information I felt I had to have. Rumors had reached me, through the dragons, of a man who killed their kind with a new magical power that was embodied in a sword. And other word had reached me, through other means, of other swords that were said to have been made by the gods . . . I have good reason to want to know about these things."

Nestor thought that possibly he was becoming used to the burden of that dark gaze. Now he could meet it once again. "You are a friend of dragons, then, and talk to them."

The giant hesitated. " 'Friend' is perhaps not the right word for it. But in some sense I talk to them, and they to me. I talk with everything that lives. Now, I would ask you to answer a few more questions for me, in turn."

"I'll try."

"Good. There is an old prophecy . . . what do you know of the Gray Horde?"

Nestor looked back blankly. "What should I know? I have never heard the words before. What do they mean?"

His interrogator considered. "Come with me and I will show you a little of their meaning." With that, the towering figure turned and paced away toward the temple. Nestor followed, sword in hand. He smiled briefly, faintly, at the enormous furred back moving before him; the other had not thought twice about turning his back on a strange man with a drawn sword. Not that Nestor was going to think even once about making a treacherous attack. Even if he'd had something to gain by it, he would as soon have contemplated taking a volcano by surprise.

The front entrance of the temple was high enough for the giant to walk into it without stooping. Now, once inside, Nestor observed that the building had indeed been constructed of some hardened and pre- served wood—traces of the grain pattern were still visible. He thought that it must be very old. Much of the roof had fallen in, but the ceiling was still intact in some of the rooms. So it was in the high chamber where Nestor's guide now stopped. Here it was already quite dark inside. As Nestor's eyes adapted to the gloom, the fantastic carvings that filled the walls seemed to materialize out of the darkness like ghosts.

The giant, his body outlined in the night by his own faintly luminous fur, had halted beside a large open tank that was built into the center of the floor. The reservoir was surrounded by a low rim of the same preserved wood from which the floor and walls were made, and Nestor thought that it was probably some kind of ritual vat or bath.

Moving a little closer, he saw that the vat was nearly filled with liquid. Perhaps it was only water, but in the poor light it looked black.

From a shelf his guide took a device that Nestor, having seen its like once or twice before, recognized as a flameless Old World lantern, powered by some force of ancient technology. The giant focussed its cold, piercing beam down into the black vat. Something stirred beneath that inky surface, and in another moment the shallowness of the tank was demonstrated.

The liquid it contained was no more than knee-deep on the smallish, man-shaped figure that now rose awkwardly to its feet inside. Dark water, bright-gleaming in the beam of light, ran in rivulets from the gray naked surface of the figure. Its hairless, sexless body reminded Nestor at once of the curved exoskeleton of some giant insect. He did not for a moment take it as truly human, though it was approximately of human shape.

"What is it?" Nestor demanded. He had backed up a step and was gripping his sword.

"Call it a larva." His guide's vast voice was almost hushed. "That is an old word, which may mean a ghost, or a mask, or an unfinished insect form. None of those are exact names for this. But I think that all of them in different ways come close."

"Larva," Nestor repeated. The sound of the word at least seemed to him somehow appropriate. He observed the larva carefully. Once it had got itself fully erect, it stood in the tank without moving, arms hanging at its sides. When Nestor leaned closer, peering at it, he thought that the dark eyes under the smooth gray brow fixed themselves on him, but the eyes were in heavy shadow and he could not be sure. The mouth and ears were tiny, puckered openings, the nose almost non-existent and lacking nostrils. Apparently the thing did not need to breathe. Nestor thought it looked like a mummy. "Is it dead?" he asked.

"It has never been alive. But all across the Great Swamp the life energies of the earth are being perverted to produce others like it. Out there under the surface of the swamp thousands of them are being formed, grown, raised by magical powers that I do not understand. But I fear that they are connected somehow with the god-game, and the swords. And I know that they are meant for evil."

The god-game again. Nestor had no idea what he

ought to say, and so he held his peace. He thought he could tell just from looking at the figure that it was meant for no good purpose. It did not really look like a mummy, he decided, but more like some witch's mannikin, fabricated only to facilitate a curse. Except that, in Nestor's limited experience at least, such mannikins were no bigger than small dolls, and this was nearly as big as Nestor himself. Looking at the thing more closely now, he began to notice the crudity of detail with which it had been formed. Surely it would limp if it tried to walk. He could see the poor, mismatched fit of the lifeless joints, how clumsily they bulked under the smooth covering that was not skin, or scale, or even vegetable bark.

The giant's hand reached out to pluck the figure from the tank. He stood it on the temple floor of hardened wood, directly in front of Nestor. As the hand released it, the figure made a slight independent movement, enough to correct its standing balance. Then it was perfectly still again. Now Nestor could see that its eyes under the gray brows were also gray, the color of old weathered wood, but still inanimate as no wood ever could have been. The eyes were certainly locked onto Nestor now, and they made him feel uncomfortable.

And only now, with an inward shock, did Nestor see that the figure's arms did not end in hands but instead grew into weapons; the right arm terminated in an ugly blade that seemed designed as an instrument of torture, and the left in a crude, barbed hook. There were no real wrists, and the weapons were of one piece with the chitinous-looking material of the forearms. And the bald head was curved and angled like a helm.

With a faint inward shudder Nestor moved back another step. Had he not been carrying the sword, he might have retreated farther from the figure. Now he made his voice come out with an easy boldness that he was far from feeling: "I give up, oh giant who wishes to be nameless. What is this thing? You said 'a larva,' but that name answers nothing. I swear by the Great Worm Yilgarn that I have never seen the like of it before."

"It is one cell of the Gray Horde, which, as I said, is spoken of in an old prophecy. If you are not familiar with that prophecy, believe me that I cannot very well explain it to you now."

"But thousands of these, you say, are being grown in the swamp. By whom? And to what end?"

The giant picked up the two-legged thing like a toy and laid it back into the tank again. He pressed it down beneath the surface of the liquid, which looked to Nestor like swamp-water. No breath-bubbles rose when the larva was submerged. The vast figure in glowing fur turned off the bright light and replaced the lantern on the shelf. He watched the tank until its surface was almost a dark mirror again. Then once more he said to Nestor: "Come with me."

Nestor followed his huge guide out of the temple. This time he was led several hundred paces across the wooded island and into the true swamp at its far edge. A gibbous moon was rising. By its light Nestor watched the furred giant wade waist deep into the still water, seeking, groping with his legs for something on the bottom. He motioned unnecessarily that Nestor should remain on solid ground.

For a full minute the giant searched. Then he suddenly bent and plunged in an arm, big enough to have strangled a landwalker, to its fullest reach. With a huge splash he pulled out another larva. It looked very much like the one in the tank inside the temple, except that the two forearms of this one were connected, grown into one piece with a transverse straight gray shaft that went on past the left arm to end in a spearhead.

The larva let out a strange thin cry when it was torn up from the muck, and spat a jet of bright water from its tiny mouth. Then it lay as limp as a broken puppet in the huge furry hand.

The giant shook it once in Nestor's direction, as if to emphasize to the man the fact of its existence. The larva made no response to the shaking. "This outh cannot breathe," the giant said. "Or even eat or drink, much less speak, or sing. It can only whine as you have just heard, or howl. It can only make noises that I think are intended to inspire human terror."

Nestor gestured helplessly with the sword that he still carried. "I do not understand."

"Nor do I, as yet. I had feared for a time that the gods themselves, or some among them, were for their own reasons causing these things to come into existence. Just as, for their own reasons, some of the gods decided that you should be given great power to kill dragons. But so far I can discover no connection between the two gifts. So I do not know if it is the gods who are raising these larvae, or some magician of great power. Whoever is doing it, I must find a way to stop it. The life energies of the land about the swamp will be exhausted to no good purpose. Already the crops in nearby fields are failing, human beings are sickening with hunger."

Nestor, looking at the larva, tried to think. "I believe I can tell you one thing. I doubt that the gods had any hand in making these. Because the swords made by the gods are beautiful things in themselves, whatever the purpose behind them may be." And Nestor raised the weapon in his right hand.

The giant, looking at the sword, rumbled out what might have been a quotation:

> *"Long roads the Sword of Fury makes*
> *Hard walls it builds around the soft . . ."*

Nestor waited for more that did not come. Then he lowered the sword, and suddenly demanded: "Why do you deny that you are a god yourself?"

The enormous furred fist tightened. The gray carapace of the larva resisted that pressure only for a moment, then broke with an ugly noise. Gray foulness in a variety of indistinct shapes gushed from the broken torso. What Nestor could see of the spill in the moonlight reminded him more of dung than of anything else. The gray limbs twitched. Wildly, the spear waved once and was still.

The giant cast the wreckage from him with a splash, then washed his hands of it in the black water of the swamp. He said: "I am too small and weak by far, to be a proper god for humankind."

Nestor was almost angry. "You are larger than Hermes was, and I did not doubt the divinity of Hermes for a moment once I had seen him. Nor have I any doubts about you. Is this some riddle with which you are testing me? If so, I am too tired and worn right now to deal with riddles." And too much in need of help. Indeed, the feeling of strength and well-being that Nestor had experienced when the giant first touched him was rapidly declining into weariness again.

The other gazed at him for a moment in silence, and then in silence waded out of the swamp. The mud of the swamp would not stick to his fur, which still glimmered faintly, radiant on the edge of vision. He paced back in the direction of the center of the island, where stood the temple.

Nestor, following, had to trot in his effort to keep up. He cried to the giant's back: "You are no demon, surely?"

The other answered without turning, maintaining his fast pace. "I surely am not."

Nestor surprised himself, and ran. Almost staggering with the effort, he got ahead of the giant and confronted him face to face. With his path thus blocked, the giant halted. Nestor was breathing hard, as if from a long run, or as if he had been fighting. Leaning on his sword, he said: "Before I saw Hermes face to face, I did not believe in the gods at all. But I have seen him, and I believe. And now when I see — well, slay me for it if you will —"

Surprising himself again, he went down on one knee before the other. He had the feeling that his heart, or something else vital inside him, was about to burst, overloaded by feelings he did not, could not, understand.

The giant rumbled: "I will not slay you. I will not knowingly kill any human being."

" — but whether you admit you are a god or not, I know you. I recognize you from a hundred prayers and stories. You are the Beastlord, God of Healing, Draffut."

CHAPTER 10

The high gray walls of Kind Sir Andrew's castle were growing higher still, and darkening into black against the sunset. Mark watched their slow approach from his place in the middle of the wagon's seat. Barbara, slumping tiredly for once, was at his right, and Ben at his left with driver's reins in hand.

Now that their road had emerged from the forest and brought the castle into view, Barbara stirred, and broke a silence that had lasted for some little time. "I guess we're as ready as can be. Let's go right on in."

No one else said anything immediately. From its battered cage back in the wagon's covered rear, the battered dragon chirped. Ben looked unhappy about their imminent arrival, but he twitched the reins without argument and clucked to the team, trying to rouse the limping, weary loadbeasts to an enthusiasm he

obviously did not feel himself. Earlier in the day Ben
had suggested that they ought to travel more slowly
though they were late already, delaying their arrival at
Sir Andrew's fair for one more day, giving Nestor one
more chance to catch up with them before they got
there. But Ben hadn't argued this idea very strongly.
Mark thought now that neither Ben nor Barbara really
believed any longer that Nestor was going to catch up
with them at all.

As for Mark himself, he pretty well had to believe
that Nestor was going to meet them somewhere, with
Townsaver in hand. Otherwise Mark's sword was truly
lost.

It had been pretty well established, in the few days
that the three of them had been traveling without
Nestor, that Barbara was now the one in charge. She
was little if any older than Ben was—Mark guessed
she was about seventeen—and probably not half Ben's
weight. But such details seemed to have little to do
with determining who was in charge. Barbara had
stepped in and made decisions when they had to be
made, and had held the little group and the enterprise
together.

Before they'd left the place where the wagon had
tipped, she'd had them cut off the ears of the freshly
dead landwalker, and nail them to the front of the
wagon as trophies to show their hunting prowess.
Later she'd got Ben and Mark to tighten up all the
loosened wagon parts as well as possible, and then to
help her wash and mend the cloth cover. All their
clothes had been washed and mended too, since the
great struggle in the mud. Mark thought that the outfit
looked better now that it had when he'd joined up.

After the fight they'd traveled as fast as they could
for some hours. Then, when they'd reached a secluded
spot along a riverbank, Barbara had decreed a layover
for a whole night and a day. The animals had been

given a chance to eat and drink and rest, and their hurts had been tended. Medicine of supposed magical power had been applied to Mark's burned face, and it had seemed to help, a little. That night Ben had made his one real effort to assert himself, deciding that he wanted to sleep in the wagon too. But it had been quickly established who was now in command. Ben had wound up snoring on the ground again.

A small hidden compartment directly under the wagon's seat held a secret hoard of coin, tightly wrapped in cloth to keep it from jingling when the wagon moved. Ben and Barbara knew already of the existence of this cache, and during that day of rest they'd brought out the money in Mark's presence and counted it up. It amounted to no fortune, in fact to less than Mark had sometimes seen in his father's hands back at the mill. Nestor's success in hunting dragons evidently hadn't paid him all that well in terms of money—or else Nestor had already squandered the bulk of his payment somehow, or had contrived to hide it or invest it somewhere else. He had been paying both Ben and Barbara small wages, amounts agreed upon in advance. They said that beyond that he had never discussed money with either of them.

As soon as the coins were counted, Barbara wrapped them tightly up again and stuffed them back into their hiding place and closed it carefully. "We'll use this only as needed," she said, looking at the others solemnly. "If Nestor comes back, he'll understand."

Ben nodded, looking very serious. All in all it was a solemn moment, a pledging of mutual trust amid shared dangers; at least that was how it impressed Mark. Before he had really thought out what he was going to do, he found himself telling Ben and Barbara his own truthful story, even including his killing of the seneschal, and his own right name.

"Those soldiers of the Duke's were really after me,"

he added. "And my sword. Maybe they got the sword;
I still keep hoping that Nestor has it, and that he's
going to meet us somewhere. Anyway, even if we're
over the border now the Duke will probably still be
after me. You two have a right to know about it if I'm
going to go on traveling with you. And I don't know
where else I'd go."

The other two exchanged looks, but neither of them
showed great surprise at Mark's revelation. Mark
thought that Ben actually looked somewhat relieved.

Barbara said: "We were talking about you—Mark—
and we kind of thought that something like that was
going on. Anyway, your leaving us now wouldn't help
us any. We're going to need you, or someone, when we
get to the fair, to help us run the show. And if we still
manage to get a hunting contract we're going to need
all kinds of help."

Ben cleared his throat. "I know for a fact that the
Duke wanted to get his hands on Nestor, too. I don't
know exactly why, but Nestor was worried about it. It
made him nervous to cut through the Duke's territory,
but we didn't have much choice about that if we were
going to get down to Sir Andrew's from where we were
up north."

And here they were at Sir Andrew's now, or very
nearly so. Just ahead, vague in the twilight, was the
important intersection that the castle had been built to
overlook. And just beyond that intersection, which at
the moment was empty of traffic, a side road wound
up to the castle, and to the broad green where the fair
sprawled like something raised by enchantment in the
beginning twilight. The fairgrounds were coming alive
with torches against the dusk. They stirred with a
multitude of distant voices, and the sounds of competing musicians.

As the wagon creaked its way toward the crossroads,
Mark left his seat and went back under the cover. He

had agreed with the others that it would be wise for him to stay out of sight as much as feasible until they knew whether or not the Duke was actively seeking him this far south. He felt the change in the wheels' progress when Ben turned off the main road. Then, looking forward through a small opening in the cover, Mark saw that people were already trotting or riding out from the fairgrounds to meet the wagon when it was still a couple of hundred meters down the side road that wound up from the intersection.

One of those riding in the lead was the marshal of the fair, a well-dressed man identifiable by the colors of his jerkin, Sir Andrew's orange and black. The marshal silently motioned for the wagon to follow him, and rode ahead, guiding it through the busy fairgrounds to a reserved spot near the center. Mark, staying in the wagon out of sight, watched the blurred bright spots of torches move past, glowing through the wagon cover on both sides. Sounds surrounded the wagon too—of voices, music, animals, applause. Barbara had thought that the end of daylight would signal the fair's closing for the day, but obviously she had been wrong.

When the marshal had led them to their assigned site, he rode close to the wagon and leaned from his saddle to peer inside. Mark went on with what he was doing, feeding the captive dragon from the replenished frog-crock—if the authorities here were really going to search for him, he would have no hope of hiding. But the marshal only stared at Mark blankly for a moment, then withdrew his head.

Mark heard the official's voice asking: "Where's Nestor?"

Ben gave the answer they had planned: "If he's not here somewhere already, he'll be along in a day or two. He was dickering over some new animals. A team, I mean."

"Looks like you could use one. Well, Sir Andrew wants to see him, mind you tell him as soon as he gets here. There's a hunting contract to be discussed."

Barbara: "Yessir, we'll remind him soon as we see him. It shouldn't be long now."

The marshal rode away, shouting at someone else about garbage to be cleaned up. The three who had just arrived in the wagon immediately got busy, unpacking, tending to the animals, and setting up the tent in which they meant to exhibit the dragon. Their assigned space was a square of trodden grass about ten meters on a side, and the wagon had to be maneuvered into the rear of this space in order to make room for the big tent at the front. Their neighbor on one side was the pavilion of a belly-dancer, with a crowd-drawing preliminary show that went on every few minutes out front — Ben's attention kept wandering from his tasks, and once he tried to feed a frog to a loadbeast. In the exhibitor's space on the far side, a painted lean-to advertised and presumably housed a supposedly magical fire-eater. The two remaining sides of the square were open, bordering grassy lanes along which traffic could pass and customers, if any, could approach. Along these lanes a few interested spectators were already gathering, to watch the dragon-folk get settled. They had hoped to be able to set up after dark, unwatched, but there was no hope of that now. Nor of Mark's remaining unobserved, so he did not try.

The tent in which the dragon was to be shown was made of some fabric lighter and tougher than any that Mark had ever seen before, and gaudily decorated with painted dragons and mysterious symbols. Ben told Mark that the cloth had come from Karmirblur, somewhere five thousand kilometers away at the other end of the world.

As soon as the tent had been put up and secured,

and a small torch mounted on a stand inside for light, the three exhibitors carried the caged dragon into it without uncovering the cage; the bystanders were going to have to pay something if they wanted to catch even the merest glimpse. The three proprietors were also planning to keep at least one of their number in or beside the wagon as much as possible. All obvious valuables were removed from the wagon, some to be carried in purses, others to be buried right under the dragon's cage inside the tent. But Nestor's sword remained within the vehicle, concealed under false floorboards that in turn were covered with a scattering of junk. Barbara, at least, still nursed hopes of being able to put the sword to use eventually, even if Nestor never rejoined the crew. Several times during the last few days Ben had argued the subject with her.

He would be silent for a while, then turn to her with a lost, small-boy look. "Barb, I don't see how we're going to hunt dragons without Nestor. It was hard enough with him."

Barbara's mobile face would show that she was giving the objection serious consideration, even if she had answered it before, not many hours ago. "You know best about that, Ben, the actual hunting. Maybe we could hire some other hunters to help us?"

"Wouldn't be safe. If we do that they'll find out about the magic in the sword. Then they'll try to steal it." Despite the fact that it had taken Ben himself more than long enough to notice. But Mark didn't think that Ben was really slow-witted, as he appeared to be at first. It was just that he spent so much of his mental time away somewhere, maybe thinking about things like minstrelsy and verse.

At last, after several arguments, or debates, Barbara had given in about the hunting, at least temporarily. "Well then, if we can't, we can't. If Nestor never shows up at Sir Andrew's, we'll just act more surprised than

anyone else, and wonder aloud what could have
happened to him. Then we'll wait around at Sir
Andrew's for a little while after the fair's over, and if
Nestor still isn't there we'll pack up and head south
and look for another fair. At least it'll be warmer down
south in the winter. Anyway, I don't suppose Sir Andrew
would be eager to hire us as hunters without Nestor."

"I don't suppose," Ben agreed with some relief.
Then he added, as if in afterthought: "Anyway, if Sir
Andrew takes me on as a minstrel, you'll be going
south without me."

He looked disappointed when Barbara agreed to
that without any comment or hesitation.

Mark didn't have any comment to make either. He
suspected that if Nestor didn't appear, Barbara meant
to sell the sword if she couldn't find a way to use it.
He, Mark, would just have to decide for himself when
the time came what he wanted to try to do about that.
This sword wasn't his. But he felt it was a link, of
sorts, to his own blade, about the only link that he still
had. If Nestor came back at all, it would be with the
idea of recovering his own sword, whatever other
plans he might have.

Of course, he might not have Mark's sword with
him when he showed up. And if he did have it, he
might not be of a mind to give it back.

Any way Mark looked at the current situation, his
chances of recovering his sword, his inheritance, looked
pretty poor.

Three hours after the dragon-people had arrived,
the carnival was showing some signs of winding down
for the night, though the grounds were by no means
completely quiet as yet. Barbara still had the dragon-
exhibit open, though business had slowed down to the
point where Ben was able to put on his plumed hat,
collect his lute, and announce to his partners that he

was going out to try his hand at minstrelsy.

Mark's help was not needed at the showtent for the moment either, and he had retired to the wagon, where he meant to get something to eat, meanwhile casually sitting guard over the concealed sword.

The inside of the wagon looked about twice as big now, with almost everything moved out of it. From where Mark was sitting he could just see the entrance to the tent, which had been erected at right angles to the wagon. Barbara had just finished conducting one small group of paying customers into the tent to see the dragon and out again, and she was presently chatting with a prospective first member of the next group. This potential customer was a chunkily-built little man, evidently of some importance, for he was dressed in fancier clothes than any Mark had seen since the seneschal, the Duke's cousin, went down.

Mark was chewing on a piece of boiled fowl—Ben had laid in some food from a nearby concession before he left—and thinking gloomy thoughts about his missing sword, when he heard a faint sound just behind him, right inside the wagon. He turned to see a man whom he had never seen before, who was standing on the ground outside with his head and shoulders in the rear opening of the wagon. Knotted on the man's sleeve was what looked like the orange-and-black insignia of an assistant marshal of the fair. He was looking straight at Mark, and there was that in his eyes that made Mark drop his drumstick and dive right out of the front of the wagon without a moment's hesitation. Only as Mark cleared the seat did it fully register in his mind that the man had been holding a large knife unsheathed in his right hand.

Mark landed on hands and knees on the worn turf just outside the wagon. He somersaulted once, and came up on his feet already running. As he reached the doorway of the tent he was drawing in a deep breath to yell for help. Inside the tent, the small dragon was already yowling continuously, and this perhaps served as a subliminal warning; Mark did not yell. When he looked into the tent he saw by the light of the guttering single torch how Barbara lay limp in the grasp of a second man in marshal's insignia, how the dragon's cage had been tipped over backwards, and how the well-dressed stranger, who a moment ago had been chatting innocently with Barbara, was now frantically digging with his dagger into the ground where the cage had been, uncovering and scattering fine valuable crossbow bolts and bits of armor.

Mark did not yell. But the men inside the tent both yelled when they saw him, and turned and rushed in his direction. He was just barely too quick for them, as he darted away and then rolled under the flimsily paneled side of the fire-eater's construction on the adjoining lot.

The inside of that shelter was as dark as the toe of a boot; no flames were being ingested at the moment. But there came a quick stir in the blackness, an alarmed fumbling as of bedclothes, an urgent muttering of voices. Mark somehow stumbled and crashed his way through the darkness, once tripping over something and falling at full length. When he had come to the opposite wall he went out under it, in the same manner he had come in. There was no one waiting in the grass outside to seize him; for the moment he had foiled his pursuers. But for the moment only; he could hear them somewhere behind him, yelling, raising an alarm.

He made an effort to get in under the wall of the next shelter, which was a tent, found his way blocked, and slid around the tent instead. Now a deep ditch offered some hope of concealment, and he slid down into the ditch to scramble in knee-deep water at the bottom. When he had his feet more or less solidly under him he followed the ditch around a turn, where he paused to look and listen for pursuit. He heard none, but realized that he'd already lost his bearings. This fairground was certainly the biggest of the two or three that Mark had ever seen. There, the dark bulk of the castle loomed, enormous on its small rise, with lights visible in a few windows. But to Mark in his bewildered state the castle was just where it ought not to have been, and at the moment it gave him no help in getting his bearings.

Now people were yelling something in the distance. But he couldn't tell whether or not the cries had anything to do with him. What was he going to do now? If only, he thought, Kind Sir Andrew himself could be made to hear the truth . . .

Mark followed the ditch for a few more splashing strides, then climbed from it into the deeper darkness behind another row of tents and shelters. He was moving toward lights and the sounds of cheerful music. It was in fact better music than Ben was ever going to be able to make, if he practiced for a hundred years. If only he could at least find Ben, and warn him . . .

With this vague purpose of locating Ben, Mark looked out into the lighted carnival lanes while keeping himself as much as possible in the shadows. He crawled under someone's wagon, then behind a booth, seeking different vantage points. In another open way were clowns and jugglers, drawing a small crowd, laughter and applause. Mark tried to see if Ben was in the group somewhere, but was unable to tell. He moved briefly into the open again, until orange and black tied on a sleeve ahead sent him crawling back into hiding, through the partly open back door of a deserted-looking hut. Once more his entry roused an unseen sleeper; a man's voice muttered alarm, and half-drunken, half-coherent threats.

Mark darted out of the hut again, and went trotting

away from people, along a half-darkened traffic lane.
Brighter torchlight shone round the castle's lowered
drawbridge, now not far ahead of him. More suits of
orange and black were there, gathered as if in conference.
To avoid them, Mark turned a corner, toward more
music. This time there were drums, and roistering
voices. Maybe this crowd would be big enough to hide
him for a while. And there, a few meters ahead, stood
Ben, plumed hat tipped on the back of his head, his
lute temporarily forgotten under one arm. His stocky
figure was part of the small crowd gawking at the
belly-dancer's outside-the-tent performance. Mark realized that he had unconsciously fled in a circle, and
was now back near the place where he had started
running.

He took another step forward, intending to warn
Ben. And at that same moment, the chunky dandy
reappeared, approaching from the direction of the
dragon-tent beyond. He saw Mark, and at once raised
a fresh outcry. Mark yelped and turned and sped
away. He didn't know whether Ben had even noticed
him or not.

Now, several more of the marshal's men were blocking the lane ahead of Mark. He turned on one toe, to
dash in at right angles under the broad banner advertising the Maze of Mirth, past a startled clown-face
and into a dim interior. The stuffed figure of a demon,
crudely constructed, lurched at him out of the gloom,
and a mad peal of laughter went up from somewhere
behind it. The inside of this place was a maze, furnished
with crude mirrors and dark lanterns flashing suddenly,
constructed of confusingly painted walls all odd shapes
and angles. The head of a real dragon, long since
stuffed and varnished, popped out at Mark from behind
a suddenly open panel.

Mark could feel the burn on his face throbbing.
Now another panel opened unexpectedly when he

leaned on it, and he spun in confusion through a dark opening. A mirror showed him a distorted image of the chunky dandy, coming after him, perhaps still two mirrors away. The man's mouth was opening for a yell.

An arm, banded in orange and black, came out of somewhere else to flail at Mark, and then was left behind when yet another panel closed. The very walls were shouting as they moved, roaring with mad laughter . . .

A new figure loomed before Mark, that of a tall, powerful clown in jester's motley. The clown was holding something out to Mark in one hand, while at the same time another hand, invisible, pushed at the jester's painted face. The face moved. It became a mask that slid back, revealing —

The mask slid back from the face of the one-armed clown. The face revealed was fair and large and smiling. It was lightly bearded, as Mark had never seen it before, but he had not an instant's doubt of just whose face it was.

"Father!"

Jord nodded, smiling. The shape he was holding out was half-familiar to Mark. It was the shape of a sword's hilt. But this time the weapon was sheathed in ornate leather, looped with a leather belt. As Mark's two hands closed on the offered hilt, and drew the weapon from its sheath, his father's face fell into darkness and away.

"Father?"

Now someone's hands were moving round Mark's waist, deftly buckling a swordbelt on him. "Mark, take this to Sir Andrew. If you can." It was half the voice of Jord as Mark remembered it, half no more than an anonymous whisper.

"Father . . . "

Mark turned, with the drawn blade still in his hands, trying to follow dim images that chased each other

away from him through mirrors. He saw the form of a
lean carnival clown, two-armed and totally unfamiliar,
backing away. Mark tried to follow the figure through
the dim mad illumination, the light of torchflames
beyond mirrors, glowing through mirrors and cloth.
This time Mark could feel power emanating from the
blade he held. But the flavor of the power was different,
somehow, from what he had expected. *Another* sword?
It fed Mark's hands with a secret, inward thrumming—

With a terrific shock, something came smashing
through thin partitions near at hand. It was an axe,
no, yet another sword, this one quite mundane though
amply powerful. Enchantment seemed to vanish, as it
was supposed to do when swords were out. A nearby
mirror fell from the wall, shattering with itself the last
image of the retreating clown.

And now hard reality reappeared, in the form of the
chunky little man in dandy's clothes. He was all
disarranged and rumpled with triumphant effort. His
face, as he closed in on Mark, displayed his triumph.
His mouth opened, awry, ready to bawl out something.
The dandy lifted a torch toward Mark—and then
recoiled like one stabbed. Still staring at Mark, he
made an awkward, half-kneeling gesture that was
aborted by the narrowness of the passage. The orange-
and-black armbands who now appeared behind him
also stared at Mark, in obvious stupefaction.

Mark could see now, without knowing quite how he
saw it, that they were not what their armbands
proclaimed them.

The stocky leader said to Mark: "Your Grace . . . I
am sorry . . . I never suspected that you would be . . .
which way did he go?"

Mark stood still, clutching the naked sword, feeling
the weight of its unfamiliar belt around his waist. He
felt unable to do anything but wait stupidly for whatever might happen next. He echoed: "He?"

"That boy, Your Grace. It was the one that we are after, I am sure. He was right here."

"Let him go, for now." Magic's mad logic had taken hold of Mark, and he knew, as he would have known in a dream, that he was speaking of himself.

"I . . . yes, sire." The man in front of Mark was utterly bewildered by the order he had just heard, but never dreamt of disobedience. "The flying courier should have the other sword at any moment now, and will then depart at once. Unless Your Grace, now that you are here, wishes to change plans—?"

"The other sword?"

"The sword called Dragonslicer, sire. They must have hidden it there somewhere, in their wagon or their tent. Our men will have it any moment now. The courier is ready." The stocky man was sweating, and not only with exertion; it bothered him that it should be necessary to explain these things.

Mark turned away from him. A great anger at this gang of thieves was building in him. Holding his newly acquired sword before him like a torch, he burst his way out through the hacked opening that made a new solution to the Maze of Mirth. Feeling the rich throb of the weapon's power steady in his wrists, he ran along the grassy lane outside, past men in orange and black who stumbled over each other to get out of his way. He heard their muttered exclamations.

"His Grace himself!"

"The Duke!"

Mark ran in the direction of the dragon-hunters' tent and wagon. The wagon had been tipped on one side now, and men were prying at its wreckage, while a large gray shape with spread wings squatted near them on the ground. Before Mark was able to get much closer, the large winged dragon rose into the air. Mark heard the windmill-creaking of its voice, and he saw that it was now carrying a sword, clutched close against its body in one taloned foot.

Once again a sword was being taken from him. Mark, incapable at the moment of feeling anything but rage, ran under the creature as it soared, screaming at it to come down, to bring the stolen weapon back to him. In the upward glow of the fairgrounds' varied lights, Mark saw to his amazement how the dragon's fanged head lowered in midflight. Its long neck bent, its eyes searched half-intelligently for the source of the voice that cried at it. It located Mark. And then, to his greater amazement still, it started down.

The people who were standing near Mark scattered, allowing him and the dragon ample room to meet. At the last moment Mark realized that the creature was not attacking him. Instead it was coming down as if in genuine obedience to his shouted order.

Feeling the sword surging in his hands, he stepped to meet the dragon. In rage grown all the greater because of his previous helpless fear, he stabbed at the winged dragon blindly as it hovered just above the grass. The attack took it by surprise, and Mark felt his thrust go home. The dragon dropped the sword that it was carrying, and Mark without thought bent to pick it up.

For just an instant he touched both hilts at the same time, right hand still following through his thrust, left fingers touching the hilt that had fallen to the ground.

For an instant, he thought that a great wind had arisen, and was about to blow him off his feet. For that heartbeat's duration of double contact, he had a sense that the world was altering around him, or else that he was being extracted from it . . .

The rising movement of the flyer pulled from Mark's extended hand the hilt of the sword with which he'd stabbed it. The dragon was taking off with the blade still embedded in its side. Mark, on his knees now,

squinting upward as if into dazzling light, lost sight of
the sword that went up with the dragon. But before
his eyes the dragon's whole shape was changing, melting
and reforming. He saw first a giant barnyard fowl in
flight, then an enormous hawk, at last a winged woman
garbed in white. Then the shape vanished, climbing
beyond the effective range of the fairgrounds' lights.

Slowly Mark stood up straight, still holding the
sword that the dragon had dropped in front of him. It
was Dragonslicer—by now, he found, he was able to
tell one from another by the feeling, needing no look at
the hilt.

The world that had been trying to alter around him
was now trying to come back. But its swift shifting
had been too violent for that to be accomplished in an
instant.

The stocky man who had attacked Barbara and had
been chasing Mark had now caught up with him once
more. But the man only stood in front of Mark in
absolute consternation, gazing first at Mark and then
up into the night sky after the vanished courier.

From somewhere in the gathering crowd, Barbara
came stumbling, staggering, screaming incoherent
accusations. The dandy, bemused and rumpled, turned
on her with his dagger drawn. Before Mark could
react, a huge hand reached from behind the man to
grab him by one shoulder and turn him, spinning him
into the impact of a fist that seemed to break him like
a toy.

Men in orange and black had Ben surrounded. But
now, from the direction of the drawbridge, another
small group of men in black and orange came charging.
These were half-armored with helms and shields, and
held drawn swords. Led by a graybeard nobleman,
they hurled themselves with a warcry at the first
group.

Mark knew that his own hand still held a sword. He

told himself that he should be doing something. But the sense that his place in the world had changed still held him. It was not like anything he had ever felt before. He thought that he could still feel the two hilts, one in each hand.

And then he could feel nothing at all.

CHAPTER 11

"Yes, I am Draffut, once called by humans the Lord
of Beasts. And now they call me a god." In the deep
voice were tired tones that mocked the foolishness of
humans. "Stand up, man. No human being should
kneel to me."

All around Nestor and the giant the night creatures
of the swamp were awakening, from whatever daytime
dreams they had to noisy life. Nestor stood up. His
emotional outburst, whether or not it had been based
on some misconception, had relieved something in
him and he felt calmer. "Very well," he said. "What
shall I call you, then?"

"I am Draffut. It is enough. And you are Nestor,
who kills dragons. Now come with me, you will need
food and rest."

"Rest, first, I think." Nestor rubbed at his eyes;

exhaustion was rapidly overtaking him. The sword dragged down whichever hand he held it in.

Draffut led the way back to the ancient temple. Standing beside the building, he raised a shaggy arm to indicate a place where, he said, Nestor should be able to rest in safety. This was a half-ruined room on an upper level, in a portion of the structure that once had had a second floor. The stairway nearby had almost entirely disappeared, but Nestor was agile and he found a way to scramble up. His assigned resting place was open to the sky, but at least it should offer him some degree of isolation from creeping things. When Nestor turned from a quick inspection of the place to speak to Draffut again, he saw to his surprise that the giant had disappeared.

Neither the hard floor of his high chamber, nor the possibility of danger, kept Nestor from falling quickly into a deep sleep, that turned almost at once into a vivid dream.

In this dream he beheld a fantastic procession, that was made up partly of human beings, and partly of others who were only vaguely visualized. The procession was marching through brilliant sunlight to the temple, at some time in the days of that building's wholeness and glory. At first the dream was quite a pleasant experience. Then came the point when Nestor realized that in the midst of the procession was being borne a maiden meant for sacrifice—and that the prospective victim was Barbara.

In the dream Barbara was straining at the bonds that held her, and crying out to him for help. But in terror Nestor turned away from her. Clasping the hilt of his precious sword, which he knew he must not lose no matter what, he ran with it into the jungle surrounding the temple closely. This was a dream-growth of spectacular colors, very different from the scrubby woods that his waking eyes had beheld covering most of the island. But as soon as Nestor had reached the jungle, the sword-hilt in his hand turned into something else—and before he could understand what it had become, he was waking up, gasping with his fear.

Night-creatures were being noisy at a little distance, yet the darkness round him was peaceful enough, though he was breathing as hard as if he had been fighting. The gibbous moon was by now almost directly overhead, in a sky patched with clouds; it was some time near the middle of the night.

The image of Barbara remained vividly with Nestor for some time after he had awakened. Ought he to have stood by the spilled wagon, sword in hand, to fight for her and for the others?

Nonsense. Before he'd managed to get his hand on a sword, they'd all run away, scattering and hiding as best they could. He would have been killed, and it would have done no one any good at all.

Maybe he knew that he would have run away, even if the others hadn't. But it was nonsense, dredging up such theoretical things to worry about.

Though the unpleasantness of the dream lingered, Nestor soon fell asleep again. He woke with the feeling that no time at all had passed, though the sun was now fully up in a bright sky, and monkbirds were exchanging loud cries in branches not far above his head.

Nestor sat up, reflecting on how well he felt, how rested. He rubbed the shoulder that yesterday had been—he was sure of it—broken. It felt as good as the other shoulder now.

He vaguely remembered having some disagreeable dream, but he no longer remembered what it had been about.

The sword was at his side, just where he had put it down. What had Draffut said, that sounded like quoted verse? *Long roads the Sword of Fury makes, Hard*

walls it builds around the soft . . . Nestor would have
given something to hear the rest.

Beside the sword now was a pile of fresh fruit, that
certainly had not been there when he last fell asleep.
Nestor sniffed at something yellow and round, then
nibbled cautiously. Then, suddenly ravenous, he fell
to. The sword made a convenient tool to slice and peel.

Before Nestor had fully satisfied his appetite, Draffut
appeared, walking tree-tall from among the trees. The
giant exchanged rather casual greetings with Nestor,
and claimed credit for the provision of the man's
breakfast, for which Nestor thanked him. In the bright
morning Draffut's fur glowed delicately, just as it had
in twilight and after dark, holding its own light. As
Draffut stood on the ground outside the temple his
face was approximately on a level with Nestor's, who
was standing on what had once been a second floor.

This morning Nestor felt no impulse to kneel. He
realized that his awe of Draffut was already fading
into something that approached familiarity, and in an
obscure way the man partially regretted the fact. As
soon as a few conversational preliminaries had been
gone through, he asked: "Draffut, will you tell me
about the gods? And about yourself. If you maintain
you are not one of them, I don't intend to argue with
you. But perhaps you can understand why I thought
you were."

Draffut answered thoughtfully. "I understand that
humans often show a need for beings greater than
themselves. But I repeat that I can tell you very little
about the gods. Their ways are often beyond my
understanding. As for my own story, it is very long
and I think that now is not the time for me to begin to
tell it. Right now it is more important that I learn
more about your sword."

"Very well." Nestor looked down at the blade with
which he had been halving fruit, that was not really

his. He sighed, and shook his head, thinking of the one he'd lost. Then he explained as briefly as he could how the wagon he had been driving had been pursued, and had tipped over, and what had happened to him after that, and what he surmised might have happened to his companions. "So, the landwalker, which I suppose was your creature too, attacked Duke Fraktin's men in the vicinity of the wagon—or at least that's what it sounded like. I could not stay to see who won the fight, for your messenger came to invite me to be your guest. So, that boy may have my sword now. Or the Duke might have it, or some of his soldiers. As for this blade here, the boy told me that it can kill fighting men with great efficiency. I've never put it to the test."

Draffut stared as if he thought a particularly interesting point had been raised. Then the giant asked: "You have fought against other men at some time in the past, though? And killed them sometimes?"

Nestor paused warily before he answered. "Yes, when it seemed to me there was no way of avoiding such a fight. Soldiering is not a profession that I'd choose to follow."

"It is no more dangerous than hunting dragons, surely."

"Less so, perhaps, most of the time. Still I'd not choose it." And at the same time, Nestor could not help wondering again what might have happened back at the wagon if he had turned with this sword in hand to fight the Duke's patrol. Probably if he'd survived that by some magic, he would have had to fight the dragon too. Almost certainly he'd now be dead, magic swords or not, just like the brother that young Einar—if that was his real name—had spoken of. Well, he was sure he was going to die in some kind of a fight, sometime, somewhere. But there was an inescapable fascination about the particulars.

Meanwhile Draffut stood in thoughtful silence, con-

sidering Nestor's answer. Once the giant reached with
two fingers to the pile of fruit, and popped several
pieces into his mouth at once, chewing with huge
fangs that appeared much better suited to a carnivo-
rous diet. To Nestor, this mere fact of eating somehow
added force to Draffut's disclaimer of divinity—though
if he thought about it, he recalled that the deities were
often described as feasting.

Nestor at last broke the silence with a question:
"What do you plan to do with me?"

Draffut roused himself from thought with a shake of
his head. "I am sorry now that I sent dragons to bring
you here, at risk of your being killed or injured. For it
seems that you can tell me little that is useful."

"I would if I could."

"I believe it. I could arrange for the flying dragon to
carry you out of the swamp again."

"Thank you, no. I think I would rather remain here
as your guest for the next twenty years or so. Is there
some other alternative?"

"The number of alternatives is quite limited. Still, I
can probably arrange something to get you out of the
swamp. In which direction would you prefer to go?"

"I was headed with my companions toward the
domain of Kind Sir Andrew, with whom I had a
hunting contract to discuss. If my friends somehow
managed to survive both the dragons and the Duke's
men, they are probably there now, looking for me."

"And if they should still have with them your own
sword . . ."

"Dragonslicer. Or, the Sword of Heroes, so Hermes
told me. Yes, it may be there too."

Draffut took a little time to consider before he spoke
again. "Would you be willing to make the trip on the
back of a large landwalker? I can influence them, as
you have already seen. But they are somewhat less
docile and dependable than the flying dragons. Also I

fear that the journey would probably take longer that way, several days at least."

"Are there no boats to be had here in the swamp? No people living here at all?" Nestor was sure that there were at least a few, grubbing around in savage conditions. "If it comes down to the choice, I'll try to carve my own boat out of a log and paddle it out, rather than depend again on the whim of any dragon. Regardless of what spells you may be able to put on them."

"I put no spells on dragons," said Draffut almost absently. "I am no magician."

"You spoke of influencing them . . . "

"As for making your own boat, I do not think that you would live for many hours in the swamp, traveling alone in any boat you could build for yourself under these conditions. And unfortunately I cannot spare the time it would take to escort you to safe land myself. But I will see what I can do to help you."

You cannot spare the time from what? Nestor wondered. But he kept the question to himself; the giant had already turned and was walking purposefully away. In a few moments Draffut had vanished from Nestor's view behind a screen of trees. His head briefly reappeared, topping a screen of shorter trees in the middle distance. Then it sank abruptly below the treetops' level, as if he had stepped into the swamp.

Left to himself, Nestor out of curiosity soon undertook a more or less complete exploration of the temple. In several of the rooms he examined the carvings on the walls fairly closely. These reliefs depicted men, women, and unidentifiable other beings engaged in what Nestor took to be a variety of ritual activities; it was difficult to make out any details of what they were about.

In the room where Draffut had shown him the odd thing he called a larva, Nestor peered again into the tank. The surface of the water was once more mirror-quiet. On the shelf nearby waited the Old World lamp, but Nestor made no move to take it down. He had no wish to raise the larva again.

He continued his explorations. He was in another large chamber, pondering what appeared to be a row of empty closets, when his thoughts were interrupted by a noise. This was a sudden outburst of shrill cries, delivered in an inhuman voice that sounded as if it were somewhere close outside the temple. Nestor went to a doorway, sword in hand, and cautiously peered out.

A flying dragon was hovering nearby, above the courtyard. Somewhat smaller than the one that had earlier kidnapped Nestor, it looked at him but kept its distance. It circled a few more times, hovered some more, and shrilled at him. It was almost as if, he thought fancifully, the beast had something it was trying to communicate.

It kept on making noise until Nestor at last spoke to it, as a man alone speaks to a thing or an animal, not expecting understanding. "If it's Draffut you're looking for, he's not here. He stalked off into the swamp, to the southwest, more than an hour ago. No telling when he'll be back."

To Nestor's considerable surprise—after years of dealing with dragons, he considered their intelligence to be about on a par with that of barnyard fowl—the creature reacted as if it had in fact understood him. These flying creatures must indeed be a subspecies he had never heard of. At least it ceased its noise and flew away at once. Whether it really headed southwest Nestor could not tell, but it flapped its way around the bulk of the temple and might have gone in that direction.

Nestor, shaking his head, went slowly back inside the building, intending to explore some more. Looking around the place gave him something to do while he waited for Draffut, and the more he knew about his immediate environment the more secure he felt. On the ground level he discovered one large chamber whose floor was padded with heaps of fronds and springy vines; he wondered if this was the place where Draffut rested. Everyone agreed that gods could eat, but did they have to rest?

Pondering, or trying to ponder, the mysteries of Draffut, and of the multiple swords of magic, and of what the god-game might be, Nestor made his way outside again. This time he exited through the place where a wall had tumbled, to emerge on a slope leading to an upper level of the temple. He climbed across a high ruined section, that was littered with tilted slabs of fallen roof. From here it was possible to see above the island's treetops, or most of them, but there was apparently nothing but more swamp and trees beyond.

The morning sun had climbed, but it was not yet too hot to make it uncomfortable to stretch out on a fallen slab of roof and bask. Relaxation sometimes helped a man to think.

But soon, instead of concentrating on the intriguing questions that had arisen, Nestor was almost dozing. In his thoughts images came and went, pictures of Draffut and the swords. Then Barbara and the imagined gods. Somehow, thought Nestor, the world ought to fit together, and basically make sense. People always hoped it would. But, as far as he knew, the human race had never been given any such guarantee . . .

He was almost asleep when a faint sound caught at his attention. A light tap first, like a cautious footfall, and then a small scraping or sliding sound. It was repeated, tap and slide, tap and slide. Nestor listened, heard the sound no more, and went briefly back to his dozing thoughts.

Then it came again: tap-slide. Tap-slide. Almost like

footsteps. But limping footsteps. Almost like—

He leaped up, just as a shadow fell across him. And he snatched up the sword barely in time to parry the first blow of the crude barbed hook.

CHAPTER 12

First Mark was moving through a world of dreams, then he was not. The vision of many swords was gone, but now he was not at all sure at just what point the transition from sleep to waking life had taken place.

His eyes opened to a view of a ceiling of vaulted stone. Quickly raising himself on one elbow, he could see that he was for the first time in his life inside a real castle. This large and richly furnished room could be part of nothing else. And he was lying in a real bed, with sunlight that had a morning feeling to it coming in through the room's single narrow window.

On a table in the center of the room, the Sword of Heroes rested — Mark could make out the small white dragon in the decoration on the black hilt. Lying on the bare wood beside the weapon were the belt and the scabbard that had been given to Mark — last night? —

along with a different sword.

Sharp as a dagger's stroke, the memory returned now of his father's face, bearded as Mark had never seen it before, but unmistakable. The smiling kindness, the look of recognition in the eyes. That face in the Maze of Mirth had been so real—

On a small lounge beside the single bed, Barbara was sleeping. She appeared to be wearing her ordinary clothes, but a rich shawl had been thrown over her. It was as if she had been watching over Mark and had fallen asleep, and then perhaps some other watcher had covered her for warmth. And now Mark saw where his own clothes were draped over another chair, with a set of much handsomer garments beside them. Was the finery meant for him? He'd never worn such things.

A familiar snore disturbed the air, making Mark turn his head. In a far corner of the room, almost lost behind more furniture, Ben lay snoring on a heap of fancy pillows. He too was covered with a rich, unfamiliar robe.

As soon as Mark sat up straight in bed, Barbara stirred too. She opened dark eyes and looked at him for a moment without comprehension. Then, wide awake in another instant, she smiled at him. Then she had thrown the shawl aside and was standing beside the bed to feel Mark's head for fever. She asked: "Are you all right?"

"I think so. What happened? Who brought us into the castle? I remember there was a fight . . . "

"And you fell over. Then Sir Andrew had us all brought in. Ben and I have told him just about everything. We were all worried about you, but the enchantress said she thought you'd just sleep it off. Dame Yoldi's her name, and I'm supposed to call her as soon as you wake up. Just stay there and I'll go get her."

Barbara went out of the room quickly. Mark, disregarding her orders, got up and began to dress, choosing his own old clothes though the elegant new ones beside them appeared to be of a suitable size. Meanwhile Ben snored on peacefully in the corner.

When Mark was dressed he looked out the window briefly at distant fields and forests beneath the rising sun. Then he stood over the table that held the sword, looking at the weapon but not touching it. He was trying to remember, to reconstruct the experience that must have made him lose consciousness the night before, evidently many hours ago. He could not remember suffering any blow to the head or other injury. Only touching, for a moment, two swords at the same time, and then feeling strange. He didn't seem to be wounded now, or hurt in any way, except for the old, half-healed mark of dragon's fire on his left cheek.

The voice came from the doorway behind him: "You are Mark. Son of Jord, who is a miller in Arin-on-Aldan."

Mark whirled at the first word. He found himself confronted by the man who last night had led the charge of men armed with swords from the drawbridge, and who could only be Sir Andrew himself. Beside the knight was an elegantly dressed woman who must be his enchantress. Mark stuttered something and started to go down on one knee.

"No, stand up." Sir Andrew's voice was powerful, but so far not threatening. He was frowning as he stood with hands clasped behind him. "Duke Fraktin sends me word that he considers you a thief and a murderer."

"I am not, sir." The tone in which the accusation had been passed along had seemed to encourage a bold denial. In the far corner of the room, Ben was now waking up, trying to remain inconspicuous even as he lumbered to his feet.

"I hardly thought that you were," Sir Andrew agreed.

"I know Duke Fraktin is guilty of both charges himself, and perhaps worse . . . and last night the agents he sent here showed they were no better. They've committed what amount to acts of war against me. They—"

The beautiful woman who was standing beside Sir Andrew put a hand on the knight's arm, gently interrupting him. When he had let himself be silenced, she spoke urgently to Mark: "What do you remember of last night?"

Haltingly at first, then gaining confidence as he was granted a patient hearing by both the highborn folk, Mark recounted his experiences at the fair as he remembered them. He began with his arrival in the wagon with Ben and Barbara, and went on to the moment when the dragon-courier of Duke Fraktin had soared away, the sword Mark had stabbed it with still wedged into its scales.

"As the dragon went up, it looked—changed. It looked unreal to me. Like it was one different creature after another. And then I lost sight of it, and people were fighting all around me. As you must know, sir, ma'm. And then I think that something must have struck me down. But just before that I was feeling—strange."

The enchantress came toward Mark, and stood in front of him looking at him very closely. At first he was frightened, but something soon drained away the fear. She said to him: "You were not wounded, were you?"

"No ma'm, I wasn't wounded. But . . . I just had the feeling that something was . . . happening to me."

"I don't doubt you did." Dame Yoldi finished her long look at Mark, and sighed. She looked around at each of the other people in the room. "I was watching from a castle window, while most of the rest of you were out in the fairgrounds. There was a magic in that stolen sword, that made the creature carrying it seem to change. We each of us saw it as something different when it rose up through the air—but each of us saw it as something harmless, or as a being that ought to be defended. Just as everyone saw you, Mark, as someone to be obeyed, protected, served—as long as you were carrying that sword."

Mark nodded solemnly. "Once I had it, the man who had been chasing me called me 'Your Grace' —what became of him?"

Sir Andrew grunted. "Hugh of Semur was among last night's dead." The knight glanced momentarily toward Ben, who was continuing to stand in his corner, still wrapped in his blanket and trying to look small. "And my own men fought well, once we understood that we were required to fight. Some of those who were pretending to be my marshals got away from us, I fear. But some are dead, and one or two are in my dungeon now. I fear they'll be a bad influence on my one honest criminal." To Mark's further bewilderment, the knight here shook his head, apparently over some private worry.

Dame Yoldi asked: "Mark, who gave you that other sword, the one that's now flown away? You've just told us that the man who did so appeared to be your father, as long as he had the sword. But what did he look like afterward, when he'd passed Sightblinder over to you?"

"When I had the sword, I saw him only as a masked clown. Lady, I do not understand these things of magic."

There was a pause before the enchantress answered. "Nor do I, all too often." As she turned quickly away from Mark, he thought he caught a glimpse of some new inner excitement in her eye. Again she took the lord of the castle by the arm. "Andrew, send out men to search for the carnival clowns. They're scattered now, I'm sure, after last night, along with all the merchants and the visitors. But if we could only find him . . ." For the moment Dame Yoldi appeared to be lost in some wild private speculation.

Sir Andrew stared at her, then went to the door where he barked out orders. In a moment he was back. "They must be scattered like chaff, as you say. But we can try."

"Good." The enchantress was contemplating Mark again, now with something enough like awe to make him feel uncomfortable. "I do not know much yet, lad, about these magic swords. But I am learning. I do know the names of some of them, at least. It was Sightblinder that you stabbed the dragon with, last night. It is also known as the Sword of Stealth. He who carries it is disguised from all potential enemies — and perhaps from his friends as well. And the man who gave it to you . . . did he say anything?"

"Yes." Mark blushed for his forgetfulness. "He said that I was to give it to Sir Andrew. If I could."

"Did he, hah?"

"And I meant to, sir. But then they told me that the other sword was being stolen. And — and I had to do something."

"And so you did something. Yes, yes, I like having folk about me who sometimes feel that something must be done. I do wish, though, that we still had Sightblinder here. I suppose it's in the Duke's hands now, and I don't like to think what he might do with it." The knight looked at Dame Yoldi, and his worried frown was deeper than before. "My own flyers have all come back now, Yoldi. They couldn't catch his courier in the air, or even see it. Luck is with Fraktin at present."

"In the form of Coinspinner, yes," Dame Yoldi said. She nodded tiredly, and spoke to Mark again. "Is it possible, boy, that for one moment last night you had your hands on two swords at the same time?"

"Yes ma'm, it's more than possible. It happened that way. And that was when the — the world started to go strange."

"I thought as much. And now the Duke, with his luck augmented by Coinspinner, is going to have the Sword of Stealth in hand as well. No one else in the world has ever owned two of those swords since they were made . . . Mark, I have learned that the smith who helped Vulcan forge them was your father."

Mark could feel himself standing, a small figure, alone, beside the table that held the sword called Townsaver. "I knew that he helped make this one. But, until I left home, I never heard that Vulcan had forged other swords at the same time. My father never liked to speak of it at all. And now he's dead. I saw him die, the same day my brother died, and Duke Fraktin's cousin in our village.

"Last night when I thought it was my father—" Mark covered his eyes briefly with his hands. "But I know it was only some piece of magic."

Two sentries, armed and alert, had arrived at the room's door, and now one of them entered to whisper something to Sir Andrew.

"Bring her in," the knight ordered grimly.

Before whoever it was could be brought in, Dame Yoldi moved to the table near Mark's side. With a small piece of black cloth that might have been a handkerchief she draped the hilt of the sword that lay on the table, so that the little white design of decoration could not be seen. Then she stepped away from the table and nodded to the guards.

A moment later, a dark lady appeared in the doorway, of elegant appearance and malevolent expression. Her air of arrogance made the soldiers at her sides appear to be a guard of honor.

She glared at each person in the room in turn. Her gaze lingered longest on Mark, and he had the sensation that something invisible, but palpable and evil, had passed near him. Then, with her lifted chin turned to Sir Andrew, the lady said: "I demand to be released."

"Most likely you soon will be." The knight's voice had turned cold, much changed from what it had been. "My investigation of what your agents did at the fairgrounds last night is almost complete. If you were not here on business of diplomacy, woman, you'd likely be down in my dungeon now."

The lady chose not to hear this. She tossed back dark hair imperiously. "And where is Hugh of Semur?"

"That dog is dead. Diplomat or not, he succeeded in earning himself a broken neck last night."

The dark lady demonstrated shock. "Dead! Then his killers must be placed in my custody, that I may take them to face the Duke's justice. As I must take him." She pointed a long fingernail at Mark. "And that sword on the table. It belongs to His Grace too."

"I think, m'lady, that you'll take precious little out of my territory but yourself."

The lady started to pretend surprise at this refusal, then shrugged lightly and gave it up. "It will go ill for you, Sir Andrew, if you refuse the Duke his property, and his just vengeance. Who will guarantee the security of your frontiers if he does not?"

"Oh, ah? Speaking of property, there's the matter of the damage done to some of mine last night, and to some of my people, too. That fine coach that brought you here, my fine Lady Marat, should fetch something on the market. Enough, perhaps, to pay some of the bills that you've run up in damages. I'll see if I can find a farm wagon somewhere, and a loadbeast or two, to furnish you and your servants transportation home. A somewhat bumpy ride, perhaps, but—"

Now indeed she flared. "Beast yourself! How dare you treat me, the Duke's emissary, in such a way? How dare you?"

"—but, as I say, it would be a long way for you to walk."

The lady now had a hard struggle to restrain her

tongue, but she managed it at last. After delivering one last glare at each person in the room, she turned between her guards with a fine swirl of glittery fabrics, and with her guards was gone.

Dame Yoldi reached to brush her fingers through Mark's hair; it was as if she were only petting him, but Mark had the sense that something, a cobweb maybe, that he had not known was there, was brushed away. The enchantress smiled at him faintly, then closed her eyes. She held Mark by the hand, as if she were learning something from the feel of his hand.

"The son of Jord," she said, her eyes still closed. "Of Jord who was a miller — and before that, a smith."

"Aye, ma'm."

"Aye, and aye. But I wonder what else your father was?" Dame Yoldi's eyes opened, large and gray and luminous. "Mark, in all the world, your father Jord is, or was, the only human being ever to have handled more than one of the swords. And only you yourself have ever handled as many as three of them, since their steel was infused with the gods' magic. And a question that has nagged at me was answered here, last night, in part: what would happen if a person, a being of any nature, were to touch and use more than one of the swords at the same time?"

Dame Yoldi paused, looking around at all the people in the room. "And what if two or more of the gods' swords were to touch each other? What if they should be used directly against each other in battle?"

No one could answer her.

All were thinking that Duke Fraktin soon would have two swords, unless his courier were somehow stopped.

Mark met Barbara's expressive eyes, and knew what she was thinking: In our old wagon we had two swords at once, and never tried . . .

CHAPTER 13

Nestor, after making that first parry in time to save his life, got quickly to his feet and stepped back from the attacking larva. As it came after him he backed away. It continued to advance, limping even as he had imagined it must move. Nestor was backing up with cautious steps that took him along the jagged edge of a broken roof. On his left was the paved courtyard, seven meters below; sloping upward on his right was the jumble of tilted, fallen slabs, which would be sure to offer abominable footing.

The thing that limped after Nestor blew little moaning cries at him out of its absence of a face, as if it might be in agony, or perhaps in love. On the almost featureless front of its head only the dark eyes moved a little, staying locked on Nestor. The larva was advancing with its bent arms raised, both its weapons held up near its head, ready to parry a swordstroke or to swing at him again. Not only were those forearms armed with barbed hook and torture-knife, but they were in themselves as hard as bronze. Nestor had a good gauge now of that metallic hardness; his first edged parry had nicked and dented the thing's right wrist, but no more than dented it. A human arm would almost certainly have been completely severed.

After backing up only a few steps along the rim of the roof, Nestor decided retreating was more dangerous than standing his ground would be. He was a competent swordsman, and the blade in his hand a superb weapon, even when, as now, whatever magic it might possess was in abeyance. Why then had he automatically retreated, and why did deep terror still lie in his stomach like a lump of ice? The terror must come, he realized, only from the peculiar nature of his enemy, and not from any powers that it had so far demonstrated. The movements of his foe showed speed and strength—but no more speed or strength than many human opponents might have shown. And the larva was fighting with one considerable, obvious disadvantage—though its weapons were two in number, they were no longer than its arms. If Nestor could keep his nerve and his footing, and use his own magnificent weapon as it deserved to be used, such an attacker ought not to be able to defeat him.

On the other hand, it was already plain that the larva had certain advantages as well: devilish persistence, and a horrible durability. When Nestor stood his ground and struck back, landing a hard chop on its torso, he had the sensation of having hewn into frozen mud. The gray shell cracked at the spot where the blow landed, and substance of a deeper gray began oozing out. But the larva was not disabled, and it seemed to feel nothing. It still came after Nestor, nor was it minded to seek its own safety after what the sword had begun to do to it.

Nestor feinted a high blow, and then hit his opponent in the leg. And now the limp that he had so accurately forecast became more pronounced. When Nestor experimentally retreated a step again to see what the thing would do, it followed. Its gait was now a trifle slower.

Of course it might be keeping speed in reserve, something to surprise the man with at a critical moment. But somehow Nestor doubted that. He had trouble imagining that there could be much in the way of cleverness behind that lack of face. The larva blew its whistling, forlorn whine at him, and advanced on him implacably.

He hit it again, this time in the arm, stopping its advance. This was a harder blow, with much of the swordsman's weight and strength behind the driving edge, and now one of the larva's wrists and weapons dangled from a forearm that had been almost severed for all its hardness. The cut was leaking slow gray slime instead of blood.

Nestor, gaining confidence now, made up his mind and charged the larva suddenly. He caught it with its weight on what seemed to be its weaker leg, and it went back and over the edge of the roof under the impact of a hard swordthrust that only started to pierce its tough breastplate. As it went back and over, the larva made grabbing motions, trying to seize the blade, but it lacked the hands with which to grab anything, and anyway one of its arms was almost severed, its weapon flapping like some deadly glove. Still, Nestor had one horrible moment, in which he feared that the sword was stuck so firmly into the chitinous armor that it might be pulled from his hands or else pull him after the larva as it fell. But the point tugged free when the weight of the gray body came on it fully.

No skill or magic broke that fall, and the paved court was a full seven meters down. Looking over the edge of the roof at the inert, sprawled figure after it had bounced, Nestor could see that the whole gray torso was now networked with fine cracks. More of the varied grayness that must serve the thing as life was oozing from inside.

Nestor had no more than started his first easy breath when the thing stirred. Slowly it flexed its limbs, then got back to its feet. It tilted its head back to let its eyes find its human enemy again. Then, moving deliberately, it limped back into the temple on the level below Nestor. He felt sure that it was coming after him again.

He was sweating as he stood there on the broken roof, though heavy clouds were coming over the sun. He had the feeling that he had entered the realm of nightmare. But the urgency of combat was still pumping in his veins, and before it could dissipate back into fear he made himself start looking for the stairway where the thing would logically come up if it was coming. He was going to have to finish it off.

They faced each other, Nestor at the top of a flight of half-ruined, vine-grown stairs, the larva at the bottom. A monkbird screamed somewhere, still mocking the noise that they had made. With scarcely a pause, the larva started up, dragging one foot after it in its methodical limp, dripping spots of grayness from its cracked carapace. It raised the twisted little knife that was its one remaining weapon.

Nestor, watching with great alertness, saw a tiny tip of something appear like a pointed tongue just inside the larva's small round mouth. He ducked, swiftly and deeply, and heard the small hiss of the spat dart going past his head. Then Nestor leaped forward to meet his enemy halfway on the stair. He piled one swordstroke upon another, driving the thing backwards down the stairs again, and then into a stone corner where it collapsed at last.

Though it went down, Nestor kept on hacking at his foe. When both of the larva's arms had been disabled, and one leg taken off completely, he went for the torso, which at last burst like a gray boil. Nestor had to fight down the urge to retch; the smell that arose was of swamp mud and putridity.

"And no heart, by all the demons," he muttered to himself. "No heart to stop in the damned thing anywhere." Indeed, nothing that he could recognize as an internal organ of any kind was visible, only thicker and thinner grayness that varied in its consistency and hue.

Still, the broken arms of the thing kept trying to hit at Nestor's feet, or grab his legs. The attached gray leg still wanted to get the body up. Nestor, reciting all the demons' names he knew, swore that he was going to finish the horror off, and he went at it like a wood-chopper, or rather a madman, abandoning skill. Some of his strokes now were so ill-aimed that the sword rang off the flagstones of the paved yard.

Taking the head completely off settled the thing at last. With that, whatever spells had given the larva the semblance of life were undone. The gray chitin of its outer surfaces immediately started to turn friable. It crumbled at a poke, and the inner grayness that ran out of it thinned out now and spread like mud and water.

Which, as Nestor could now see, what all it was.

Some huge raindrops had already begun to fall. These now multiplied in a white rush. Parts of what had been the larva were already dissolving, washing away into the ground between the paving stones.

Nestor deliberately remained for a time standing in the rain, letting it cool him. He raised his face to the leaking skies, wanting to be cleansed. The downpour grew fiercer, yet still he remained, letting it wash the sword as well. From his experience with Dragonslicer, he did not think that this blade was going to rust.

When Nestor felt tolerably clean again he went back into the temple. Just inside the doorway he leaned against the wall, dripping rainwater from his hair and clothing, watching the continuing rain and listening to it. The thing he had just destroyed with his sword was already no more than a heap of wet muck, rapidly losing all shape as it was washed back into the earth.

"Draffut—god or not, Beastlord, healer, whatever you may or may not be—I am sorry to have destroyed your pet. No, that's doubly wrong. It wasn't your pet, of course. Your experiment in magic, or whatever. And naturally I'm not really sorry, it was a hideous thing. When something comes sneaking up and attacks a man with a hook and a peeling knife, he really has no choice—what's that?"

What it had sounded like was human voices, a small burst of excited conversation. Nestor waited in silence, listening, and presently the voices came again. They were in the middle distance somewhere. He couldn't make out words, but they sounded like the voices of panicked people who were trying to be quiet.

What now?

The sounds came again. Nestor still could not make out any of the words. Some language that he did not know. Most likely that meant some of the savages of the swamp.

Muttering a brief prayer that he might have to do no more fighting, to gods whose existence he still partly doubted, Nestor took a good grip on his sword and went to see what he could see, through a ruined room and out into the slackening rain again. He would move, then wait until he heard the voices and move again.

Climbing a tumbled corner of the temple, past a

tilted deity with rain dripping from his nose, Nestor had a good view out to the northeast. In that direction an arm of the swamp came in closer to the center of the island than in any other. This inlet was visible from the high place where Nestor crouched, and he could see that a handful of dugout canoes had just arrived there. The last of them was still being pulled up on the muddy shore. There were about a dozen people, with straight black hair and nearly naked coppery skins, already landed or still disembarking. It wasn't a war party. Among them they were armed with no more than a couple of small bows and a few clubs—not that they were carrying much of anything else. There were women and children among them, in fact making up a majority of the group. Everything they had looked poor—the Emperor's children, these were, born losers if Nestor had ever seen any.

One of the women pointed back into the swamp, away from Nestor and the temple, and made some statement to the others in the language that Nestor did not know. Then the whole small mob, now gathered on shore, turned inland and began hurrying through low bush toward the temple. They were certainly not aware of Nestor yet, and he crouched a little lower, concealing himself until he could decide what he ought to do next.

Before he could make a plan, something that looked like a large, low-slung lizard came scrambling up out of the swamp behind the people. Though it was mostly obscured by bushes, Nestor could tell it was moving with an awkward run in the same general direction as the humans—but it was not pursuing them. It passed them up and they ignored it. A general migration of some kind? A general flight . . . ?

Farther back to the northeast, in the depths of the swamp, another shape was approaching, with Nestor's view of it still dimmed by rain. Presently he made it out to be another canoe, paddled by two more copper-skinned men. Two women crouched amidships, slashing at the water with their cupped hands as if determined to do everything possible to add speed. The people on shore ceased their progress inland to turn and watch.

When the craft was just a little nearer, Nestor could see a horizontal gray shape coming after it. For a moment he thought this new form was some kind of peculiar wave troubling the water of the swamp, bearing dead logs on its crest. But then he realized that what he had first taken for a wave was really an almost solid rank of larvae like the one he had just destroyed, marching, swimming, clambering forward through the swamp. Beyond this first jumbled rank there appeared a second; Nestor, looking to right and left, could not see the end of either. Scores of the things at least were coming toward the island, and more probably hundreds. He could hear them now, what sounded like a thousand whistling utterances that could not be called voices; he could hear the multitudinous splash of their advance, and the forest of their dead limbs, knocking together softly like tumbled logs in a flood.

Now more animals and birds, large and small together, came fleeing the swamp, as if before a line of beaters in a hunt. The approaching terror came closer, and Nestor's view of it grew less blurred by rain. Now he could see, all along the advancing lines of larvae, how arms ended in spears, in flails, in maces, clubs, and blades. No two pair of raised arms appeared quite alike, but all of them were weapons.

A hundred meters to Nestor's right, he saw a man-sized dragon climb from the muck onto a hummock and turn at bay before the advancing horde, snarling defiance. In an instant the dragon was surrounded by half a dozen of the dead-wood figures. It hurled one back, another and another, but more kept crowding in, their deadly arms rising and falling. Somewhere farther in the distance, a great landwalker bellowed, and Nestor wondered briefly whether it too would choose to stand and fight, and what success it might have if it did.

The people who had already reached the island were waving their arms and calling now, trying to cheer on the last canoe. Its paddlers appeared to Nestor to be gaining on the pursuing horror. But then the bottom of their craft scraped on some large object, log or mud-hump, under water. The next moment, despite all their frantic paddling, they were stuck fast.

Nestor could see now that both of the women in the canoe were carrying, or wearing, infants strapped to their bodies. All four of the adults in the canoe were working frantically to free it, and they seemed on the point of success when the gray wave overtook them, and the first handless arms reached out. To the accompaniment of human screams the canoe tipped over, and its passengers vanished.

Those who had already gained the shore turned from the scene in renewed panic. Crying to one another in a fear that needed no translation, they ran for the temple.

Nestor hesitated no longer over whether to show himself, but jumped up into their full view. He was not going to be able to outrun the oncoming threat, particularly not on a small island; nor were the refugees from the boats. In union lay their only possible chance of making a successful stand against it; and that possible of course only if Townsaver's latent powers could somehow be called into action, and if they were as great as Nestor had been led to expect. The mental map that he had formed during his exploration of the temple showed him another key factor in his hope: a certain high room, open only on one side, that would perhaps be defensible by three or four determined fighters.

The people Nestor was calling to now, who paused in their frightened flight at the sight of his figure in their path with a sword, probably did not understand his language any more than he knew theirs. But they were ready to follow shouts and gestures, to grasp at any straw of hope. In obedience to Nestor's energetic waves, they came running to him now, and past him. Then they let him get ahead and lead them, at a run over piled rubble and up tilted slabs and collapsing stairs, to reach the place he had in mind.

This was one of the highest surviving rooms of what had once been a towering structure. The only way to approach it now was up a long, rough slope of rubble. When Nestor had led the whole group toiling up this ascent, and had them gathered in the high room, they came to a reluctant stop, looking about them in bewilderment.

He gestured with sword and empty hand. "I'm afraid this is it, my friends. This is the best that we can do."

He could see the understanding growing in the adults' faces, and the renewed terror and despair that came with it.

Nestor turned away from those looks, facing downslope and to the north as he looked out of the room's open side. Not a very large width to defend, hardly more than a wide doorway; but it was a little more space than any one man with any one sword could cover. From this high place he could see now that which made his heart sink: the ranks of the larvae, that had come sweeping across the swamp from the north, extended to both east and west across and beyond the entire width of the island, and farther, for some indeterminate but great distance out into the swamp. There must certainly be thousands of them,

There was movement among the people behind Nestor, and he turned around. Slowly the four or five males of fighting age among the group of refugees were taking their places on his right and left, their bows and clubs as ready as they were ever going to be. Nestor looked at them, and they at him. Fortunately there seemed to be no need to discuss strategy or tactics.

The wave of the enemy had some time ago reached the island, and was now sweeping across it. The gray ones had swarmed into the temple, perhaps in extra numbers because of fleeing prey in sight; the ranks looked thicker than ever when they came into Nestor's view at the foot of the long slope of rubble. They paused there, continuing to thicken with reinforcements behind the steady upward stare of a hundred faceless heads, that gazed upslope as if already aware of determined resistance waiting at the top. What sounded like a thousand larval voices were whistling, whining, mocking, making a drone as of discordant bagpipes that seemed to fill the world.

The ranks of the Gray Horde paused briefly to strengthen themselves at the foot of the long hill of rubble. Then they began to mount.

The women behind Nestor, brought to bay now with their young, were arming themselves too. He glanced back and saw them picking up sharp fragments from the rubble, ready to throw and strike. Something flashed across Nestor's mind about all the concern that warriors, himself included, had for their own coming deaths, all the wondering and worrying and fretting that they gave the subject whether they talked about it or not. And these women, now, had never had a thought in their lives about image and honor and courage, and they were doing as well as any . . .

As for Nestor himself, the thousand voices of the larvae assured him that his time was now, that he was never going to have to worry about it again.

Just behind Nestor, a baby cried.

And at the same moment something thrummed faintly in Nestor's right hand. The swordhilt. His own imagination? Wishful thinking? No . . .

The gray wave was coming up on limping, ill-made legs, brandishing its dead forest of handless arms, aiming its mad variety of weapons, shrieking its song of terror.

Nestor opened his mouth and shouted something back at them, some warcry bursting from he knew not what almost-buried memory. And now around him the bowmen loosed their first pitiful volley of arrows, that stuck in their targets without effect. Other men murmured and swung their clubs. Nestor realized that he was holding the sword two-handed now, and he could feel the power of it flowing into his arms, as natural as his own blood. Now the blade moved up into guard position, in a movement so smooth that Nestor could not really tell if it had been accomplished by his own volition or by the forces that drove the sword itself. And now with the blade high he could see the threaded vapor coming out of the air around it, seeming to flow into the metal.

He had not a moment in which to marvel at any of these things, or to try to estimate his chances, for now a dart sang past his shoulder, and now the awkwardly clambering gray mass of the enemy was almost in reach.

He yelled at them again, something from the wars of years ago, he knew not what. *Townsaver*, pronounced a secret voice within his mind, and he knew that it had named the sword for him.

Townsaver screamed exultantly, and drew the line of its blade through a gray rank as neatly as it had sliced the fruit. It mowed the weapon-sprouting limbs like grass.

CHAPTER 14

"This is it, Your Grace," said the lieutenant in blue and white. "This is the place where the dragon-pack attacked us."

Duke Fraktin halted his riding-beast under a tree still dripping from the morning's rain, and with an easy motion dismounted from the saddle. He made a great gesture with both arms to stretch the muscles in his back, stiffening somewhat after hours of riding. He looked about him.

He did not ask his lieutenant if he were sure about the place; there was no need. From where the Duke now stood, surrounded by a strong force of his mounted men, he could see and smell the carcass of a giant landwalker. The dead beast lay forty meters or so away among some more trees, and now that the Duke looked carefully in that direction he could see a dead man lying close to the dead dragon, and a little farther on one of his own cavalry mounts stiffened with its four feet in the air.

The pestilential aftermath of war, thought the Duke, and stretched again, and started walking unhurriedly closer to the scene of carnage. With a war coming, indeed at hand already, he decided it would be wise to reaccustom his senses as soon as possible to what they were going to be required to experience.

As he walked, with his right hand he loosened Coinspinner in its fine scabbard at his side. "And where," he asked his lieutenant, "is the wagon you were chasing? Did you not tell me that it tipped over in the chase, and then the dragons sprang out and attacked you before you could gather up the people who were in it?"

"That's how it was, Your Grace." And the pair of survivors of that ill-fated patrol who were now accompanying the Duke began a low, urgent debate between themselves as to just where that cursed wagon had been and ought to be. The Duke listened with impatient attention, meanwhile using his eyes for himself though without result. According to the best magical advice he had been able to obtain, that wagon might well have had another of the swords hidden in it somewhere—possibly even two of them.

Before his subordinates' argument was settled, the Duke's attention was drawn away from it by a rider who came cantering up with the report that another kind of wagon was arriving on the road that led from the southwest. This, when it presently came into sight, proved to be a humble, battered vehicle, a limping farm-cart in fact, pulled by a pair of loadbeasts even more decrepit than itself. The Duke at first was mystified as to why some of his advance guard should have doubled back to escort this apparition into his presence.

And then he saw who was riding in the middle of

the one sagging seat, and he understood, or began to understand.

"Gentle kinsman," said the Lady Marat, as she held out her hand for the Duke's aid in dismounting. His voice and gesture were as casual as if her humiliation did not concern her in the slightest. But her words indicated otherwise. "I want you to promise me certain specific opportunities of vengeance, on the day that the castle that I left yesterday lies open to your power."

Fraktin bowed his head slightly. "Consider the promise made, dear lady. So long as its fulfillment does not conflict with my own needs, with the necessities of war. And now, I suppose it likely that you have something to report?"

But before he could begin to hear what it might be, a trumpet sounded, causing the Duke to turn away from the lady momentarily. He saw that the head of the long column of his main body of infantry, approaching at route step along the road from the northeast, had now come abreast of the place where they were talking. Duke Fraktin returned the salute of the mounted officer who led the column, then faced back to his discussion with the Lady Marat. And all the while that they were talking there, the ragged, heavy tramp of the infantry kept moving past them.

The Duke offered the lady refreshment. But she preferred to wait until, as she said, she had made her preliminary report, and thus a beginning toward obtaining her revenge. She had plans for everyone in that castle, but particularly for the knight who had stolen her coach and treated her with such total disrespect.

Duke Fraktin listened with close attention to her report, learning among other things that the dragon-hunters' wagon had indeed gone on to Sir Andrew's rather than being destroyed by dragons here.

He asked: "My courier did get away from Sir Andrew's castle with one sword, though? You are sure of that?"

"Yes, good cousin. Of that fact I am very sure. Though I cannot be sure which sword it was."

The Duke, not for the first time, was beginning to find this lady attractive. But he put such thoughts aside, knowing that right now he had better concentrate on other matters. "Then where is this flying courier now? It has never reached me."

The lady could offer no explanation. The Master of the Beasts, when summoned from his place among the Duke's staff officers, gave his opinion that such a dragon ought to be able to fly easily and far, even after being stabbed once or twice with an ordinary sword. The Master of the Beasts had no explanation for the absence of the courier either, except that, as everyone knew, dragons could be unreliable.

Now the Duke turned to consult with yet another figure, who had just dismounted. "What have you to say about my luck now, Blue-Robes? What of the supposed power of this sword I wear?"

The magician spread his hands in a placating gesture. "Only this, Your Grace: that we do not know what your luck might be now, if you did not have Coinspinner there at your side."

"I find that answer something less than adequate, Blue-Robes. I find it . . . what are you gawping at, you fish?" This last was directed aside, at one of the retainers of the Lady Marat. This man had been driving the farm wagon when it arrived. Having been somewhat battered in the lady's service over the past few days, he was now receiving treatment for his wounds from the Duke's surgeon.

The surgeon looked up at the Duke's voice, and stilled his hands. The man who had been addressed started to say something, took a second look at the

Duke's face, and threw himself prostrate, bandages trailing unsecured. "A thousand pardons, Your Grace. I was remembering that I . . . that I thought I had seen you at the fair."

"What? At . . . ' "And even as the Duke spoke, there came in his brain the remembered echo of the voice of someone else, telling him that he had been seen in some other place where he had never been. "Explain yourself, fellow."

The man began a confused relation of what had happened at Sir Andrew's fair, on the night when he and the Duke's other secret agents had got their hands on Dragonslicer. He told some details of that sword's subsequent loss, and of the uncanny, magically changing appearance of the courier dragon as it had soared away.

The Duke nodded thoughtfully. "But me? Where did you think that you saw me?"

"Right there in the fairgrounds, sire. As surely as I see you now. I understand now that what I saw must have been only an image created by magic. But I saw you running toward the courier when it first flew up, and I heard your voice calling it down. And then I saw you stab it."

The Duke turned to look at the Lady Marat, who nodded in confirmation. She said: "Those are essentially the details that I was about to add in my own report."

Next the Duke looked at his wizard, whose eyes were closed. The blue-robed one muttered, as if to himself: "We knew there was another of the swords involved, located at Sir Andrew's castle. And now we know which one it was. That called Sightblinder, or the Sword of Stealth. It is—"

The Duke jogged his arm, commanding silence. "Wait."

Something was going on, up in the vaguely dripping

sky. The Master of the Beasts, with head tilted back, was calling and gesturing. Now a reptilian messenger of some kind—the Duke was unable to distinguish the finer gradations of hybrid dragons and other flying life—could be seen in a descending spiral. Alas, thought Duke Fraktin, watching, but this creature was too small to be the courier that had disappeared with one of the swords. This was some smaller flying scout reporting.

In fact it was small enough to perch upon the Master's wrist when it came down. He carried it to some little distance from the gathering of other humans, that the Duke might be able to receive its news, whatever it might be, with some degree of privacy.

In a hoarse whisper the Master translated the report for the Duke a few words at a time, first listening to the dragon's painfully accomplished, almost unintelligible half-speech, then turning his head to speak in human words. "Your Grace, this concerns the dragon-hunter, the man whose human name is Nestor."

"Aye, aye, I know of him. He wronged me once. But what has he to do with our present situation?" Passing this query on to the dragon was a slow and difficult process also. Sometimes the Duke thought that his Beast-Master, indispensably skilled though the man was, had grown half-witted through decades of conversation with his charges.

At length a reply came back. "It is that this Nestor has been carried off into the Great Swamp, sire. By a great flying dragon, not one of ours."

"A grown man, carried off by a flyer? Preposterous. And yet . . . but what else is it trying to say?"

Another guttural exchange took place between trainer and beast. "It says, the Gray Horde, sire. It tells me that the Gray Horde is raised, and marches toward Sir Andrew's lands."

There was silence, except for the drip of water from

the trees, and the eternal background tramp of marching soldiery. At last the Duke breathed: "Someone has taken a great gamble, then. Raised by whom?" Although he thought that he could guess.

There was another exchange of bestial noises. Then the Beast-Master said: "By humans who follow a woman, sire. A woman mounted on a warbeast, and leading a human army through the swamp."

Duke Fraktin nodded slowly, and made a gesture of dismissal. The Master rewarded his charge with a small dried lizard, laced with a drug that would give the flyer a sleep of delightful dreams.

Meanwhile the Duke, walking the short distance back to where his staff and the Lady Marat were waiting for him, prepared to call a major conference. Things had changed. What confronted him now was no longer the simple conquest of a smaller power that he had planned.

It appeared to him that the gods were once more actively entering the affairs of humankind.

CHAPTER 15

The screaming of the sword had seemed to Nestor to go on at its full voice for centuries. But then at last it had declined to a low whine, and now it was dying down to silence. And the life, the power, that still flowed from the hilt into Nestor's shaking hands was gradually dying too.

Gasping with exhaustion, his skin slippery everywhere with sweat and in places with his own blood, he took one staggering step forward. The long, sloping hill of rubble was still before him, and he still stood at the top of it alive. He looked round him for something, some deadwood figure, to strike at with the sword. But none of those that were still in sight were still erect.

He could still hear, starting to fade with distance now, the myriad whining voices of the larvae-army.

Those gray ranks had split around the temple and gone on. But not all of them. Over a broad, fan-shaped area of the slope immediately in front of Nestor, the hill had gained a new layer of rubble. It was the debris of a hundred gray bodies, hewn by Townsaver into chunks of melting mud.

Those fallen bodies were all quiet now. Nothing but the returning rain moved on the whole slope.

Stray drops of rain touched Nestor's face. And he turned round slowly in his tracks, looking dazedly at the equally dazed people who had been fighting beside him, and covering his back. He saw that two of the men had gone down, their clubs still in hand. And one of the women had been butchered, along with her small child. But all of the other people were still alive. They were mostly cowering in corners now, and some of them were hurt. Townsaver's shrieking blur had covered almost the whole wide doorway.

— hard walls it builds around the soft —

Only now did Nestor become fully aware of the small wounds he himself had sustained, here and there. He had tried when he could to use the sword to parry, to protect his own skin as much as possible. But the magic power that drove the sword in combat had been in ultimate control, and it had been less interested in saving him than in hacking down the foe.

A dart was still stuck loosely in Nestor's shirt, scratching him when he moved, and drawing blood. As he pulled the small shaft loose and threw it away he wondered whether it might be poisoned. Too late now to worry about it if it was.

At least he could still move; in the circumstances, he could hardly ask for more. He looked once more at the stunned survivors, who remained where they were, numbly looking back at him. Then he scrambled down across the slope that was littered with the bodies of his foes, and up another hill of ruins. He was heading for the highest remaining point of the temple's roof. From up there he should be able to see a maximum distance across the swamp in every direction.

Clinging to that precarious remnant of a roof, Nestor could see in the distance the waves of the larvae-army that had broken on his strongpoint and then rolled on, rejoining like waves of water when they were past the temple. The sight gave him a strange feeling. The hundred larvae that he had destroyed were suddenly as nothing.

From this high place Nestor could see something else as well. It was a sight that made him hurry down, passing as quickly as he could the people he and the sword had saved, and who had now decided that they wanted to prostrate themselves before him as before a god. His body shaking now with fatigue, relief, and perhaps with poison, Nestor made his way down to the ground level of the temple, and then out of the building to the south.

In another moment, Draffut, who in Nestor's view from the roof had been only a distant, toylike figure, was coming around a corner of the temple from the southwest. The giant moved in vast strides, his two-legged walk covering ground faster than any human run. A flying dragon of moderate size, perhaps the very one that Nestor had earlier spoken to, was flitting along near Draffut's head, almost as if it were planning to attack him. But Draffut ignored the flying thing, and it did him no harm.

The small mob of refugees had followed Nestor down to ground level. Draffut was obviously known to them, and a very welcome sight; Nestor supposed it was hope of the giant's protection that had brought them fleeing to the island in the first place. Now they offered Draffut worship, and clamored to him at length. The giant answered them in their own language. With his huge hands he raised them from their knees, and touched their wounds and healed them.

Then one of his enormous hands reached out for Nestor, who once more felt its restoring power. As his touch healed, Draffut said to him: "You have fought well here. And with the use of more than ordinary powers, if what these people tell me is correct."

"It probably is. Thank you again, Healer-who-is-not-a-god." The shaking was gone from Nestor's body, and the places where his small wounds had been were whole. He felt healthy, to a degree that made the long fight just past seem as unreal as a dream. He was surprised at a passing feeling that, along with the fear and pain, something valuable had been wiped away.

"Yes," Nestor went on, "there were very many of them. Very many, including your pet that rose up in advance of the others and tried to kill me. The sword gave me no more than ordinary service against that one."

Abstractedly Draffut lifted one of his huge wrists, and the flying dragon perched on it like a falcon. "My airborne scouts," the giant rumbled, "tell me that the Great Swamp is being invaded from the west by a large human army. Its soldiers wear the black and silver of Yambu, and it may be that the queen herself is leading them."

"Ah." Nestor felt shaken by the news; he bent to take up again the sword he had cast down when Draffut reached out to him. Nestor like everyone else had heard of that queen and of her power. "I suppose that her objective is not the conquest of the swamp."

"And I suppose that it is probably the domain of Kind Sir Andrew. The sorcerers of her army chant their spells as they march, and all across the swamp the larvae that they have cultivated from afar rise up and form in ranks to follow them."

"So," said Nestor. "We know now who is responsible for the larvae. And why is this army being led against Sir Andrew in particular? And why just now?"

Draffut made a motion of his arm, so that the dragon flew up from his wrist; it had rested, and now with vigorous wing-strokes went off on its own business. Draffut said: "Two of the god-swords, at least, are there now. A tempting booty to be taken, would you not agree?"

Nestor looked at the refugees, who were following the talk with reverence if little understanding. He said to Draffut: "One sword at least is there, and that one mine. I suppose if the Queen of Yambu knew where it was, and its importance, she might risk much to take it. As would Duke Fraktin, or a hundred others, I am sure. So what are we to do? I'd risk much myself to get it back."

Draffut said: "You should go to Sir Andrew, and warn him. And do what you can, with that you have there in your hand, to help him. Now that we know who is raising the Gray Horde, and where it is being led, I no longer feel that I must remain in the swamp. In fact, there is somewhere else I want to go now, and we can go part of the way together."

Again Draffut held brief conversation with the surviving swamp-folk. Then he explained to Nestor: "I have told them that they can return to their village now, on another island not far from here. They will be safer there than here, if powers should come seeking here for followers of mine."

"What powers might those be?"

"I mean to go," said Draffut, "and start an argument with the gods. Or with some of them at least. Are you ready to depart?"

Nestor had no baggage to bring with him except the sword. Which was, he now observed, an awkward thing to have to carry in one's hand for any length of time. This difficulty loomed larger when he realized that he was going to have to ride a long way on

Draffut's shoulders, and that he might at times want both hands free to hang on with. Draffut, suggesting a solution, sent Nestor to rummage in a certain room of the temple that he had not found in his own explorations, a long-abandoned guardhouse or arsenal. Much of the weaponry stored therein had rusted and rotted away, but Nestor turned up a copper scabbard that fit Townsaver tolerably well. To make the necessary belt, he used the sword itself to cut a length of tough vine from the temple wall.

The surviving swamp-people and their canoes had already disappeared back into their native habitat when Draffut, with Nestor clinging to his back, left solid land behind and strode into the morass, heading to the northeast. Draffut's long wading strides soon overtook the paddlers; the people in the canoes made way for him, waving as they pulled aside.

For half an hour or so, Draffut made steady and uneventful progress. If any of the multitude of life-forms large and small that inhabited the marsh ever considered molesting the Beast-Lord in his passage, Nestor at least was not aware of it. Draffut never went more than waist-deep in the water and mud, and Nestor was easily able to keep himself dry. Now and then he had to dodge a tree-branch, but that was his most serious immediate problem. He clung with both hands to his mount's glowing fur, and was actually beginning to enjoy himself. It seemed to Nestor that sometimes even the thorntrees bent aside before the giant reached them.

This pleasant interval ended abruptly just as Draffut was mounting a ridge of dry, comparatively high ground. At that point a large warbeast, armored and collared in the colors of Yambu, sprang in ambush at the Beast-Lord from a brake of reeds. The giant's reaction was practically instantaneous; before Nestor could draw his sword, Draffut had caught the attacker in midair, as if he were playing with a kitten. But then the giant threw the warbeast violently, so that the flying, screaming body broke tree branches and vanished behind a screen of trees some thirty meters distant before it splashed into the swamp.

Almost as if in response, there came a distant, whistling call, that sounded like some hunter's cry. Nestor had heard similar signals used to control warbeasts. Draffut paused for a moment, turning to gaze over the treetops to his left; then he moved swiftly off to his right, walking at a greater speed than ever. Now Nestor had to clap his half-drawn sword back into its scabbard and once more hold tight with both hands.

"The advance guard of Yambu," said Draffut over his shoulder, in what he used for a low voice. "We will outspeed them if we can."

Looking back, Nestor saw more warbeasts already in pursuit. He counted three, and there might well be more. Hundreds of meters farther back, beyond the great catlike creatures, he could see the first advancing elements of a human army, some of them mounted and some in boats. He announced this to Draffut's ear, but the giant did not bother to answer. Draffut was almost, but not quite, running now. Maybe, thought Nestor, his size and build made a real run an impossibility for him. Nestor had considerable conference in Draffut's powers; but at the same time the man could almost feel those huge warbeast talons fastening on him from behind . . .

The chase went on. From time to time Nestor reported, in a voice he strove to keep calm, that their pursuers were catching up. Then abruptly Draffut stopped, and calmly turned to stand his ground.

"It is no use," he said. "They are too fast. And they are maddened with the lust to fight, and will not listen to me." With one hand he lifted Nestor from his shoulders, and placed the man in a high crotch of a dead tree. "Defend yourself," the Beast-Lord laconically advised him, and turned to do the same.

A moment later, half a dozen warbeasts, hot on the trail, came bounding out of the brush nearby. Draffut cuffed the first one to come in reach, grabbed and threw another by its tail, and had to pick a third one from his fur when it was actually brave enough to leap on him. He hurled it into the remaining three. With that all of the warbeasts that were still able to move scattered in flight, emitting uncharacteristic yelps. Nestor, his sword drawn and ready though showing no special powers, had nothing to do. Which, under the circumstances, was quite all right with him.

Draffut had just retrieved Nestor from his high perch when a new figure appeared. It was the form of a woman with long black hair, her body clothed in light armor of ebony and silver, on another ridge or island of dry land about a hundred meters distant to the west. She was mounted on a gray warbeast of such a size that Nestor for an instant thought it was a dragon.

Beneath the cloudy sky, the woman's armor flashed as if it were catching desert sunshine. She brandished a silver needle of a sword, and she was shouting something in their direction.

The words came clearly in her penetrating voice: "Remove yourself from my army's path, great beast, or I will set men to fight against you! I know your weakness; they'll kill you soon enough. And who is that you carry?"

Nestor had heard of people who rode on warbeasts, but never before had he seen it done. As he resumed his seat on Draffut's shoulders, the giant roared back: "Rather remove your blood-mad warbeasts from my path! Or else I will send you dragons enough to make your march through the swamp much more interesting." Without waiting to see what effect his words might have, he turned and stalked away, resuming his passage to the north.

There was no observable pursuit.

"That was the Silver Queen herself. Yambu," said Nestor to Draffut's ear a little later. The comment was undoubtedly unnecessary, but the man was unable to let the encounter pass without saying something about it.

"Indeed." The huge voice came rumbling up through Draffut's neck and head. "There are elements of humanity that I sometimes wish I were able to fight against."

Once more they were traversing bog and thicket at what would have been a good speed for a riding-beast on flat, cleared ground. Some time passed in silence, except for the quick plash and thud of Draffut's feet, while Nestor pondered many things. Then he asked: "You said that you are planning to go and start an argument with the gods?"

"I must," said Draffut. And that was all the answer to his question that Nestor ever got.

But little further conversation was exchanged. Nestor welcomed the comfort of his ride, and watched the sun move in and out of clouds in the western sky. By the time Draffut stopped again, some hours had passed and the reddening sun was almost down. Imperceptibly the land had changed, continuous marsh giving way to intermittent bogs bridged by dry land. Once Nestor saw herdsmen watching from a distance.

The giant set Nestor down carefully on dry ground, and said to him: "Go north from here, and you will find Sir Andrew. From here on north the land is solid enough for you to walk, and savage beasts are fewer. My own way from here lies to the east."

"I wish you good luck," said Nestor. And then, when he had looked to the east, he would have said something more, for never until now had he known the sunset fires of Vulcan's forge to be so bright that they could be seen from this far west.

But Draffut was already gone.

CHAPTER 16

When Dame Yoldi took Mark for the first time to her workroom, he discovered it not to be the dismal, forbidding chamber that he had for some reason expected. Rather it was open, cleanly decorated with things of nature, and as light as the dying, cloudy day outside could make it, entering narrow windows.

The enchantress lighted tapers, from a small oil lamp that was already burning. She distributed a few of these in the otherwise dark corners of the room, and placed two more on the central table where Dragonslicer now rested on a white linen cloth. Most of the floor space in the room was open, while shelves round all the walls contained an armament of magic, arrayed in books and bottles, boxes, jars, and bags. One set of open dishes held grain and dried fruit, another set what looked like plain water and dry earth.

Yoldi made Mark sit down at the table near the sword, where she made him comfortable, and gave him a delicious drink, not quite like anything he had ever tasted before. Then she began to question him closely about his family, and about the several god-swords he had seen, and about what he thought he would do with his own sword if he could ever get it back. Her questions suggested new ideas to Mark, and made him see his own situation in what seemed like a new light, so that when he looked at the sword before him on the table now he saw it as something different from the weapon he had once held in his own two hands and used to kill a dragon. The more he talked with Yoldi the more fearfully impressive the whole business grew. But somehow he was not more frightened.

Their chat was interrupted by an urgent tapping at the door. Yoldi went to open it, and listened briefly to someone just outside. A moment later, with a solemn face, she was beckoning to Mark to follow her out of the room. She led him up many stairs, and finally up a ladder, which brought them out onto what proved to be the highest rooftop of the castle. This was a flat area only a few meters square, copper-sheeted against weather and attack by fire, and bounded by a chest-high parapet of stone. Sir Andrew's Master of the Beasts, a dour young man who gave the impression of wanting to be old, was on the roof already, doing something to one of a row of man-sized cages that stood under a shelter along the northern parapet. In these cages were kept the flyers, the inhuman messengers and scouts, temporarily before launching and when they had returned from flights.

When Dame Yoldi and Mark appeared on the roof, the Beast-Master silently pointed to the east, into the approaching night. In that direction a large arc of the horizon was sullenly aglow, with what looked like an untimely dawn, or distant flames.

"The mountains," Mark said, understanding the origin of the glow. And then: "My home."

Dame Yoldi, standing behind him, held him by the shoulders. "In which direction exactly is your village, boy?" Her voice at first sounded almost eager. "Can you point toward it? But no, I don't suppose that's possible. It's somewhere near those mountains, though."

"Yes." And Mark, continuing to stare at the distant fires, lapsed into silence.

"Don't be afraid." Yoldi's tone turned reassuring, while remaining brisk, refusing to treat volcanoes as a disaster. Her grip was comforting. "Your folk are probably all right. I know these foothill people, ready to take care of themselves. It might actually be a good thing for them, make them get out of Duke Fraktin's territory if they haven't done so already." The enchantress turned away to the dour man, asking: "When is your next scout due back from the east?"

Mark did not understand whatever it was that the man answered. He was intent on wondering what might be happening to his home, on picturing his mother and his sister as stumbling refugees.

"I wonder," Dame Yoldi was musing to herself, "if anyone's told Andrew about this yet. He ought to be told, but he's down there talking to the fellow from Yambu — probably wouldn't do to interrupt him now."

And now Mark saw that one of the airborne scouts was indeed coming in against the fading sky; coming from the south and not the east, but approaching with weary, urgent speed.

Baron Amintor, who was Queen Yambu's emissary to Sir Andrew, was a large man, the size of Sir Andrew himself but younger. The Baron with his muscles and his scars looked more the warrior than the diplomat. He had the diplomat's smooth tongue, though, and Sir Andrew had to admit to himself that the man's man-

ners were courteous enough. It was only the substance of what the visitor had to say that Sir Andrew
found totally objectionable.

The two men were conversing alone in a small
room, not far above the ground level of the castle, and
within earshot of Sir Andrew's armory, where the
clang of many hammers upon metal signalled the
process of full mobilization that the knight had already
put into effect. It was a sound he did not want his
visitor to miss.

Not that the Baron appeared to be taking the least
notice of it. "Sir Andrew, if you will only hand over to
me now, for delivery to the Queen, whichever of these
swords you now possess, and grant the Queen's armies
the right of free passage through your territory—which
passage you will not be able to deny her in any case—
you will then be under her protection as regards these
threats you have lately been receiving from Duke Fraktin.
And, I may add, from any similar threats that may
arise from any quarter. *Any* quarter," Amintor repeated,
with a sly, meaningful look, almost a wink. At that
point he paused.

Sir Andrew wondered what particular fear or suspicion that near-wink had been calculated to arouse in
him; but no matter, he was worrying to capacity already,
though he trusted that it did not show.

Baron Amintor went on: "But, of course, Her Majesty cannot be expected to guarantee the frontiers or
the safety of any state that is unfriendly to her. And if
for some misguided reason you should withhold from
her these swords, these tools so necessary to Her
Majesty's ambitions for a just peace, then Her Majesty
cannot do otherwise than consider you unfriendly." At
this point the Baron's voice dropped just a little. It
seemed that, bluff soldier that he was, it rather shocked
him to think of anyone's being unfriendly to Yambu.

"Ah," Sir Andrew remarked. "The tools necessary

for a just peace. I rather like that. Yes, that's quite good."

"Sir Andrew, believe me, Her Majesty has every intention of respecting your independence, as much as possible. But, to be unfriendly and small at the same time—that is really not the policy of wisdom."

"Wisdom, is it? Small, are we?" Bards would never repeat such words of defiance; but Sir Andrew felt that the man standing before him did not deserve anything in the way of fine or even thoughtful speech. And anyway he felt too angry to try to produce it.

"Good sir, the fact is that your domain *is* comparatively small. Comparatively weak. Duke Fraktin is of course as well aware of these facts as you and I are, and the Duke is not your friend. The people of your lands—well, they are brave, I am sure. And loyal to you—most of them at least. But they are not all that numerous. And they are widely scattered. This castle—" and here the Baron, being bluff and military, thumped his strong hand on the wall "—is a fine fortress. The noise from your armory is entertaining. But, how many fighting men have you actually mobilized so far, here on the spot and ready to fight? Two hundred? Fewer, perhaps? No, of course you need not tell me. But think upon the number in your own mind. Compare it to the numbers that are ready to cross your borders now, from two directions, east and west. You can prevent neither the Queen's army crossing, nor the Duke's. And then think upon the people in your outlying villages that you are never going to be able to defend. At least not without Her Majesty's gracious help."

Sir Andrew stood up abruptly. He was so angry that he did not trust himself. "Leave me now."

The Baron was already standing. He turned, without argument, without either delay or evidence of fear, and took a couple of steps toward the door. Then he paused. "And have you any further message for the Queen?"

"I say leave me for now. You will be shown where to wait. I will let you know presently about the message."

As soon as Sir Andrew was alone, he left the small chamber where he had been talking with Baron Amintor, and walked into another, larger room, where most of his old books were kept. There by lamplight he picked up a volume, fingered it, opened it, closed it, and put it down again. When was he ever going to have time to read again? Or would he die in battle soon, and never have time again to read another book?

After that, he took himself in a thoughtful, silent, solitary walk down into the dungeon. There he stood in front of the one cell that held a human being, gazing thoughtfully at the prisoner. Kaparu his captive looked back at him nervously. Down the side corridor, workers were busy opening the cells where birds and animals were confined, preparing to set the small inmates free. War was coming, and luxuries had to go, including the dream of a vivarium in the castle grounds.

At length the knight spoke. "You, Kaparu, are my only human prisoner. Have you meditated upon the meaning of my last reading to you? I do not know when, if ever, it will be possible to read to you again, and try to teach you to be good."

"Oh, yes, indeed I have meditated, sire." Kaparu's hands slipped sweatily on the bars to which he would have clung. "And—and I have learned this much at least, that you are a good man. And I was quite sure already that those who are planning to invade your lands are not good people. So, I—I would give much, sire, not to be in this cell when . . . that is, if . . . "

"When my castle is overrun by them, you mean. A natural and intelligent reaction."

"Oh, if you would release me, sire, if you would let me out, I would be grateful. I would do anything."

"Would you go free, and rob no more?"

"Gladly, sire, I swear it."

Sir Andrew, hesitating in inward conflict, asked him: "Is your oath to be trusted, Kaparu? Have you learned that it is no light thing to break an oath?"

"I will not break mine, sire. Your readings to me . . . they have opened my eyes. I can see now that all my earlier life was wrong, one great mistake from start to finish."

Sir Andrew looked long at Kaparu. Then, with a gentle nod, he reached for the key ring at his own belt.

A little later, when the knight had heard the latest message from the flying scouts, and had begun to ponder the terrible news of the raising of the Gray Horde, he sent away Yambu's ambassador with a final message of defiance. There seemed to him to be nothing else that he could do.

After that, Sir Andrew went up to the highest parapets of his castle, which at the moment were otherwise unoccupied, there to lean out over his battlement and brood. Everywhere he looked, preparations for war and seige were being made, and he had much to ponder.

Presently he was aware that someone else had joined him on the roof, and he looked up from his thoughts and saw Dame Yoldi standing near. From her expression he judged that she had no urgent news or question for him, she had simply come in his hour of need to see what else she might be able to do to help.

"Andrew."

"Yoldi . . . Yoldi, if the power in these god-forged swords is indeed so great, that these evildoers around us are ready to risk war with each other, as well as with us, to obtain even one of them—if it is so great, I say, then how can I in good conscience surrender to them even one source of such power?"

Dame Yoldi nodded her understanding, gently and sadly. "It would seem that you cannot. So you have already decided. Unless the consequences of refusing to surrender strike you as more terrible still?"

"They do not! By all the demons that Ardneh ever slew or paralyzed, we must all die at some time, but we are not all doomed to surrender! But the people in the villages haunt me, Yoldi. I can do nothing to protect them from Fraktin or Yambu."

"It would give those village people at least some hope for the future—those among them who survive invasion—if you could stand fast, here in your strong place, and eventually reclaim your lands."

"If I try to stand fast, here or anywhere, then I must say to my people: 'March to war.' We know, you and I, what war is like. Some of the young ones do not know . . . but it apears that the evil and the horror of war are coming upon them anyway, whatever I decide. No surrender will turn back such enemies as these, once they are mobilized upon my borders, or moderate what they do to my people. Regardless of what they might promise now. Not that I have asked them for any promises, or terms. Why ask for what I would never believe from them anyway?"

A silence fell between the knight and the enchantress, the world around them quiet too except for the distant chinking from the armorers. "I must go back to my own work," Yoldi said at last, and kissed the lord of the castle once, and went away.

"And I must go down," said Sir Andrew aloud to himself, "and inspect the defenses."

A little later when he was walking upon the castle's outer wall, near one of the strong guard-towers that defended the main gate, Sir Andrew encountered one of his old comrades in arms, and fell into conversation with him.

"A long time, Sir Andrew, since we've had to draw our swords atop these walls."

"Yes, a long time."

At some point the comrade had turned into quite an old man, white-haired and wrinkled, and Sir Andrew, not remembering him as such, could not quite shake the feeling that this aged appearance was some kind of a disguise, which the other would presently take off. The talk they had sounded cheerful enough, though most of the matters they talked about were horrible, seige and stratagem, raid and counterattack and sally.

"That kept 'em off our backs a good long time, hey sir?"

"Not long enough." Sir Andrew sighed.

And presently he was once more left alone, still standing on the wall near the main gate. This was a good vantage point from which to overlook the thin, intermittent stream of provision carts, fighting men, and refugees that came trickling up the winding road that led from the intersection of the highways to the castle.

Here came some priests and priestesses of Ardneh, white-robed and hurried, who had just passed an inspection at the checkpoint down the way. They were driving two carts, that Sir Andrew could at least hope were filled with medical supplies. Sometimes, in time of war, Temples of Ardneh stood unscathed in the midst of contending armies. Each leader and each fighter hoped that if he were wounded, he would be cared for if there were room. But evidently it would not be that way this time. Ardneh, in a sense, was coming to Sir Andrew's side; and, medical supplies aside, the troops were sure to take that as a good omen.

Sir Andrew closed his eyes, and gripped the parapet in front of him. He thought of praying to Ardneh for more direct help—although with part of his mind he knew, knew better than almost anyone else in the world, that though Ardneh had once lived, he had now been dead for almost two thousand years. Sir Andrew knew it well. And yet . . .

And this mystery regarding Ardneh called to mind another, that had long troubled Sir Andrew and that none of his studies had ever been able to solve: If Ardneh was dead, why were all the world's other gods and goddesses alive? The common opinion was that all of them had been living since the creation of the world, or thereabouts, and that of course Ardneh was still alive with all the others. But Sir Andrew had the gravest doubts that the common opinion was correct.

He tended instead to trust certain historical writings, that spoke in matter-of-fact terms of Ardneh's existence and his death, but did not so much as mention Vulcan, Hermes, Aphrodite, Mars, or any of the rest — with the sole exception of the Beast-Lord Draffut. And Draffut was not assigned the importance of Ardneh, or of their evil opponent Orcus, Lord of Demons.

And whatever Sir Andrew might think of gods, he had no doubts at all about the reality of demons.

At some time in his long years of study and deep thought, a horrible suspicion had been born, deep in his mind: That the entities that who now called themselves gods, were recognized by humanity as gods, and who claimed to rule the world — whenever they bothered to take an interest in it — that these beings were in fact demons who had survived from the era of Ardneh and of Orcus. But there were, comfortingly, important difficulties with that theory too.

After all Sir Andrew's study of the gods, all he could say about them with absolute certainty was very little: That most of them were real, here and now, and very powerful. The swords were testimony enough to the real power of Vulcan.

Yoldi was a fine magician, and a brave one. But

there were limits to the ability of any magician to reach and control the ultimate powers of reality.

Why in the names of all the gods and demons did the universe have to be such a complicated, confused, and contrary place? Sir Andrew thought now, not for the first time, that if he had been put in charge of the design, he would have done things differently.

Sir Andrew had opened his eyes for a while, closed them again, and was trying to decide whether he was really praying to Ardneh now or not, when he heard his name called from below. Looking down, he saw that one man had stepped aside from the continued trickle of traffic approaching the castle, and was now standing just below Sir Andrew on the shoulder of the road. The man was in his late youth or early middle age, rather slight of build, and with a traveled look about him. He wore a large sword, belted on with what looked like rope or twine, that immediately drew Sir Andrew's attention.

The man had to speak again before Sir Andrew recognized the dragon-hunter, Nestor. "Sir Andrew? I bring you greetings from the Beast-Lord, Draffut."

CHAPTER 17

Even traveling almost without pause, at the best speed made possible by his enormous strides, it had taken Draffut a day and a half to get from the temple island near the middle of the Great Swamp east as far as the high plains. And night was falling again before he reached the region in Duke Fraktin's domain where the upward slope of land began to grow pronounced. The volcanic fires that had lighted the eastern sky when seen from hundreds of kilometers away were at this close range truly spectacular.

Almost immediately upon leaving the swamp behind, Draffut had begun to encounter refugees from the eruption. These were mainly folk from Duke Fraktin's high villages, where a mass evacuation had obviously started. The villagers were fleeing their homes and land in groups, as families, as individuals, moving

251

anywhere downslope, most of them lost now in unfamiliar territory. Some of these people, passing Draffut at a little distance, shouted to him word of what they considered Vulcan's wrath—as if Draffut should not be able to see for himself the flaming sky ahead.

Draffut was not sure whether these folk were trying to warn him, to plead for his intercession with the gods, or both. "I will speak to Vulcan about it," he said, when he said anything at all in answer. Carefully he avoided stepping on any of the people. For the most part of course they said nothing to him. They were astonished and terrified to see him, and in their panic would sometimes have run right under his feet, or would have driven their livestock or their farm-carts into him. Draffut made his way considerately around them all, and went on east, and up.

He had no such need to be careful with the small units of Duke Fraktin's army that he encountered along the way, some of them even before he had entered the Duke's domain. Whether mounted or afoot, these always scattered in flight before Draffut's advance, as if they took it for granted that he would be their deadly enemy. Draffut could not help thinking back to the time when soldiers had cheered him and looked to him for help. But that had been many ages and wars ago, and halfway around the world from here.

In a lifetime that had spanned more than fifty thousand years, Draffut had often enough seen swarms of human refugees, and even burning skies like these. But seldom before had he felt the earth quiver beneath his feet as it was quivering now.

When he got in among the barren foothills he continued climbing without pause. Now the rumbling towers of fire loomed almost above his head, and fine ash drifted continuously down around him. He thought that there were forces here that could destroy him, that he was no longer immune to death, as he might once have been. His own powers, absorbed over ages, were fading as slowly as they had been gained, but they were fading. Yet he could feel little personal fear. By his nature, Draffut could not help but be absorbed in larger things than that.

The shuddering, burning agony of the mountains against the darkening sky brought back more old memories to Draffut. One of these recollections was very old indeed, of another mountain, upon another continent, that once had split to spill the Lake of Life . . . that had been in the days of Ardneh's greatest power. Ardneh, whom Draffut had never really known at all, despite the current human version of the history of the world. It hardly mattered now, for now Ardneh was long dead . . .

The question to be answered now was, where had these new creatures of power sprung from, these upstart entities calling themselves gods? Ardneh in his days of greatest strength had never claimed to be a god, nor had the evil Orcus. Indeed, it seemed to Draffut looking back that for thousands of years the very word *god* had been almost forgotten among humanity.

If he tried to peer back too far into his own past, he reached an epoch where all memory faded, blurring into disconnected scenes and meaningless impressions. He knew that these were remnant of a time when his intelligence, brain, and body had been very different from what they were now. But certainly Draffut's memory of the past few thousand years was sharp and clear. He could recall very well the days when Ardneh and Orcus had fought each other. And in those days, not one of these currently boasting, sword-making upstarts who called themselves gods and goddesses had walked the earth. They bore names from the remote past of human myth, but who were they? By what right did they plan for themselves games that involved for humanity the horror of wars? Draffut could no longer delay finding out.

He had climbed only a little way up the first slopes of the real mountain when he found his way blocked by a slow stream of lava, three or four meters wide. The air above the lava writhed with heat. And in the night and the hellglow on the far side of the molten stream, visible amid swirling fumes and boiling air, there stood a two-legged figure far too large to be human, even if a human could have stood there and lived. The figure was roughly the same size as Draffut himself, and it was regarding Draffut, and waiting silently.

In the raging heat he could see nothing of the figure clearly but its presence. He stopped, and called a salutation to it, using an ancient tongue that either Ardneh or Orcus would have understood at once. There was no reply.

Now Draffut summoned up what he could of his old powers, concentrating them in his right hand. Then he bent down and thrust that hand into the sluggish, crusting, seething stream of lava. Without allowing himself to be burned, he scooped up a dripping handful of the molten rock. With another exertion of his will he gave the handful of magma temporary life, so that what had been dead rock quickened and soared aloft in the hot, rising air, making a small silent explosion of living things exquisite as butterflies.

Still the figure that waited beyond the lava-stream would not move or speak. But now another like itself had joined it, and as Draffut watched yet another and another one appeared. The gods were assembling to watch what he was doing, to judge him silently.

He wanted more than that from them. He stood erect and brushed his hands clean of smoking rock. It was impossible to tell from the silent observation whether the onlookers were impressed by what he had done.

In a carrying roar he challenged them: "Why do you not tell humanity the truth? Are you afraid of it?"

There was a stir among the group, images wavering in the heat. With the noise of the earth itself pervading all, Draffut could not tell what they might be saying among themselves. At last a voice, larger than human, boomed back at him: "Tell them yourself, you shaggy dog."

Another voice followed, high clear tones that must be those of a goddess: "We know well what you used to be, Beast-Lord, when first you followed your human masters into the cave of the Lake of Life, fifty thousand years ago and more. Do not pretend to grandeur now."

And yet another voice, belligerent and male: "Yes, tell them yourself—but will they believe what they are told by a dog, the son of a bitch? Never mind that some of them now think you are a god. We can fix that!"

Draffut could feel the fervor of his anger growing, growing, till it was hotter than the lava that made the earth burn just in front of him. He roared back: "I have as much right to be a god as any of you do. More! Tell the human world what you really are!"

Beyond the wavering heat, their numbers were still increasing. Another voice mocked him: "*You* tell them what we really are. Ha, haaa!"

"I would tell them. I will tell them, when I know."

"Ha, haaa! We are the gods, and that is all ye need to know. It is no business of a son of a bitch to challenge gods."

In a single stride Draffut moved forward across the stream of lava. And now he could see the last speaker plainly enough to be able to recognize him. "You are Vulcan. And now you are going to give me some answers, about the swords."

Vulcan answered boldly enough, with an obscene

insult. But at the same time he appeared to shrink back a little within the group. There was wrangling and shoving among the deities, amid a cloud of smoke and dust. Then another figure, pushing Vulcan aside, stepped forward from behind him. Now the shape of a gigantic and muscular man, carrying a great spear, his head covered with a helm, stood limned against a fresh flow of red-hot lava spilling down a slope.

"I am traveling west from here," said Mars. His voice was one that Draffut had not heard before, all drums and trumpets and clashing metal. "War draws me there. I see a beseiged castle, and one in the attacking army who offers me sacrifice with skilful magic. I think it is time for me to answer the prayers of one of my devoted worshippers."

From the group behind the speaker there came a discordant chorus of varied comments on this announcement. Draffut noted that they ranged from applause to enthusiastic scorn.

Mars ignored them all. He did not turn his terrible gaze from Draffut, who stood right in his way. Mars said: "I am going to that castle, there to spend some time in killing humans for amusement."

Draffut said simply: "No, that you will not do."

At this point someone in the rear rank of the gods threw a burning boulder straight at Draffut. It seemed to come with awesome slowness through the air, and it was accurately aimed. Catching it strained his great strength, but from some reserve he drew the power to hurl it back—not at its unseen thrower. Instead Draffut aimed it straight for Mars, just as the long spear leveled for a throw. Rock and spear met in mid-air, to explode in a million screaming fragments.

Another spear already in his hand, the God of War strode forward to do battle.

CHAPTER 18

Dame Yoldi herself had told Mark several times that she considered his survival vitally important, and that she meant for that reason to keep him in comparative safety at her side as much as possible when the fighting started. Thus it happened that they were together on the high roof of Sir Andrew's castle, in early morning light, when the first attack of the Gray Horde broke like a dirty wave against the walls.

The defenders were as ready as they could be for the assault, for there had been no way for the attackers to achieve surprise. On the previous day, Sir Andrew's enchantress had announced that the speed and direction of the larvae's advance could be only approximately controlled by the magicians of Yambu. For the past few days, Yoldi and several of her assistants had attempted to interfere with the enemy magic, and turn

257

the larvae against those who had raised them. But that effort had failed, and Dame Yoldi was necessarily concentrating upon other matters now. She said that in any case the larvae would not be able to remain active for more than a few days, Once raised from the swamp, they drew no nourishment, no energy of any kind, from their environment. This made them difficult to interfere with, and almost impossible to poison, but also awkward for their masters to control. However, for the few days that their pseudo-life endured they were an almost invincible army, immune to weariness and fear.

Their massed howling, like distant wind, could be heard in the castle for more than an hour before their first charge at the walls. Therefore the defenders were alerted and in place when the hundred scaling ladders of the Horde were raised.

As the light grew full, Mark could see from his high vantage point how Ben was taking part in the fighting atop the eastern wall, using his great strength behind a pole to topple scaling ladders back as fast as the handless, clumsy larvae below could prop them up; there were no humans to be seen at all in the first wave of attackers.

And Barbara was on the wall west of the guard towers and the main gate, one of a company of men and women armed with bows and slings. Their missiles went hailing thickly down into the sea of the attackers, but Mark could not see that they did much damage. An arrow might penetrate a larva's shell, but the thing kept advancing anyway, pushing up another ladder and then climbing to the attack. A slung stone might crack a carapace, but the hit figure came on anyway, until a leg joint was broken too badly to let it walk, or its arms disabled to the point where it could no longer climb a ladder.

The hundred ladders carried forward to the walls in

that first attack, Mark decided, must have been made for the larvae by their human masters and allies. Last night he had heard Nestor talking in the castle, describing in detail what he had seen of the larvae at close range, and what kind of fighting might be expected when their horde swept to the assault on the castle walls.

Sir Andrew had listened very carefully to the same account. The knight had then sat alone for a while, the picture of grim thought, and then had issued orders, disposing of his defense forces as best he might. Mark had got the impression, listening, that all the experts on hand knew that the walls were going to be under-manned.

Then Sir Andrew had had Nestor speak to the defenders also of Draffut, of how the Lord of Beasts had seemed to favor their cause, and to hint of active intervention on their side. This raised the hopes of everyone somewhat, though Nestor was careful not to claim that any such promise had been made by Draffut.

Nestor, as he had explained to a smaller gathering of his old companions of the wagon, had decided he had no real choice but to take part in the fighting, once he had decided to come to Sir Andrew's castle with the sword.

"Besides, where would I have gone to get away? From here all roads lead ultimately to Fraktin or Yambu, except those that go back into the swamp, or to the northwest; and I expect that even those are closed by now."

Armed with the Sword of Fury, and wearing the best armor that Sir Andrew had been able to fit him with at short notice, Nestor was somewhere in one of the central guard-towers when the first attack began. The strategy was for him to wait there until close combat provided a suitable chance to bring the sword's powers into use. But though the sword whined restlessly

when the attack began, and drew its threads of vapor
from the air into itself, that chance did not come with
the first assault.

Not that there was much of a break between the
first and second. The Gray Horde did not retreat from
the foot of the walls to reform, as a human army
would certainly have done. Instead its thousands milled
around, indifferent to slung stone and arrow.

And then surged forward behind the ladders once
again.

By now it had been discovered that large stones
dropped on the attacking larvae below the walls were
somewhat more effective than slings and arrows, but
that fire was disappointingly inefficient. The dead-
wood figures were not really dry, and they would have
to be burnt into ashes to be stopped.

"A breach! A breach!"

Mark heard the cry go up some minutes after the
second surge with ladders against the walls began.
Looking down at the top of the west wall, to his right,
he saw that gray mannikins were on it, their arms
windmilling as they fought.

"The sword comes!"

"Townsaver!"

Through the defenders' thin reserves the figure of
Nestor, recognizable in his new armor, was moving
into action. Above and through the banshee-howling
of the enemy sounded the high shriek of the blade.
The sound called up for Mark his last day in his home
village, and he felt a surge of sickness.

The hand of Dame Yoldi pressed his arm. "It comes
awake, and timely too. We have a holding here, and
unarmed folk in it to be defended. The gods cannot bw
wholly evil, to have forged a weapon of this nature."

Mark could not think beyond that screaming sound.
Nestor had reached the foe now, and the blade in his
hands blurred back and forth, faster than sight could

follow it, and the first gray rank went down.

This was Duke Fraktin's first chance to hear Townsaver scream, and he was greatly interested. He watched from a distance as the small blur in one man's hands cleared the west wall of larvae. The Duke was impressed, but not particularly surprised.

He watched also, with fascination, how gracefully and angrily Queen Yambu rode her prancing warbeast in front of her own ranked army of human men, even as he himself paced near the center of his own. The bulk of the Duke's forces were now disposed in a semicircular formation, with its right wing on the lake almost behind the castle, left wing anchored just about where the winding road came up the hill to find Sir Andrew's fortified main gate. Upon that gate a hundred larvae were now battering with a ram fashioned from the trunk of a huge tree. Their feet slipped and slid in mud that had been their predecessors' bodies, while stones and fire decimated their ranks from above. Meanwhile, along the road, rough battalions of replacements jostled forward, howling dully, ready without fear or hope to take their turn beneath the walls.

From the winding road around west to the lake again, the human forces of Yambu held the field. They were arrayed, like the Duke's army, in a rough halfcircle. The Duke like everyone else was well aware that the two armies of attackers were watching each other closely and uneasily, even as both watched the progress of the swarming preliminary attack on the castle by Yambu's auxiliaries.

The Duke turned to his blue-garbed wizard, who was waiting nearby clad in incongruous-looking armor. "At least," His Grace remarked, "a good part of the Horde is going to he used up against those walls, and particularly by that sword. We can hope that most of those dead-wood monsters will be out of the way before it comes our turn to fight Yambu, for the spoils."

"Indeed, sire."

"I'm convinced now, Blue-Robes, that it was *she* who tried to kidnap my cousin. Obviously she's got word of the swords somehow . . . what word is there from the east?"

This last was spoken to the Duke's staff at large. None of them had any real news to report from that direction. At night there were the reddened eastern skies for all to see, and by day the distant plumes of smoke. When the Duke had dispatched a flying scout with a message for the small garrison at Arin-on-Aldan, the scout had come back with a report of being unable to find the village or its garrison, in the altered landscape and foul air. (The message had been an order for the family of Jord the Miller to be brought into the Duke's presence for some serious interrogation, milder methods having failed.) Indeed it appeared now that communications with the foothill region had broken down completely. Reports, scattered and uncertain, indicated that the whole civilian population of that area was now in flight, and military patrols were at best disrupted. The Duke sighed, for his vanished family of subjects for interrogation. But he had a battle to fight here, and could spare no extra manpower for search operations of doubtful utility over there.

Still, the blue-robed wizard did not appear entirely unhappy when this subject came up for discussion. He had the air of holding good news in reserve, and, sure enough, at his earliest good chance he announced it.

"Sire, I am pleased to be able to report that my private project has achieved a measure of success."

"What other project?" The ducal brow creased with a slight frown. "Oh. You are speaking now of . . . of what you spoke to me about last night in secret."

"Exactly so, sire." The wizard bowed, a small dip with an air of triumph. "We now have reason to hope that Mars himself is soon going to come directly to our aid. Then, what will our rivals have gained from their paltry success in raising the Horde?"

"By the Great Worm Yilgarn." Duke Fraktin was indubitably impressed. But he was suddenly somewhat worried as well. "Do you think, Blue-Robes, that such a raising is . . . the *god*? *Mars*? Are you sure you're serious?"

"Oh, entirely serious, sire."

A hundred people or more might be watching, even if probably none of them were close enough at the moment to hear. The Duke made himself smile. "Do you think it entirely wise?"

At this the wizard began to look downcast; he had surely been expecting more enthusiasm from his master. He was somewhat relieved when their talk was interrupted. A close-ranked body of men had surrounded, and were now bringing into the Duke's presence a man who (it was reported) insisted on speaking to the Duke himself, who swore that he had been within the past day inside the beseiged castle, and who claimed to know a way by which it would be possible to enter secretly with a body of armed men.

Presently, after the man was thoroughly searched, and tested for magical powers, the Duke confronted him. "Well? Spit it out, fellow."

The fellow before him was poorly garbed, and young, with a lean, hunted look. "My name is Kaparu, Your Grace. I have worked as an agent of Queen Yambu in the past, but I'll be pleased to work for a prince as well-known for generosity as yourself instead."

Throughout the whole morning the fighting continued with scarcely an interruption. What small pauses there were resulted not from any weariness or unwillingness on the part of the inhuman mob that tried to swarm upon the walls, but from their need for new ladders, as numbers of the old ones burned or broke under the impact of rock or fire or molten lead. And even when the fighting ebbed for a time, the howling of the Horde went on without pause. The volume of sound did not seem to diminish much with their necessarily diminishing numbers.

As Mark came down from the roof to the level of the top of the outer walls, he heard a stalwart swordsman mutter: "We have cut down thousands of them, and yet still they come." The man was not exaggerating.

Presently Mark was making his way across the crowded main courtyard of the castle, passing hastily arranged stockpiles of supplies, tethered animals, a row of moaning wounded being cared for. He had come down from the roof with Dame Yoldi's permission, in response to a wave from Barbara. A longer break in the fighting than any previous had set in, and the magicians of Yambu had even summoned the Horde back from the walls, out of reach of fire and hurled rock, till more ladders could be got ready. Inside the castle, those who had borne the burden of the battle were being relieved now, wherever possible, for food and rest. Still it seemed to Mark that the yard was crowded mostly with noncombatant refugees, all of whom seemed to be muttering complaints that too many others had been let in. Mark heard several people assuring others that whatever food supplies Sir Andrew had available could not possibly be enough to see this crowd through a long seige.

Mark repeated this saying to his old companions, when he came to the place against a damp-stoned wall where Barbara, and now Ben as well, were waiting for him.

Barbara sat leaning against the wall, but Ben was standing, as if his nerves and muscles were still on alert, tuned to too high a pitch to let him rest. He was not tall, but neither was he as short as his thick build sometimes made him look. The mismatched breastplate and helmet he had scrounged somewhere now gave him an almost clownish look.

Looking at Barbara, Ben laughed tiredly. "I only hope we have the chance to try out a long seige. I think we'd like it better than..." He didn't finish, but let himself slump back against the wall, and then slide down till he was sitting beside her.

Now Mark could see Nestor, swordless at the moment but still wearing most of his new armor, picking his way wearily across the crowded court toward them.

Nestor said nothing until he had come up to where they were, and had let himself down with a great sigh, that seemed to have in it all the exhaustion of war. He tipped his head back and kept it that way, gazing up into the gray sky which dropped a little rain from time to time. Only occasionally did he lower his gaze to look at any of his companions.

"The fighting..." Nestor began to say at last. And then it appeared that he did not mean to finish either.

For some time there was a silence among them all. Mark knew, or at least felt, that there were things that needed saying, but he had no feeling for how to begin.

He kept expecting at any moment to hear the call to arms, but it did not come. The respite in the fighting was growing unexpectedly prolonged. From the distance came the repetitive, soothing chants of the lesser magicians of Yambu—it was said that the Queen there was her own best wizard. The chanting was being used to keep the Horde treading in place or marching in a circle until a greater number of ladders could be made and distributed for the next assault.

... Mark roused with a start, and realized he had been dozing, his back against a wall. Dame Yoldi had appeared in the midst of their resting group. It was early afternoon now, and she was bending over Nestor, talking to him. "Are you hurt?"

"No, lady. Not much. But tired. And stiffening now. I've had a fair rest, though. I'll be ready to take back the Sword and use it when the fighting starts again."

Yoldi, straightening up, nodded abstractedly. She said: "Whoever has Townsaver in hand, fighting to protect unarmed folk in a held place, cannot die so long as he keeps on fighting, no matter how severe his wounds. But if he is badly hurt, he will fall as soon as the fighting slackens."

Nestor said nothing, but continued gazing at the sky. After a time he nodded, to show that he had heard.

Mark, happening to look toward a far part of the courtyard where vehicles were gathered, saw something that made him speak without thinking.

"Look," he said. "Our old wagon."

The others looked. "My lute is there," Ben said.

"I wonder," asked Barbara, of no one in particular, "if the money's still under the front seat."

Mark had nodded into sleep again, only to waken to a heart-pounding shock. It was late in the day, very late now, and long afternoon shadows had come over them all.

"Listen!" Nestor ordered, urgently.

Mark sat bolt upright.

The distant chanting of the sorcerers of Yambu had fallen into silence.

There was no time for farewells or good wishes. Mark rushed to rejoin Dame Yoldi on the roof, as she had bidden him do if an alert sounded. On his way to the first ascending stair, Mark ran past Sir Andrew. The knight's armor was dented here and there from the earlier fighting. He was exhorting his troops, in a huge voice, to make another winning effort.

It was a long climb back to the roof. When he emerged on it at last, Mark found Dame Yoldi already there, her arms raised to a darkening sky and her eyes closed. A pair of her helpers, a man and a woman, arranged things on the parapet before her, things of magic in bottles and baskets between two burning candles.

Looking down, Mark saw the next surging attack of the larvae strike against the walls on a broad front, and wash up like a wave upon a hundred scaling ladders. He could draw some encouragement from the fact that the creatures' reserve force, that in the morning had stretched endlessly across the fairgrounds, was much compacted now. Their legions had been hacked and broken into a vast mud-flat that stained the ground for meters in front of every wall they had assaulted.

But, beyond those thinning deadwood ranks, the human armies of Fraktin and Yambu were both readying themselves for an attack. Mark realized that the human onslaught would be timed to fall upon an exhausted and weakened defense, just as the last of the larvae were cut down—if indeed the last of the larvae could be defeated. Already the defenders' ranks, thin to begin with, had suffered painful losses.

Sir Andrew's voice, now distant from Mark's ears, roared out from a wall-top: "Save your missiles! We'll need them to hit men!"

And the slingers and the archers on the battlements held their fire. Mark supposed that Barbara had rejoined her group there, though he could not pick her out.

The sun was setting now, beams lancing between dark masses of cloud, red-rimmed like some reflection of the renewed red glow in the east. Torches were being lighted on the walls, for illumination and weapons both, and they shone down on the advancing, climbing Horde. Darts and arrows flew up at the defenders from below the walls, but in no great numbers. The Horde was not well supplied with missile weapons.

Dame Yoldi still stood like a statue on the high roof, her arms raised, her eyes closed, a rising wind moving her garments. She appeared to be oblivious to what was happening below. She would be trying to strike back at the enemy somehow, or else to ward off some new harm from them—Mark was unable to tell which.

The attack this time was on a broader front than before, along almost the entire accessible rim of wall, and just as savage as the previous attacks had been. It prospered quickly. Two calls for Townsaver went up at the same time, from opposite directions on the walls.

Was it Nestor again, the helmed figure Mark saw now, running out from a guard-tower with the sword? Mark could not be sure. Whoever it was, he could fight in only one place at a time.

Again the screaming of the Sword of Fury rose above the eternal whistle-howling of the foe. Again Mark watched Townsaver's blade carve a dead-wood legion into chunks of mud and flying dust. Again the sword built a blurred wall through which the invaders could not force their way, press forward as they might.

But, again, Townsaver prevailed only where it could be brought to bear.

Now, Mark could hear despairing cries go up, from the defenders on the wall where the sword was not. The enemy had gained a foothold there, at last, and was now pouring in reinforcements. Dame Yoldi, rousing herself from what had seemed a trance, abruptly abandoned her work, snapping orders to her assistants. Then she grabbed Mark by one arm and began to tow him to the trapdoor that led down. In his last glance from the high roof at the fighting, he could see warbeasts starting to mount some of the scaling ladders far below.

And, across what had once been the fairgrounds,

the human troops of Fraktin and Yambu were answering to trumpets, marshalling for their own move to attack.

The enchantress, still clutching Mark tightly by the wrist, left the stair at the level of the castle where her own workroom was. Already there was panic in the corridors, folk running this way and that bearing weapons, children, treasures great and small that they had hopes of saving somehow. Yoldi ignored all this, moving almost at a run to her own chambers. There, without ceremony, she lifted Dragonslicer from the table, and grabbed a belt and scabbard from a shelf.

She began to buckle the sword on her own body — then, with a rare display of hesitation, paused. In an instant she had changed her mind and was fastening it round Mark's waist instead.

"It will be best this way," she murmured to herself. "Yes, best. Now let us get on down."

Once more they hurried through hallways, then down flight after flight of stairs.

"If anything should happen to me on the way, lad, you keep going. Down as far as you can, to the bottom of the keep, to where the dungeons are."

"Why?"

"Because we can't hold the castle now, and the last way out is down there. And you are the one, of all of us, who must get out."

Mark wasn't going to argue about it. Still he couldn't help wondering why.

When they reached ground level inside the castle, uproar and confusion swept in at them from a courtyard, where the sounds of fighting were very near. Voices were crying that Sir Andrew had been wounded.

Dame Yoldi halted abruptly, and when she spoke again her voice had changed. "I must go to him, Mark. You go on. Down to the dungeons and out. Our people down there will show you the way."

She hurried out. Mark turned toward the doorway

she had indicated. He had almost reached it when a mass of struggling soldiers knocked him down.

Duke Fraktin and his handpicked force of fifteen men were following their volunteer guide, Kaparu, toward the castle. It had been a quick decision on the Duke's part, made when the larvae had won success atop the walls, and it looked as if the citadel might after all fall quickly.

The Duke would not have trusted any of his subordinates to lead a mission like this one, not when he wanted to be sure that the prize gained reached his own hands. He had faced war at close range many times before, when the prizes at stake were far less than these Swords. And now, secret but most powerful encouragement, Coinspinner was giving signs that he took to mean its powers were fully active. Just as the small force had started out toward the beleagured castle, the Sword of Chance had begun a whispering thrumming in its scabbard, so soft a sound that the Duke was sure no one but he could hear it. He could hear it himself only when he put a hand upon the hilt. Even then the thrum was more to be felt than heard; but it was steady, and it promised power. The Duke kept one hand on the hilt as he walked.

The small body of men, seventeen in all, had moved out from the lines of the ducal army about an hour after dark, just as soon as the Duke had convinced himself that Kaparu's offer represented a worthwhile gamble. The gamble had to be taken soon if it was to be taken at all, for it was impossible to count on the defenders of the castle being able to hold out much longer, and at any moment the human army of Yambu might move as well.

Moving toward the castle, the Duke's small force traversed a slope of worn grass, cut by ditches, that Kaparu said had been a fairground only a few days

ago. The ditches afforded a certain amount of cover—
not that the castle's defenders had any attention to
spare right now for this little group of men. Torches
still burning on the walls ahead showed that parts of
them were still held by Sir Andrew's troops, but new
assaults against those sections were being readied to
left and right, where now the regular troops of Fraktin
and Yambu alike were moving forward, following the
larvae.

But, just ahead, where the keep itself almost became
a part of the outer wall, that wall rose to a forbidding
height. Until now, no direct attack had been attempted
at this point.

When his party was halfway across what had been
the fairgrounds, the Duke stopped. He warned Kaparu
yet once again, with Coinspinner's edge against his
throat: "You will be first to die, if there is any treachery here."

The fellow took the threat calmly and bravely enough.
"There'll be no treachery from me, Your Grace. I look
forward too eagerly to receiving the generous reward
that you have promised."

Silently the Duke pushed him forward.

When he and his men had topped the outer lip of
the almost waterless moat, they could see rectangular
patches of faint light in the castle wall, now just a few
meters in front of them.

"The windows," breathed Kaparu. "As I promised. I
tell you the old man is a soft-brained fool; I only
wonder that his defenses held out as long as they did."

The Duke had to admit that the rectangles certainly
looked like windows, open and undefended. Any castle
lord who came to be known as Kind could hardly
expect to keep his castle . . .

The group easily forded the muddy moat, and easily
climbed its inward wall, which was badly eroded and
had obviously been neglected for years. As they came

at last in reach of the castle wall itself, Kaparu leaned a hand upon the giant stones, and paused for a final whisper: "As I have already warned you, there will be ponderous iron bars inside. Once through the wall, we'll be inside a large dungeon cell, whether locked or unlocked I do not know."

The Duke nodded grimly. "Bars we can deal with," he said, and glanced at some of his men who carried tools, and at Blue-Robes in his incongruous armor. They silently nodded back. The wizard had volunteered half-willingly to accompany this expedition, as a sort of penance; Mars had not, after all, made his appearance as predicted.

In a voice barely audible, the Duke hissed at Kaparu: "Just so there are no tricks."

The guide Kaparu was made to be the second man in through one of the tunnel-like windows, with Duke Fraktin right behind him. The Sword of Chance, throbbing faintly with the risks its master was taking, was touching its needle point to the guide's back.

Once inside, through the five or six meters of the wall's thickness, the Duke dropped down from window-sill to stone floor, following closely the men ahead of him and moving to make room for those who followed closely after. Yes, they were in a cell, all right. The bars were visible as dark outlines against some illumination of ghostly faintness that came through an arch-way atop some stairs.

As the Duke motioned his tool-workers and wizard forward, to grope in silence for the door, he found himself starting to sweat. As the last of his party dropped in through the window, and his men milled around him, he found uneasiness, queasiness, grow-ing in the center of his belly. Fear, he reminded himself, was quite natural when a man was engaged in an enterprise as dangerous as this. Even fear enough to make him feel sick . . . but this . . . this sickness had

been only in his gut at first, but now it felt as if it were
centered somewhere even more central than that, if
such were possible . . .

Beside the Duke, one of his hand-picked men cried
out in a low voice, then seemed to be struggling with
himself, trying to muffle yet another cry. Another's
weapon fell clashing on the stone floor. A third sobbed
loudly. The Duke would have struck out at them all, in
anger at their noise, but something was turning like
poison in the core of his own being, and he could
hardly move his limbs . . .

Not poison, no.

The wizard was perhaps the first to understand
what was happening to them all, and he choked out
the first words of a phrase of power. But it was too late
to be an effective counter, or perhaps too weak—
something strangled the next words in his throat.

The sensation of deadly illness had now fastened
upon all the men who were crowded into the large cell.
Blue force, no longer completely invisible, hung in the
black air around the windows, preventing any effort at
retreat. Some of the men had groped and pushed their
way to the cell bars, and hung on the bars now,
rattling them. Now blue fiery tongues, constructions
almost more of darkness than of light, were playing in
the air all around the men, tongues of force that
became more clearly visible as the wakefulness and
the hunger of their possessor grew.

With Coinspinner drawn and throbbing strongly in
his hand, the Duke managed to tear himself free of
momentarily faltering blue tongues of light. He threw
himself down on the stone floor of the cell, rolling
violently from right to left and back again. He was
trying, and managing successfully so far, to avoid that
groping, subtle touch, that was so wholly horrible . . .

Two men were hurriedly carrying Sir Andrew down-

stairs on a stretcher. They had shoved their way somehow through a melee on the first floor of the castle,
and then had slammed a door on a charging Yambu
warbeast to get down to ground level. Their intention
was to carry their master through the dungeons and
then on out through the secret passage that here, as in
so many other castles, offered one final hope when
defenses and defenders failed.

The bearers entered the long dungeon stair. The
warbeast had been evidence enough that human
attackers, coming in their own hordes on the heels of
the remnants of the Horde itself, were now battering
at the doors of the keep above. Above were screams
and murder, fire and panic; down here there was still
almost silence.

At any other time, the sight of the faint blue horror
that hazed the air inside the large end cell might well
have stopped the stretcher-bearers and sent them running back. But now they knew there could be no going
back. They set their burden down in the narrow corridor that ran between the cells, and one of them ran on
ahead, through a false cell whose secret they knew. He
meant to scout the secret way ahead and make sure
that it was still undiscovered by the enemy. The other
bearer meanwhile crouched down by the stretcher,
watching and resting with his knife drawn. He was
willing to die to protect Sir Andrew; but at the moment
the man's bloodied face showed only terror as he
gazed in between the bars of the end cell.

Sir Andrew, who was still wearing portions of his
armor under the rough blanket that covered him,
winced, and stirred restlessly on his pallet. When his
eyes opened he was facing the end cell. In there, behind
the bars, the silent blue terror wavered and grew and
faded and came back, like flickering cool flames. All of
the seventeen men in that cell were like candle wicks,
being slowly consumed, as from the inside out.

One shape among them was clinging to the bars, and the mouth of it was open in a soundless yell.

Sir Andrew recognized that face. His own voice was a weakened whisper now. "Ah, Kaparu. I'm sorry . . . I am sorry . . . but there's nothing I can do for you now."

The tortured mouth of the blue-lit figure strained again, but still no sound came out of it.

The knight's weak voice was sad but clear. "I told you you were my only *human* prisoner, Kaparu. I had one other captive, as you now see . . . no stone or steel could have held him in that cell, but Dame Yoldi's good work could . . . he had been half-paralyzed, you see, long before we encountered him. Some skirmish against Ardneh, two thousand years ago."

Kaparu looked as if he might be listening. His fingers were being slowly shredded from the bars.

"He's a demon, of course." Sir Andrew was having some trouble with his breathing. "We've never learned his name . . . no possible way we could kill him, you see, not knowing where his life is kept. And it would have been an atrocity against humanity to let him go. So . . . in there. And I had the windows of the cell made bigger, thinking . . . hopeless pride on my part, to think that I might someday teach a demon to be good. That if I let him contemplate the sunlit earth, and the people on it who were sometimes happy when I ruled them . . . well, it was a foolish thought. I've never had to worry, though, about anyone coming in those windows."

The soldier who had gone scouting ahead now came scrambling back and said a quick word to his companion. The man who had been waiting sheathed his knife and between them they lifted Sir Andrew again on his stretcher. Not heeding the knight's weak, only half-coherent protests, they bore him away in the direction of possible safety. The entrance to the secret tunnel, which was hidden in a cell wall, closed after them.

For a few moments then the dungeon was almost silent, and untenanted, save for what moved in blue light in the large cell at the end of the passage. Then suddenly the door of that cell clanged open. One man came rolling, crawling out, the grip of almost invisible blue tongues slipping from his body. The man lay on the floor gasping, a drawn sword in his hand. Blue tongues strained after him, slapped at him, recoiled from his sword, and at last withdrew in disappointment.

The door of the cell had not been locked.

Summoning what appeared to be his last strength, the man on the floor put out an arm and slammed the cell door shut behind him, which had the effect of confining the blue tongues. Then he rolled over on the floor, still lacking the strength to rise.

"Luck . . . " he muttered. "Luck . . . "

He fainted completely, and the sword that had been in his grasp slipped from his fingers. There was a pause after the first slip and then the sword moved, as if of itself, a few more centimeters from the inert hand that had let it go.

Moments later, a half-grown boy in torn clothing, with a burn-scar half healed on his face and fresher scratches on his arms and legs, came bounding down the stairs and into the dungeon. He had a swordbelt strapped round his waist, and a sword, considerably too big for him, in his right hand.

He stopped in his tracks at the sight of the blue glow, and of the man that it illuminated, sprawled on the floor. Then he darted forward and picked up in his left hand the sword that had eluded the man's grasp. The boy stood with a heavy sword in each hand now, looking from one to the other. An expression of wonder grew on his face.

Meanwhile, the man had roused himself. And now

he saw what had happened to his sword. With a strangled cry, that sounded like some words about a snake, he lunged with his drawn dagger at the boy.

In a startled reaction the boy jerked back. With the movement the sword in his left hand snapped up awkwardly, almost involuntarily. The point of it found the hairsbreadth gap in the armor of the lunging man, sliding between gorget and the lower flange of helm.

Life jetted forth, blood black in the blue light. "Luck . . . " said Duke Fraktin once again. Then he fell backward and said no more.

Mark looked down at the body. He could tell only that it was the carcass of some invader, clothed like five hundred others in the Fraktin white and blue.

Now, on the stairs, not far above, there was the sound of fighting. Quickly the clash was over, and a man's voice asked: "Do we go down and search?"

Another voice said: "No, look around up here first. I think the old fox's escape hatch, if he has one, will be up here."

There was the sound of departing feet. Then silence in the dungeon again, except for the distant drip of water. And now the faint *tink* that a sword's tip made, touching iron jail bars as its holder turned. Mark had sheathed Dragonslicer now, and was holding Coinspinner in both hands. From the moment he had picked it up he had been able to feel some kind of power flowing from its hilt into his hand. The thrumming he could feel in the sword grew stronger, he discovered, when he aimed the point in a certain direction.

By what was left of the blue glow from the end cell, he looked inside the other unlocked cell at which the Sword of Chance was pointing. Then he looked carefully at the cell's rear wall. In a moment he had discovered the escape tunnel's secret door.

With that door open, he delayed. He turned back,

and with his eyes half-closed swung Coinspinner's tip like a compass needle through wide slow arcs. Up, down, right, left, up again.

There. In that direction, he could feel the power somehow beginning to work, drawing an invisible line for him up into the castle above. Now slowly it swung again, by itself this time, toward the head of the stair.

In another moment it had brought him Ben, in bloodied armor, carrying an unconscious Barbara.

The secret passageway was narrow, and twisting, and very dark. Neither Ben nor Mark had anything with them to give light. Once they had closed the door on the dungeon and its fading demon-glow, the way ahead was inky black. Ben continued to carry Barbara, as before, without apparent effort, while Mark moved ahead, groping with hands and feet for obstacles or branchings of the tunnel. In the blackness he used Coinspinner like a blind man's cane, though the sensation of power emanating from it was gone now. As they moved, Mark related in terse phrases how he had picked up the new sword from the dungeon floor. If Ben was impressed, he hadn't breath enough to show it.

Once Mark stumbled over the body of a man in partial armor, who must also have entered the tunnel in flight and got this far before dying of wounds. After making sure that the man was dead, Mark led the way on past him, his feet in slipperiness that presently turned to stickiness on his bootsoles. Horror had already become a commonplace; he thought only that he must not slip and fall.

The sound of dripping water was plainer now, and more than once drops struck Mark on the face. The general trend of the passageway was down, though nowhere was the descent steep. Twice more Mark stumbled, on discarded objects that clanged away on

rock with startling metallic noise. And once the sides
of the tunnel pinched in so narrowly that Ben had to
shift his grip on Barbara, and push her limp form on
ahead of him, into the grasp of Mark waiting on the
other side of the bottleneck. Mark when he held her
was relieved to hear her groaning, muttering something;
he had been worried that they might be rescuing a
corpse.

This blind groping went on for a long time, that
began to seem endless. Mark developed a new worry,
that they were somehow lost in a cave, trapped in
some endless labyrinth or circle. He knew that others
must have taken the secret passage ahead of them;
but, except for one dead man and a few discarded
objects, those others might as well be somewhere on
the other side of the world by now. At least no pursuers could be heard coming after them.

Mark continued tapping his way forward with the
sword he had picked up in the dungeon; he had had to
put it down when he helped to get Barbara through
the narrow place in the tunnel, and then in pitch
darkness grope past its razor edges to pick it up again.

At last the fear of being in a circular trap bothered
Mark to the point where he had to stop. "Where are
we, Ben, where're we going to come out?"

Ben had necessarily stopped suddenly also, and
Mark could hear the scraping of his armor as he
leaned against the wall—as if he were more tired or
more badly hurt than Mark had realized.

"We got to go on," Ben grunted. Mark for some
reason was surprised to hear that his voice still had in
it the almost fearful reluctance as when he and Barbara
had used to argue about hunting dragons.

"I don't know, Ben, if we're getting any—"

"What else can we do, go back? Come on. What
does your lucky sword tell you?"

"Nothing." But Ben was plainly right. Mark turned

and led the way again.

They progressed in silence for a time. Then Ben surprised with a remark. "I think we're going west."

Mark saw immediately what that would mean. "We can't be. This far west from the castle? That'd be . . . " He didn't finish it aloud. Under the lake. Around him the water dripped. The passage floor underfoot now felt level, but there was never a puddle.

They had come to another tight place, and were manhandling Barbara through it when she groaned more loudly than before. This time she managed to produce some plain words: "Put me down."

She still couldn't walk too steadily, but her escort were vastly relieved to have her standing, asking questions about Nestor and Townsaver, trying to find out the situation as if getting ready to give orders. They couldn't answer most of her questions, and she was still too weak to take command.

But from that moment on the journey changed.

Their passageway, as if to signal that some important transformation was close ahead, twisted sharply, first left then right, then dipped to a lower level than ever. And then it rose steeply. And now the first true light they had seen since leaving the dungeon was ahead. At first it was so faint it would have been invisible to any eyes less starved for light, but as they advanced it strengthened steadily.

The light was the dim glow of a cloudy, moonless night sky, and it came down a twisted, narrow shaft. Mark, thinnest and most agile, climbed ahead, and was first to poke his head out of the earth among jagged rocks, to the sound of waves lapping, almost within reach. In the gloom he could make out that the rocks surrounding him made a sort of islet in the lake, an islet not more than five meters across, one of a scattered number rising from the water. By the lights of both common torch and arson Mark could see Sir

Andrew's castle and its reflection in the water, a good kilometer away. Flames gusted from the high tower windows even as he watched.

He didn't gaze long at that sight, but scrambled down into the earth again, between the cloven rocks that must sometimes fail to keep waves from washing into the passage. "Ben? It's all right, bring her up." And Mark extended a hand for Barbara to grasp, while Ben pushed her from below.

They crowded together on the surface, peering between sharp rocks at the surrounding lake.

"We'll have to make for shore before morning—but which direction?"

Mark held up the Sword of Chance. When he pointed it almost straight away from the castle, he could feel something in the hilt. It was impossible to see how far away the shore was in that direction.

"I can't swim," Barbara admitted.

"And I can't swim carrying two swords," Mark added.

Ben said: "Maybe I can, if I have to. Let's see, maybe it isn't deep."

The lake was only waist deep on Ben where he first entered it. He shed bits of armor, letting them sink. From that point, following the indication of the blade Mark held ahead of him, the three fugitives waded into indeterminate gloom.

The sword worked just as well under the surface of the water as above it. At one point Mark had to go in to his armpits, but no deeper. From there on the bottom rose, and already a vague shoreline of trees was visible ahead. The strip of beach, when they reached it, was only two meters wide, and waves lapped it, ready to efface whatever footprints they might leave.

The sheltering trees were close to shore, and just inland from their first ranks a small clearing offered grass to rest on.

For a moment. Then, just beyond the nearest thicket, something stirred, making vague crackling sounds of movement. Mark let Ben grab up Coinspinner from the grass, while he himself drew Dragonslicer from its sheath.

They moved forward cautiously, around a clump of bushes. An obscure shape, big as a landwalker but not as tall, moved in the night. There was a faint squeal from it, a muffled rumble . . . the squeal of ungreased axles, the rumble of an empty wagon-body draped with a torn scrap of cover.

The two loadbeasts harnessed to the empty wagon were skittish, and behaved in general as if they had been untended for some time. This wagon was smaller than the one the dragon-hunters had once owned. This one too had some symbols or a design painted on its sides, but the night was too dark for reading symbols. Barbara murmured that this must be the vehicle of some other fairgrounds performer, whose team must have bolted during the recent speedy evacuation.

There were reins, quite functional once they were untangled. With Barbara resting in the back, Ben drove forth from thickets looking for a road. Dragonslicer was at his feet, and Mark on the seat at his side with Coinspinner in hand. The Sword of Chance was coming alive again, telling him which way to go.

THE END

THE SONG OF SWORDS

Who holds Coinspinner knows good odds
Whichever move he make
But the Sword of Chance, to please the gods,
Slips from him like a snake.

The Sword of Justice balances the pans
Of right and wrong, and foul and fair.
Eye for an eye, Doomgiver scans
The fate of all folk everywhere.

Dragonslicer, Dragonslicer, how d'you slay?
Reaching for the heart in behind the scales.
Dragonslicer, Dragonslicer, where do you stay?
In the belly of the giant that my blade impales.

*Farslayer howls across the world
For thy heart, for thy heart, who hast wronged me!
Vengeance is his who casts the blade
Yet he will in the end no triumph see.*

*Whose flesh the Sword of Mercy hurts has drawn no breath;
Whose soul it heals has wandered in the night,
Has paid the summing of all debts in death
Has turned to see returning light.*

*The Mindsword spun in the dawn's gray light
And men and demons knelt down before.
The Mindsword flashed in the midday bright
Gods joined the dance, and the march to war.
It spun in the twilight dim as well
And gods and men marched off to hell.*

*I shatter Swords and splinter spears;
None stands to Shieldbreaker.
My point's the fount of orphans' tears
My edge the widowmaker.*

*The Sword of Stealth is given to
One lowly and despised.
Sightblinder's gifts: his eyes are keen
His nature is disguised.*

*The Tyrant's Blade no blood hath spilled
But doth the spirit carve
Soulcutter hath no body killed
But many left to starve.*

*The Sword of Siege struck a hammer's blow
With a crash, and a smash, and a tumbled wall.
Stonecutter laid a castle low
With a groan, and a roar, and a tower's fall.*

Long roads the Sword of Fury makes
Hard walls it builds around the soft
The fighter who Townsaver takes
Can bid farewell to home and croft.

Who holds Wayfinder finds good roads
Its master's step is brisk.
The Sword of Wisdom lightens loads
But adds unto their risk.

Sword-Play
An Appreciative Afterword
by
Sandra Miesel

But Iron—Cold Iron—is master of them all.
—Kipling

From the kindling of the first fire to the latest break-through in computer design, each technological advance opens new levels of play in an age-old game for the mastery of Life. Calling Man's struggle for control over his environment a "game" is no idle figure of speech. Ours is a species of players as well as makers. Indeed, these two intertwined qualities describe humanness. Laughter and reason alike set us apart from beasts.

Work and play are meant to reinforce each other. Sundering them is a measure of human imperfection—

the wages of original sin, some say—and their union is a sign of Eden's innocence. Yet no matter how tragically estranged labor and leisure become, we still dimly feel that matters should be otherwise and wish our work could be joyful as child's play.

Slow-paced primitive societies take time to harmonize work and play. Each new way of working has to be played about so that it can be thought about sanely. Myth and ritual put technology into context, make it "user friendly."

Consider the discovery of fire. It brought Early Man far more than light, warmth, protection, or any merely practical advantage. Fire became the focal point of the community, acquired symbolic meanings, participated in ceremonies, appeared in heroic tales, even received worship. Though we harness vaster energies now, echoes of the ways cavemen worked and played with fire resound in us at every striking of a match.

Likewise, tool-shaping, agriculture, metal-crafting— all the basic innovations—were transformed through playful celebration. These human activities became holy because making and playing were seen as divine operations. In some cultures, the world a creator-god has made is a battlefield for contending supernatural powers. In others, existence is a game the Absolute plays with Itself throughout eternity. The patterns also hold in Judeo-Christian contexts: Holy Wisdom plays beside Yaweh when He lays the foundations of the earth and Christ the carpenter has been symbolized by a clown.

Speculative thought moves beyond imagery to ponder the ethics of work and play. What limits—if any— exist on the ways we may shape matter? If a thing *can* be made, *should* it be made? How far can the quest for mastery go and by what means? If Life is a game, what are the rules? Does the outcome matter, or are victories as hollow as defeats? Who are the players and what are the pawns? Are the competing sides really different or ultimately the same? Is some supreme referee keeping score?

Fred Saberhagen is genuinely comfortable with these questions. He believes that human acts have meaning and that we can compete for an everlasting prize. His grounding in traditional Western values gives his writing the staunchness of ancient and hallowed stone.

Saberhagen's technical expertise and mythic instinct equip him to fabulize reality and rationalize fable. Scientific data quicken his imagination: he can find a story in a squash seed or a spatial singularity. His innate feeling for archetype transforms specific facts into universal images. Thus in *The Veils of Azarloc* (1978), outré astrophysics provides a unique metaphor for the blurry barriers Time wraps about us.

Examples abound in his popular berserker series (*Berserker*, 1967; *Brother Assassin*, 1969; *Berserker's Planet*, 1975; *Berserker Man*, 1979; *The Ultimate Enemy*, 1979; and *The Berserker Wars*, 1981). The berserkers are automated alien spacecraft that begin as deadly mechanisms but swiftly become symbols of Death itself. These ravening maws of Chaos, these "demons in metal disguise" are today's answer to the scythe-wielding Grim Reaper of old. "They speak to our fear of mad computers and killer machines with jaws that bite and claws that snatch." The general pattern governing the wonder-war between Life and Death is embellished with allusions to particular myths (an Orpheus sings in a cybernetic Hades) and legendary historical incidents (a Don John of Austria fights a Battle of Lepanto in space).

While Saberhagen's hard sf can soar into metaphysical realms, his fantasy has a matter-of-fact solidity about it that leaves no room for disbelief. This quality is admirably demonstrated in his Dracula series. These novels (*The Dracula Tapes*, 1976; *The Holmes-Dracula*

File, 1978; *An Old Friend of the Family*, 1979; and
Thorn, 1980) condense the murky haze of folklore and
gothic romance surrounding vampires into premises
that can stand the light of day. The Count's ascerbic
character and occult gifts are made all the more con-
vincing by the strictly authentic settings (Victorian
England, Renaissance Italy, contemporary America)
through which he moves. Furthermore, as an unforeseen
player in sundry power games, the Count is an agent
of rough justice and a witness to some higher law
governing all creation.

Fact and fancy are complimentary categories for
Saberhagen because, as indicated above, his art depends
on disciplined exchanges between the two. Since both
possible and impossible worlds have their technologies,
either applied science or practical magic, technological issues are prominent in Saberhagen's work.

His concern for making is matched by an enthusiasm for playing, perhaps because his personal hob-
bies include chess, karate, and computers. Whether
mental, physical, or cybernetic, games are a recurring
device in Saberhagen's fiction.

His gaming principles can be deduced from the
berserker series. Indeed, the berserkers themselves
were invented to serve as the antagonist that a games'
theory ploy defeats ("Fortress Ship"/"Without a
Thought," 1963). Although most of the battles are
fought between computers ("faithful slave of life against
outlaw, neither caring, neither knowing"), one killer
machine is undone by joining in a human recreational
war-simulation game ("The Game," 1977). Direct personal combat still retains its place — *Berserker's Planet*
features a rigged tournament of duels to the death —
and dialectical clashes abound. As the series expands,
its military campaigns grow more complex, ranging
across time as well as space and employing psycho-
logical and spiritual as well as physical strategems.

The initial struggle for survival gradually unfolds into a conflict of vast cosmic import.

No compromise is possible between the opposing players. The berserkers are "as near to absolute evil as anything material can be." Resisting them requires total mobilization and eternal vigilance since no victory over them is ever quite perfect or complete.

The cause of Life turns enemies into allies but alliances change to emnities in the camp of Death. Yet the contending sides are not homogeneous: humans use thinking machines and berserkers incorporate living tissue. The cyborg hero of *Berserker Man* becomes humanity's paladin without denying the machine side of his nature. In the long run, Life may be more at risk from treachery by the living than from attack by the unliving. The berserkers' "goodlife" servants are worse than their masters because they freely choose and bleakly enjoy their perversions. These worshippers of destruction are but one particular expression of sentient beings' bent toward sin. Before the berserkers came to be, Evil was.

Turns of play proceed by ironic reversals of fortune. The race is not always to the swift nor the battle to the strong. Pawns have a way of becoming kings—and vice versa. Unable to penetrate the councils of the light, darkness often falls into its own malicious snares. Even when it wields planet-shattering weapons, Evil can be defeated by a child, an animal, or even a plant. Eucatastrophe, the unexpected happy ending, is always possible when the game is bravely—and skillfully—played.

The stakes could not be higher. The very nature of the universe is being put to wager of battle. Is existence a circular parade of ants? ("What did it all matter?" asks one villain. "Was it not a berserker universe already, everything determined by the random swirls of condensing gas, before the stars were born?") Or is

it a march towards a glorious destination? Defeating
Death's legions vindicates the evolutionary potential
latent in every bit of Life.

Likewise, human art, love, holiness, even humor
and personal quirks can transcend the laws of probability that govern berserkers. Machine intelligence cannot grasp why "the most dangerous life units of all
sometimes acted in ways that seemed to contradict the
known supremacy of the laws of physics and chance."
Capacity for growth and choice is humankind's pass-
port to a paradoxical space-time region—and a bound-
less future—barred to its unliving foes.

Unto what purpose was the match held? Perhaps to
let Life win its laurels under fire. Virtue untried by
adversity is meaningless. Moreover, the game does not
end where it began. Neither players nor field will ever
be the same again. Evil has only improved what it
sought to annihilate. The berserker wars are but one
set among the contests being played out instant by
instant until the end of time. Yet whatever the odds in
Death's favor, Saberhagen stubbornly proclaims that
Life will wear the victor's crown.

The same ground rules obeyed in the berserker series
reappear in all Saberhagen's fiction because they express
his personal—and highly traditional values. Length
and continuity permit some especially engrossing refine-
ments of play in *The Empire of the East* (1979), the
revised one-volume edition of a trilogy originally
published as *The Broken Lands* (1968), *The Black
Mountains* (1971), and *Changeling Earth* (1973).

Ingenious though he is, Saberhagen has never been
wildly innovative. His strength as a writer lies in
seeing old concepts from new angles and employing
them with unswerving thoroughness. *Empire* is a monu-
ment to these qualities. It rests on that venerable
fantasy premise, "a world where magic works." In the
version pioneered by L. Sprague de Camp and Fletcher

Pratt in their *Incomplete Enchanter* (1942), magic totally replaces science. However, in Larry Niven's *The Magic Goes Away* (1978), magic is being supplanted by science. Works like Poul Anderson's *Operation Chaos* (1971) and Randall Garrett's Lord Darcy series show the two kinds of knowledge co-existing unequally in realistic twentieth century settings, but series by Andre Norton (Witch World) and Marion Zimmer Bradley (Darkover) set them at odds in archaic alien societies.

Saberhagen's *Empire* takes place in a post-catastrophe North America whose culture is vaguely medieval. Wizardry dominates this demon-ridden age while the rare bits of technology surviving from the Old World are objects of superstitious awe. Sometimes Old and New can unite, as in the temperamental person of the djinn technologist, a being as maddeningly literal-minded as a computer, who must be properly programmed to perform his magic feats.

The novelty of the situation is *why* magic has become feasible. There was no thaumaturgic breakthrough. Instead, the very nature of physical reality has been fundamentally altered by the doomsday weapons used in a past global war. The probability of occult phenomena occurring has increased enormously. "Since the Change it could scarcely be said that anything was lifeless; powers that before had only been potentialities now responded readily to the wish, the incantation, were motivated and controlled by the dream-like logic of the wizard's world." Meanwhile, the likelihood of certain physical reactions and technical aptitude itself have correspondingly declined. Or as the author himself remarks, "We are not justified in assuming that all physical laws are immutable through the whole universe of space and time."

But no matter how much else may change, the craving for mastery endures. Whether engineers or wizards build their war gear, conquerors will be conquerors still. The tyrant of the age is John Ominor ("The All-Devourer"), Emperor of the East, a man far wickeder than the demons he binds to his will. Not long before the story opens, Ominor's armies consumed the last independent bit of the continent, the Broken Lands along the West Coast. But before his world dominion can be perfectly secured, rebels calling themselves the Free Folk challenge his despotic rule. Aided by a quasimaterial power named Ardneh, they fight their way up through the feudal hierarchy, from satrap past viceroy to confront the Emperor himself.

Each volume of the trilogy has a different source of mythic inspiration. As the text itself explains, *The Broken Lands* is based on an Indian myth concerning the god Indra and the demon Namuci. The gods (*devas*) and demons (*asuras*) of India are the opposite poles of the same transcendent nature. Each side continually struggles to amass enough spiritual energy to subdue the other. Indra the Thunderer; god of storm, war, and fertility; rider of the white elephant Airavata; Guardian of the Eastern Quarter of the Universe; once swore an extravagant oath of friendship with the powerful drought demon Namuci. Later, he slipped through a loophole in the terms to slay the complacent demon. (Georges Dumézil's *Destiny of the Warrior* exhaustively analyzes this episode as a key Indo-European myth.) In other adventures, mighty Indra also slew Trísiras, a triple-headed hybrid of god and demon, and Vritra, a cosmic dragon who had impounded the waters of life.

Saberhagen works some clever and selective transformations on this raw material. Indra's discus-shaped Thunderstone appears as a practical device for making rain or war. The oath becomes a prophecy of retribution by Arneh, the mysterious presence who can manifest himself in persons, places, or things. Namuçi is the East's cruel satrap Ekuman, leigeman of demons, and the sea-spume that kills him is fire-extinguisher foam. The instrument of Arneh's justice is a youth named Rolf who has a natural affinity for technology and the courage to ride the atomic-powered elephant to victory.

The Black Mountains borrows motifs rather than specific incidents from mythology and arranges these in opposing pairs to render the next great battle between East and West. Defeated Easterner Lord Chup, "the tall broken man," is wounded and healed, slain and reborn, degraded and redeemed so that he at last stands tall and whole—on the Western side. Som the Dead, an inhuman man, is annihilated by a godlike beast, the immortal Lord Draffut. (These two fantastical characters seem to echo every remembered tale of animated corpses and kindly nature spirits—the Nazgûl king and Tom Bombadil from *The Lord of the Rings* spring to mind. Nevertheless, they are strikingly original creations.) Rolf's twin quests for his kidnapped sister and for the hidden life-principle of the demon Zapranoth end in the same place, resolved by the familiar fairytale device of the separable soul. Ultimately, demons prove as vunerable to men as men are to demons.

Ardneh's World (the retitled *Changeling Earth*) reveals the secret of that being's identity. As the war front spreads out to its widest expanse, the distinctions between the two sides reach their sharpest contrast through the use of mythic prototypes. Like the ancient battle Indra the Generous fought with Vritra the Enveloper, this is a duel to the death between mankind's Advocate and its Adversary. The personifications of Defense and Aggression meet in mortal combat.

The Demon-Emperor Orcus bears the Latin name for both Hades and its ruler. He is an Old World hell bomb turned New World hell-lord. (In the *Mahabharata*, demonic Vritra looks uncannily like a nuclear explosion's mushroom cloud: "He grew, towering up to heaven like the fiery sun, as if the sun of doomsday had arisen.") The malevolence of Orcus is sordid. This haunter of waterless places is not Milton's glamorous rebel but Meredith's bully who cringes away from starlight. Ominor, once his servant but now his master, chained him away beneath the earth for a thousand years. Now like Satan or Loki, the fiend bursts forth for the day of wrath and falls like lightning on his foe.

Ardneh, like Orcus, has a substance "only partially subject to the laws of matter." But he was born of benevolent technology as the consciousness of a defense system that "damped the energies of nuclear fire" and "freed the energies of life." (His home base may have been SAC Headquarters in Omaha.) Although he is the actual author of the Change that transformed the world, he denies being a god. Perhaps a more appropriate title for the Archdemon's counterpart is Archangel—like an angelic power, Ardneh "is where he works." By sacrificing himself to annihilate Orcus, he brings victory out of defeat while the Western army retreats to win the day.

This paradoxical resolution recalls major triumphs in the berserker wars and even the Pascal mystery. It is the capstone of all the paradoxes and ironies that shape the story. Draffut destroys Som the Dead by trying to heal him. Blows wound the one who struck them; spells rebound on the one who cast them. Tiny flaws widen and small kindnesses expand to undermine the mightiest citadels of evil. The weak can prove surprisingly strong and the strong, shockingly weak.

Westerners, even Ardneh himself, resist temptation but Easterners sink ever lower in depravity by freely chosen stages. Refusing one shameful order pivots Chup against the East. The Western cause draws persons together but the East, that "society of essential selfishness" is hopelessly divided against itself as each member scrabbles for more influence. Absolute dominion as an end in itself brings scant satisfaction to him who wields it. At best, Ominor finds mild distraction in sadism.

The white-clad supreme tyrant is "the most ordinary-looking" of the nine 'Unworthies' who sit on his council. His manner is as banal as his first name and his capital on the site of Chicago is nothing like Sauron's, its charm being marred only by a few impaling stakes among the flowerbeds. Sheer untiring wickedness has raised this *apparatchik* above the direst demons in malignant force.

Exotic Lady Charmian, on the other hand, is supernally fair but eventually boring as she slithers from bed to bed. Her monotonous scheming inevitably brings about the very opposite of what she sought to achieve, at her father Ekuman's court, in Som's stronghold, and among the leaders of the East. Although she is mired in her rut of malice, her husband Chup still claims her. The same stubbornness that saved his own integrity may yet undo the effects of her childhood pledging to the East.

Chup's regeneration stands for the transformation of his troubled world. But the future of that world belongs to Rolf and his kind. As in *The Lord of the Rings*, the major figures on both sides disappear, leaving the world to men and to powers they can control. However, magic will not entirely vanish here, although technology will slowly revive. Having won the contest for mastery, men can now make of their lives what they will, whether by sorcery or science—or both.

But what happens to that bright-seeming future? It develops its own kind of darkness. Two thousand years after *Empire*, power games continue in *The Book of Swords*. But "game" is no metaphor here for plot turns are actually stages in a formal game being played by beings who call themselves gods and simultaneously fit into a wider contest between entities that may be playing through these gods. That action begins in the Ludus ("Game") Mountains signals the artificiality of all that follows.

Game-oriented sf has almost become a sub-genre of story-telling. Saberhagen has written some himself, such as those berserker stories cited earlier and his novel *Octagon* (1981) which focusses more on the players than the game being played. (A version of the latter is now commercially available.) Original games that act both as story subjects and symbols appear in Philip K. Dick's *Solar Lottery* (1955) and *The Game Players of Titan* (1963) and in Samuel R. Delany's *Fall of the Towers* (1970) and *Triton* (1976), to cite but a few examples. Other sf writers incorporate familiar games such as chess. In "The Immortal Game" by Poul Anderson (1954), a computer activates robotic chesspieces but *The Squares of the City* (1965) by John Brunner moves real human beings around on a sociopolitical grid. Andre Norton's *Quag Keep* (1978) is based on Dungeons and Dragons™ while *Dream Park* by Larry Niven and Steven Barnes (1981) brings an adventure game to life and "The Saturn Game" by Poul Anderson (1981) demonstrates the risk in playing an improvised mental game too passionately. Many sf stories have been converted to role-playing simulation games, for instance, *Starship Troopers*, adapted from the 1959 novel by Robert A. Heinlein. Several periodicals including *Ares*, *Dragon Magazine*, *Sorcerer's Apprentice*, and *The Space Gamer* serve the sf gaming audience.

However, *The Book of Swords* intends to pioneer new territory. Aside from the reading pleasure it gives, this trilogy is being written to provide the data base for an intricate new computer game that will uniquely combine both adventure-text and interactive features for play on a microcomputer. As of this writing, the designing has not yet begun. Until it is marketed, interested readers may amuse themselves by analyzing the "playable" elements of the story. (For example, the chase scene in the Maze of Mirth obviously lends itself to rendering in computer graphics.) The quick reversals of luck, the brisk introductions, removals, and translations are appropriate for a game scenario. The tendency for the characters to draw together in small teams suggests multivalent strategic possibilities in the war for possession of the enchanted swords.

"The swords made by the gods are beautiful things in themselves," observes one character, "Whatever the purpose behind them may be." They are also wonderfully versatile plot devices. The ease with which they can be confused and the restrictions on their use multiply dramatic possibilities. (Saberhagen shrewdly builds drawbacks as well as benefits into his magic.) Although the full *Song of the Swords* inventory may not be destined to actually appear in the trilogy's text, a dozen artifacts is an ambitiously large group. (Series that use as many as six talismans are rare, one example being Susan Cooper's *Dark Is Rising* pentalogy.) Nevertheless, twelve is the traditional number of completeness and is thus an appropriate count for a pantheon.

Although Saberhagen categorically denies a schematic purpose, by curious coincidence, his list matches twelve major divine powers. These can be most conveniently discussed under their classical Greek names.

Coinspinner, giver of blind luck, belongs to Tyche, the fickle goddess of fortune. Its natural opposite, *Doomgiver*, the instrument of all-seeing justice, belongs to Zeus in his role as universal judge.

Dragonslicer, exemplifying the heroic use of force, fits Apollo, slayer of the monster Python. (Celestial heroes who kill cthonic dragons are common in both

Indo-European and Semitic myth, for instance, Thor versus Midhgardhsormr or Baal versus Yam.) But *Shieldbreaker* expresses purely brutal might and thus belongs to Ares.

Farslayer is as futilely vengeful as Hera raging over the infidelities of Zeus. On the other hand, the *Sword of Mercy* suits Demeter, the Earth-Mother who presided over the death-and-rebirth mysteries of Eleusis.

The Mindsword that beguiles the inner self recalls triple-faced Selene/Artemis/Hecate, stern Lady of Heaven, Earth, and Hell. However, *Sightblinder's* deception of the senses is one effect Dionysus produces while wandering the world unrecognized. (The ecstatic god is a more sophisticated version of the crude, coniving Trickster who looms so large in African and Amerindian myth.)

Despair, constraint, and utter sterility surround *Soulcutter* as they do the dead-god Pluto. But *Wayfinder* elates, liberates, and enlightenment as does cheerful Hermes in his capacities as god of travellers and master of occult wisdom.

Stonecutter, the Sword of Seige, is no more resistible than Aphrodite, goddess of love. (One is tempted to read unwitting double-entendres into this sword's stanza.) Its natural counterpoise is *Townsaver*, a weapon befitting the armored virgin Athena Polias, protector of her city.

Thus the swords can be assigned to six masculine and six feminine principles. (Grouping the weapons into equal positive, negative, and ambiguous sets is left to the reader's ingenuity.) Since the above assignments were not consciously intended by the author, there is no reason to expect correspondences between the swords and deities seen in this book. Hermes has nothing to do with Dragonslicer except deliver it and Vulcan matches with none of the blades he forges. The supposedly divine players may have chosen their roles by whim, but their twelve playing tokens represent fundamental categories of experience.

The neatness of these comparisons and the associations they evoke offer the strongest possible demonstration of Saberhagen's innate feeling for myth. It is a matter of instinct with him, not rote learning. (As he modestly explains, "My reading in mythology has been sporadic at best.") Nevertheless, it lays a sure and true foundation under his fiction. The great mythologist Mircea Eliade might have been describing this situation when he observed that mythic images "act directly on the psyche of the audience even when *consciously*, the latter does not realize the primal significance of any particular symbol."

The most dramatic imagery operating here centers around swords, metalworking, and fire—each a landmark achievement of *homo faber*.

Any human culture that makes swords spins fables about them. As the masculine symbol *par excellence*, swords are the essence of the gods and heroes who wield them. (The Japanese say that the sword is the soul of the samurai.) Swords have been objects of worship and emblems of fertility. As prized heirlooms, they fit into the cult of dead ancestors. They may be linked with the destiny of one hero or of an entire dynasty. They can confer invincibility—at a price. Legendary swords are fashioned by mystic means, especially through blood sacrifice to transfer the victim's life into the blade. (Damascus steel was reportedly quenched in blood and bloody offerings are a normal component of smithcraft in many primitive cultures.) Finally, because swords have distinctive personalities, they are given names.

The prowess of medieval heroes lay in their swords. (Arthur's Excalibur is, of course, the most famous example.) Aragorn's Andúril in *The Lord of the Rings* carries on this noble tradition in fantasy. Perhaps the most impressive sword of virtue in science fiction to date is Terminus Est in Gene Wolfe's *Book of the New Sun* (1980–83).

But doomswords of Norse inspiration give sf grimmer drama. The pre-eminent example is Tyrfing in Poul Anderson's *Broken Sword* (1954), the baleful brand with "a living will to harm." This is the model for Michael Moorcock's Stormbringer, the "stealer of souls" whose bloodlust cannot be slaked until the last man on earth is slain. More recently, the accursed blade motif receives a scientific rationale in C. J. Cherryh's *Book of Morgaine* (1976–79) where Changeling is an alien device that cleaves the space-time fabric.

Saberhagen's swords confer sublime power without regard for the user's fate. Their properties seem to be good, evil, or ambiguous. Made at the cost of five lives, they are destined to take countless others. Although the divine smith who forges them with earthfire within an icy peak uses the Roman name Vulcan (source of the word "volcano"), he looks and acts like a brutal giant out of Northern myth. Since the swords and Mark were created within the same week— indeed, he would not have come into existence without them—their destinies are uniquely linked. In effect, his own heirloom Townsaver chose him as its heir. He is also the only person in this book to use all four of the named blades.

It is most fitting that Vulcan makes the enchanted swords out of meteoric iron since celestial origins give this material a special mystical prestige. Intact iron meteorites have been worshipped as images of divinity, for instance the Palladium of Troy and the Ka'ba of Mecca. The oldest word for "iron" is *an-bar*, Sumerian for "star-metal" because "thunderstones" were the first accessible source of the substance used in Mesopotamia. Meteorites were hammered into objects as early as the third millenium B.C. and were also used by peoples such as the Eskimos who had no knowledge of metallurgy. Superior qualities made weapons shaped from meteoric iron legendary. Even in this century, the Bedouin believed meteoric iron swords to be invincible.

As Eliade discusses in his fascinating study *The Forge and the Crucible*, "the image, the symbol, and the rite anticipate—sometimes even make possible—the practical applications of a discovery." Since iron fallen from the sky was transcendent, so was iron mined and smelted on earth. This awe soon extended to every aspect of metallurgy.

But iron's occult power can act for either good or ill. It can ward off demons, spells, poisons, curses, sickness, or bad weather. Faerie folk cannot bear the touch of it nor enter a place protected by it: Cold Iron can inhibit magic. However, iron is also the symbol of war and the agent of violence. Many primitive cultures—especially those oppressed by better-armed foes—fear iron and all who work in it. (The Masai purify all new iron objects to remove the taint of the smith's hand.)

Thus, to some, supernatural smiths may be wise, civilizing gods, adept at song, dance, poetry, and healing. (The wonder-smiths of the *Kalevala* excel in each of these areas.) But to others, they may be the gods' vicious foes—dwarves, giants, demons, or Satan himself. (Norse sagas and fairytales abound in examples.) Human smiths display the same ambivalence. As Eliade observes, "The art of creating tools is essentially superhuman—either divine or demoniac (for the smith also forges murderous weapons)." A spiritual aura clings to the act of making, whether *homo faber* be godlike or devilish.

The smith, like the shaman, is pre-eminently a master of fire. Fire was primitive Man's earliest instrument for controlling the cosmos. As the initial means of accelerating natural processes, it commenced the conquest of Time, a campaign technology has continued ever since. By the hand or through the spirit, initiates into the mysteries of fire can break the bonds confining other beings to win mastery of their environment.

Note that Vulcan's first act in the opening line of this volume is to grope for fire. His erupting volcano glows on the game board's eastern edge like a signal lamp. The smith god represents the power to shape inorganic matter but the Beast-Lord personifies organic matter's potential for growth. Unharmed by fire, Draffut can quicken Vulcan's molten lava to momentary life. Yet Draffut's confrontation with the upstart gods is only one episode in the contest that begins, proceeds, and will end via Vulcan's swords.

The gods call the game their own, but is it? Their pretentions to divinity ring hollow yet they are clearly more than human. Given the subtle hint in the Prologue that Vulcan has been "programmed" for his task, are they perhaps some magical equivalent of the huge robotic god-figures in *Berserker's Planet*? They could be automata animated by quasimaterial beings such as djinni.

Overshadowing these meddlesome, amoral gods are the images of Ardneh and the masked figure known as the Dark King. The Demon-Slayer and Hospitaller has become more of an Apollo than an Indra, a patron of humane technology opposed to Vulcan's brutal methods. Unlike Orcus, the Dark King is suave and manlike but his title would be a suitable alias for Hell's overlord. (By an irony of history, their common antagonist Ominor has been transformed from a mirthless, plodding tyrant to a legendary buffoon.) But why are they here at all, since god and demon presumably destroyed each other in *Empire*? (The question puzzles theologically aware Sir Andrew.) Did the quasimaterial beings prove immortal after all? Or are these identities, like the names of the gods, idiosyncratic choices of the game's ultimate players?

Revelation of these and other enigmas must await publication of the second and third volumes of *The Book of Swords*. But a few observations about Mark are possible even at this early stage in the contest. His very name is packed with allusion—is he a piece of labeled property or a symbolic witness? Like *Berserker Man*'s Michael, he is a Child-Hero begotten under mysterious circumstances and born into a web of contradictory influences which will surely confound the evil forces that plan to make use of him. Like *Empire*'s Rolf, young Mark is sent off into epic adventures where he will confound both chance and fate, to learn through passages of sword-play that mastery of self is the kind most worth striving for.